CW01551176

Julie D. Jones was born in Bovey Tracey on the edge of Dartmoor and grew up near Kingsbridge in the South Hams. After high school, she spent time as an au pair in Southern Bavaria, Germany. Graduating from the Gloucestershire Royal Hospital as a nurse, Julie emigrated to Australia.

Death of Innocence is Julie's sixth novel, following on from the release in 2017 *of Bound by Polaris, Devil's Realm* in 2019, *Conspiracy of Souls* in 2021, *Aftershock* in 2022 and *A Gathering of Angels* in 2024. Julie is a classically trained flautist and enjoys sailing and horse riding.

This book is dedicated to the memory of all those American, Australian, and Japanese airmen who fought and died in the skies over the vast expanses of the South West Pacific in World War 2 and never returned. From Milne Bay to Guadalcanal. May they forever rest in peace.

Julie D. Jones

MOORLAND FORENSICS –
DEATH OF INNOCENCE

AUSTIN MACAULEY PUBLISHERS®

LONDON • CAMBRIDGE • NEW YORK • SHARJAH

Copyright © Julie D. Jones 2025

The right of Julie D. Jones to be identified as author of this work has been asserted by the author in accordance with sections 77 and 78 of the Copyright, Designs and Patents Act 1988.

All rights reserved. No part of this publication may be reproduced, stored in a retrieval system, or transmitted in any form or by any means, electronic, mechanical, photocopying, recording, or otherwise, without the prior permission of the publishers.

Any person who commits any unauthorised act in relation to this publication may be liable to criminal prosecution and civil claims for damages.

This is a work of fiction. Names, characters, businesses, places, events, locales, and incidents are either the products of the author's imagination or used in a fictitious manner. Any resemblance to actual persons, living or dead, or actual events is purely coincidental.

A CIP catalogue record for this title is available from the British Library.

ISBN 9781037111969 (Paperback)
ISBN 9781035888016 (ePub e-book)

www.austinmacauley.com

First Published 2025
Austin Macauley Publishers Ltd®
1 Canada Square
Canary Wharf
London
E14 5AA

20250521

To my husband and children for always believing in me.

Preface

Breaking News
Sydney, Australia

The body of a twenty-three-year-old German national has been discovered in rugged bushland in the Blue Mountains National Park, west of Sydney. The woman, believed to be on a working holiday, was discovered in the early hours of Sunday by a person abseiling near Blackheath in the Grose Valley.

This is the third overseas tourist to go missing in New South Wales within the past six months;, police now believe they could be connected.

This is Marcia Kipple reporting for Independent Aussie Television.

***

Outback, Australia

Christina found herself being violently yanked from the car, thrown to the ground, hands stomped on, pain soaring up her arms, bile rising in her throat.

Her peripheral vision caught a glimpse of Lisa being punched repeatedly, falling to the ground, head hitting the thick, red, dusty roadside with a sickening crack.

***

Breaking News
Sydney, Australia

Two English girls missing in the Australian outback have been found alive. Both women, badly beaten, are receiving hospital treatment.

Police are quoted as saying, 'It's too early to tell if these recent attacks are related to the abduction and murder of other overseas travellers, but we urge anyone with information to please come forward.'

This is Marcia Kipple reporting for Independent Aussie Television.

***

Exeter, Devon, England.
KC's Nightclub (after hours)

Reg Copeland glanced downwards, clutching his stomach, reeling in pain. Stumbling, he crashed into a broken chair, landing heavily on the concrete floor. Desperate to escape, Reg attempted to crawl to the storeroom door, his vision blurring, life starting to ebb away.

Albert, a few feet away, trembling uncontrollably, begged for mercy, the muzzle of a gun barrel jammed hard against his right temple.

Chapter One

Devon, England

'It makes perfect sense for us to fly to Sydney.' Lana leaned over Tom's desk, offering a pleading look. 'We'd be mad not to run with this story, Tom.'

'And who do you suggest manages the Newton Abbot Star in our absence?' Tom shot back, trying to avoid focusing on Lana's ample cleavage. 'Have you even *thought* about that?'

'Howard Burke,' Lana responded with a wry smile. 'I've already spoken with Howie; he's up for it, raring to go. He can start first thing Monday morning, before we've even touched down in Sydney.'

Tom sighed. '*If* we decide to go, the expense will blow the travel budget for the rest of the year. Flights to Australia don't come cheap, especially at this time of year. For a return economy tick—'

'Who's going economy, cramped and uncomfortable down the back with the rest of the smelly proletariat?' Lana broke in, sounding indignant. 'Not me, that's for sure. It's business class all the way, my friend.'

'Then you can kiss the trip goodbye.' Tom swivelled his chair, picking up the weekly *Sun Form Guide.*

Lana reached forward, closing the paper, moving it out of the way. 'Look, Tom, it's a no-brainer. I've run the numbers a dozen times. We'll recoup our expenses and more, running with this story.'

Tom puffed out his cheeks; Lana could be very persuasive at times. 'Pitch it to me again, this time in full.'

Lana sat down, smiling. 'Right. I'll provide as much information as I can: Christina and Lisa are in their early twenties, originally from Devon. They went out to Australia seven months ago, having secured job contracts with Advance Pharmaceuticals, a Swissbased outfit with an Asian regional office in Sydney.'

'Three weeks ago, Christina and Lisa embarked on an Australian adventure, travelling around the country in a camper van. They got as far as Bourke, an outback town, when they were brutally attacked. Both women sustained serious injuries and are in hospital; Christina's condition is now stable; Lisa remains on the critical list.'

'I don't see why this story is remarkable.' Tom broke in, not convinced a dodgy 'fishing trip' to Australia would be worth the effort. 'I mean, people get attacked all the time travelling to foreign countries. The world's a dangerous place; this stuff's on the news nearly every day.'

'Yes, but three overseas travellers, all women, have been brutally murdered in Oz over the past few months, their bodies dumped on the outskirts of Sydney. Surely, this can't be coincidental. Someone's targeting backpackers arriving in Australia on working holiday visas.'

'Look, Tom, other journos are heading to Oz, getting video footage and headline copy on these women; we need to jump on the bandwagon. Particularly with the two Brits being

Devon locals, we can sell a shitload of papers overnight, then offload some 24/7 feed to the big tabloids for their online social media posts and make a tidy fortune.'

Lana's phone pinged a message. Tom merely shrugged, trying to retrieve the racing guide, which Lana had pushed well out of reach.

'Maybe this will make you change your mind,' Lana urged, bringing up a current GB News panel discussion graphic on her phone and showing it to Markham.

Police speculate the recent homicides of three overseas nationals in Australia could be linked to the recent attack on two British women.

'There's no guarantee we'll obtain inside "exclusives" on what happened to any of these women,' Tom stated. 'It's a matter for the police, who will be reluctant to part with confidential information. We could be hanging around for days, maybe weeks, waiting for the tiniest crumbs, which probably won't be newsworthy.'

'Ah, that's where you're wrong, dear boss.'

Once more, Lana flipped open her phone, her face lighting up as another GB News grab came through.

A press conference is scheduled in Sydney early next week. NSW's Assistant Commissioner of Police is asking the public to remain vigilant until more facts emerge, confirming the backpacker murders are linked to a serial killer.

Tom's face displayed a mix of doubt, combined with annoyance. 'The UK and regional press will swarm into Sydney. What's the point in—?'

Lana threw up her hands. 'Tom, what's wrong with you? Lately, we've been covering stories about bank holiday sales, roadworks on the motorway, McDonald's latest burgers, and the woman who owns fifty-eight cats, thirty-seven dogs, forty rabbits, and endless guinea pigs. This story is on another planet compared to those huge—'

'Fifty-five cats,' Tom corrected. 'I distinctly remember it was—'

Lana covered her face, shaking her head in disbelief. 'Who gives a fuck how many cats she had? Open your eyes and listen to what I'm telling you.'

Tom sat pondering for a while. 'Fine, book flights. I could do with some warm weather.'

Lana jumped up, giving Tom a warm embrace. 'You won't regret this, I promise.'

***

Exeter, Devon, England
CID

'On leave for only three months, when I come back, my office looks like someone has thrown in a grenade,' Will Parker complained to anyone in earshot who would listen. 'What did this Wallis character do whilst I was away? He certainly didn't stick around long enough to provide me with a proper handover. Where are we with the Copeland murders? Can't find anything on my desk. Bugger all in reports.'

'Yes, a bit of a shambles,' Detective Sergeant Mallory Wakefield acquiesced. 'I believe Wallis spent an inordinate amount of time on petty crime.'

Will shoved aside his chair, marching along the corridor into the superintendent's office without bothering to knock; his mood dark, he found his immediate superior flicking through a copy of *Police News Weekly*, only briefly looking up to offer the DCI a scathing look.

'I'll remind you to knock in the future, Parker. I trust you didn't lose your manners whilst away on vacation.'

Will was momentarily taken aback from the unexpected reprimand. 'Eh, sorry.'

'Well, out with it,' Pettigrew instructed, letting out a sigh, a clear indication that he was losing patience. 'It's obvious you've not come in here to exchange pleasantries or chat about the crap weather we've been experiencing lately.'

'I can't understand why the Copeland case has not been properly investigated.'

Superintendent Clive Pettigrew rolled his eyes. 'I'll have you know, DCI Wallis conducted a thorough investigation, William. Put in long hours, I understand; you can look—'

'Frankly, Clive, it appears Wallis did a very poor job.' Will felt the heat rising under his collar, reaching to loosen his tie. 'I'm going to have to start from scratch; conduct interviews, hunt down eyewitnesses, and churn my way through all the misfiled evidence. Where did you unearth that baboon?'

'Don't push it, Parker,' Pettigrew warned. 'We run a tight ship at CID. Slagging off another police officer and particularly a fellow detective is unacceptable on my watch. I won't have the harmony of the organisation threatened. If you still have concerns, take it up with the chief superintendent. Oh, and don't forget to shut the door on your way out.'

Will took this as his cue to leave. He just might have a quiet word in the ear of Izzy Bax when an opportune moment arose. Will exited the room, searching for Mallory. He located the Det Sgt in the staff canteen, enjoying a bacon sandwich.

'How did it go with the super?' Mallory enquired, making room on the table for Will to place his breakfast tray, laden with a full English Breakfast and two pastries.

Will snorted, easing into a chair opposite Mallory, before adding three heaped teaspoons of sugar to an oversize mug of strong black coffee. 'Pettigrew has nothing but praise for that moron, Wallis. In my opinion, Wallis couldn't organise a root in a brothel, let alone determine someone's cause of death or who could possibly be involved.'

'We'd better troll through all evidence to date and see what we can come up with. I suppose this means paying a visit to Shirley Copeland, owner of KC's nightclub. Perish the thought. I could do without Shirley Copeland's incessant badgering. Once we set foot in KC's, she'll be on the blower every day for updates. Mark my words.'

'What was her relationship to the Copeland brothers?' Mallory asked, prising open a carton of apple juice. 'Wallis didn't disclose much.'

'Aunt apparently. Not that Shirley harbours much in the way of any old-fashioned maternal instinct. She'd shoot her own grandmother if she were still alive. Wait until you meet our beloved Shirley; you'll know what I mean.'

'Can't wait.'

'She's a shrewd female,' Will continued his depiction of Shirley Copeland. 'Just when you've got her coming around to your way of thinking, bam, she hits you where it hurts and doubles your workload. Six years ago, Shirley lobbied us to investigate unexplained losses and inventory discrepancies with high-value brandy and other liquors from her main store, making us believe it was an inside job.'

'Turns out it was connected to an organised ring moving large shipments of cigarettes, cigars, and booze across from the continent in an elaborate VAT and excise evasion scheme. We still believe Shirley was involved; we could never prove it. Took us eleven months to break up the racket.'

'How old is Shirley Copeland?'

'Mid-sixties now? Don't be fooled, Mallory; her brain's razor sharp. Shirl's got the drive of someone much younger.'

'We've certainly got our work cut out to try and uncover who murdered Reg and Albert Copeland,' Mallory announced. 'Wallis didn't leave much for us to go on. Seemed to be more interested in investigating that major political sex scandal in Lanzarote involving the local Tory MP.'

'Right, well, drink up; let's get a move on. We won't make progress hanging around here all day.'

Mallory quickly drained the last of her juice, rising from her chair to catch up to Will, already halfway down the stairs, heading back to the main operation room.

'Troll through that lot and see what you can find,' Will instructed Mallory, pointing to a raft of files on a refectory table. 'Take your time. I've a briefing at chambers with the Crown prosecutor team in ten minutes, back around midday.'

Mallory settled into Will's chair, oblivious to other officers filling the room, burying herself in files.

***

Devon, England

Eventually, Mallory leaned back in the chair, stretching. Peering through the office glass, she sighted Will returning from the briefing.

'What a cock-up. Our QC blatantly suggested I lie in the box next week. I'm getting too old for this game. No way am I risking my reputation. I don't give a shit if the Crown case is weak and the government is desperate for a conviction. It's painfully obvious.

'The Home Office Secretary is attempting to shut down the immigration corruption smell around this case for her pals in Westminster. From what I gather, the trail goes all the way to 10 Downing Street. It could take down the whole front bench. Looks like the British public is finally waking up.'

Will plonked two takeaway lattes on his desk. 'Yours is one sugar, right? Anyway, Mal, what have you got for me?'

Mallory sipped the latte, flicking through her notepad. 'It states both victims died of gunshot wounds. A handwritten explanation from Wallis. Lord knows where he's placed the official reports. According to Wallis, Reg and Albert Copeland were gunned down at KC's.'

'A bouncer stumbled across the bodies in a disused area behind the bar when locking up that night; the corpses must have been there a fair while before they were discovered. To be perfectly frank, not much else is documented. According to Wallis, he concludes the gunshots wouldn't have been heard. Both men were killed outright, the bodies left where they fell.'

The phone on Parker's desk rang, interrupting Mallory's discourse. She picked it up on Will's hand signal. 'DS Mallory Wakefield, can I help?'

Mallory placed her hand over the phone, mouthing it was Shirley Copeland. Will quickly indicated he was not in, for Mallory to end the conversation with Shirley.

'Right, I'll tell him,' Mallory spoke into the mouthpiece. 'I'm sure that will be fine, yes, thank you for your call.'

'She wants to see us,' Will surmised. 'Great, that's all I need after a well-deserved holiday: Shirley Copeland nagging away. What did I tell you?'

Mallory smiled. 'It's what we women do best. Up you get, boss. Shall I drive?'

Will threw Mallory the Jag's digital ignition key. 'KC's, Christ, of all places to go on a Monday morning. Things couldn't get much worse.'

***

Devon, England
KC's Nightclub

'Ah, Detective Will Parker, do come in; you got my message then.' This was more of a rhetorical question from Shirley.

Will and Mallory, entering the darkened premises of KCs nightclub in Exeter, waited for their eyes to adjust to poor lighting.

'We can talk in my office,' Shirley Copeland continued, showing the detectives up a narrow flight of stairs to a large, expensively decorated office with a bay window overlooking a grey, windswept estuary. Once positioned in chairs around a low, glass table, Will updated Shirley on what he knew.

'So, bugger all really,' Shirley shot back. 'I should have known, after chatting with that silly chap they sent whilst you were away; you lot haven't got a clue who killed my nephews.'

'Yes, well, I have to agree with you there.' Will acknowledged, taking in Shirley's appearance, trying not to smile—the expression *Mutton dressed as Lamb* sprang to mind.

Shirley Copeland liked to dress at least thirty years younger than her age; today was no exception. Her bleached blonde hair lay loose around freckled, bony, fake-tanned shoulders; on the plus side, a trim waistline and shapely legs were displayed to advantage by a tight-fitting, deep red leather mini skirt, a white casual shirt, and a candy pink jacket festooned with large silver buttons.

Balancing uneasily on stilettos three inches in height, with make-up thick and pasty; bright red lipstick, pale blue eyeshadow and a pink shade of blush; the nightclub owner, one had to admit, under all the garb, was quite an attractive woman.

Blessed with unusually large, emerald-green, oval-shaped eyes, it was patently clear Shirley slavishly subscribed to the more extreme online fashion sites for 60+ women.

'You've not been listening to a word I said,' an indignant Shirley retorted, digging Will hard in the ribs.

'Er, what—?'

'I said, what are you doing to find the killer of my gorgeous nephews, Reg and Albert?'

Will tried to hide his astonishment; describing Reg and Albert as gorgeous was a contradiction in terms. Both men were well-known around the city for violent tendencies and wild tempers. Reg spent eighteen months in the Scrubs at Her Majesty's pleasure for common assault; Albert's record included a two-year suspended sentence for theft.

Secretly, Will was elated that "the boys" no longer occupied the land of the living. Two less problems for the Devon and Cornwall CID to deal with. Turning his attention back to Shirley, Will reassured her the department was "pulling out all stops" to hunt down the perpetrators.

'Let's hope you catch them before I do.' Shirley began mixing herself a scotch and water from the drinks cabinet. 'I'd offer you one, Will, and your lovely colleague here, but I believe you don't drink on the job. Shame.'

Shirley switched focus onto Mallory. 'I should offer you a job here at KC's, very pretty. Nice, full, mature figure, perfect for our older clientele, especially in latex leather. Done any stripping, my dear? I urgently need a new pole dancer. Don't worry; we can train you.'

Mallory blushed.

'KC's pays very well,' Shirley continued, patting Mallory on the arm. 'More than you pull in pounding the beat, harassing the public for thought crimes.'

'I'm fine doing what I do,' Mallory politely replied.

'Extra money always comes in handy,' Shirley continued. 'Here's my card, should you change your mind.'

Mallory graciously took the card, popping it in her top pocket, with every intention of throwing it in the bin once she got home.

'How's the family down under?' Will asked, placing both hands behind his head.

'Yeah, well thanks, William. Business is booming with Davey at the helm.'

'Shirley's brother is part owner/director of a drug manufacturing company in Sydney,' Will enlightened Mallory. 'Been out there a while now, right, Shirl? What eight years?'

'More like nine.'

'Wow, that long.' Will wasn't a Davey fan, who he described euphemistically as "another rough diamond." Around town, Davey had earned the moniker *Dodgy Dave*, notorious for ruthless business buyouts and corrupt, high-end property developments.

Every copper in Devon was elated when news broke that Davey was migrating to Australia. Will recalled they even had a small celebration in the office one night, after work.

'That was me once,' Will heard Shirley explaining to Mallory. 'Well, I originally graduated as a pharmacist, gave it up when I met my Alfie, God rest his soul. It was Alfie who got me into this line of work, nightclubs. My Alfie was an East End lad. The Copelands dynasty owned clubs in Soho going back to before the war.'

'It made sense for me to go from one drug business to another, if you get my drift. Close your ears, Will; we don't do much dealing nowadays. I'm getting too bloody old for that.'

'Glad to hear it. Now, back to your nephews. I'm sure you have a few ideas who may have murdered them; you see a lot of what goes on in this city. What's the word on the street?'

'I'll flick you a few names,' Shirley intimated, pouring herself another drink. 'Sorry to cut you short, but I've a couple of ladies due in to audition for a position at my new lap dancing bar in Torquay. Afterwards, I'm heading over to see Margo Betteridge and collect the autopsy results on Reg and Albert. And William, before you lecture me that it's unethical, Margo and I go back a long way. She owes me a couple of favours, and I want to collect.'

Will pushed his chair back, rising to his feet. 'Don't tell me these things, Shirley and I'll be none the wiser. We'll see ourselves out.'

Clearly, he'd been drinking; she could smell it on his breath.

For now, he would leave her alone, almost forget she existed, stay slumped in a chair, falling into a deep sleep. When he sobered up, things would be different; that's when his anger would surface, and the violence would commence.

Chapter Two

Flight from London to Sydney. 08:00 hours

'Not long now,' Lana announced to Tom, half dozing in the adjacent pod. 'Quite a pleasant flight so far, not much turbulence; we've been lucky, touch wood.'

'Where are we?' Tom grunted, shifting position and adjusting his eye shields.

Lana checked the graphic on the personal entertainment screen and threw a glance out the window. 'Just crossed over the coast near a place called Broome, officially in Australia. Gee, lots of blue sea, red desert, and, er, empty.'

'Can I get anything for your husband before breakfast is served?' The blonde hostess enquired, coming to stand next to Lana.

Lana, aware of Tom's scowl, immediately turned towards him. 'Darling, this lovely flight attendant wants to know if you'd like a drink.'

'A large gin and tonic.' The scowl remained on Tom's face. 'Plus, some nibbly things. I don't care what.'

'Certainly, sir.' The hostess handed Lana a glass of champagne, already aware of her order.

'Er, if I could have a full bottle, I won't have to disturb you later. I realise you can be rushed off your feet on these long hauls. If it's no bother, of course.'

The flight attendant obliged, reaching for an unopened bottle of French champagne and passing it across to Lana. 'Enjoy.'

'You've some nerve,' Tom commented, once the hostess had departed along the aisle.

'Chill, you need to chill,' Lana instructed, offering Tom a sickly smile. 'Can you really believe it? Here we are, ensconced in business class, an abundance of alcohol, and heading to sunnier climes. What could you possibly have to whinge about?'

'You,' Tom muttered.

'That's not nice. You'll be thanking me, Thomas, once our little tabloid gets the kudos and acknowledgement from the mainstream media for running this Aussie story. Fame and fortune; here we come.'

**

Bovey Tracey, Devon, England
Moorland Forensic Consultants Laboratory

James Sinclair, PhD, placed the unopened pizza boxes on the reception desk, pulling up a few extra chairs. 'Help yourselves, guys; there's white wine in the fridge if anyone fancies a drink; glasses are over there, on the grey filing cabinet.'

A ravenous Katie reached forward, opening one of the boxes, savouring the aroma of a thin crust BBQ chicken.

'Wow, this is a first, bro, holding a team meeting and shouting us all dinner; you must be seriously ill or something.'

'It's my way of welcoming Javier to the business,' James responded. 'If it weren't for our new staff member, the rest of you would be rummaging in the fridge for the mouldy cheese and stale leftovers.'

'Hell's bells, and I'm marrying into this,' Matt jibed, coming to sit next to Katie, reaching for her hand and giving it a gentle squeeze. 'Is it too late to back out?'

'You'll never see him; my brother's always too busy working. He feels personally responsible for Moorlands; it's his baby, has been since day one when he first floated the idea to myself and Fiona ten or so years ago; come on, you know the family background; besides, it's me you're marrying, not him.'

'Thank Christ for that.' Matt laughed.

'Better get started.' James took up position on the side of a vacant desk. 'Javier, don't stand there; help yourself to pizza.'

Hearing the buzzer alert, Katie looked up at the courtyard CCTV, noting the lights of a silver, vintage Mercedes 280SL waiting outside the gates, and pressed open. 'Excellent, here's Nick.'

Nick entered through the main office door, cradling a six pack of beer and a bottle of rosé. 'Shove the beer and wine over there, mate,' James directed. 'The meeting's about to start.'

Nick obliged before removing leather driving gloves and edging closer to the electric heater. 'It's bloody cold out there. Reminds me of growing up in New Zealand, thrashing my uncle's old Morgan Plus 4 around treacherous roads on the high plateau out of Dunedin. The Met's saying snow flurries are 70% probable on the high moors. Take it easy heading back to the farmhouse tonight, Mr Tyler; the roads might be lethal.'

Matt saluted. 'No worries, old boy. Just a leisurely drive around the block for my half cab turbo diesel.'

'What a joke. Here we are freezing to death, and Fiona's basking in warm sunshine, undoubtedly on the golden sands of Bondi Beach or somewhere.' Katie grumbled, a pang of jealousy creeping to the surface. 'Bet she's not regretting that move down under. Some people have all the luck.'

James switched on his smartphone to record the minutes before officially declaring the meeting open. 'First, I would like to officially welcome Dr Javier Quintano to Moorland Forensics; to recap, Javier is originally from the Philippines and grew up in Luzon, right, Javier?'

'Has a B.Sc. from Texas A&M, following that with a Bachelor of Medicine from Tulane. Javier specialised in forensic pathology with extensive hands-on law enforcement experience in Madrid and London. I understand, Javier, you've been on a research grant for the last two years, studying problems associated with the new controversial Messenger RNA "vaccines." I certainly hope you enjoy your time with us in England.'

James paused to sample a pinot grigio. 'Javier is replacing Fiona, who, as Katie just mentioned, has relocated to Australia. For Javier's benefit, I'll introduce the team here tonight: Catherine Sinclair, our forensic psychologist—just call her Katie. Nicholas Shelby, M.D., chief scientist and pathologist, home office forensic services for the southwest.

Don't hold it against him, Javier, but as previously mentioned, Nick is originally from the Shaky Isles, poor sod.'

Nick gave James a firm shove, almost causing him to spill his drink.

James jibed, 'Hey, watch it, mate, this wine was expensive. Then, we have Matthew Tyler, an IT and cyber expert who carries out specialised stuff for the MOD and contracts with Nick and local law enforcement. You'll get to see Matt around here often. MFC also pays for his expertise.'

'What was that? You pay me. That's news,' Matt interrupted jokingly.

James ended the introductions, switching on the digital whiteboard and picking up a laser pointer. 'Currently, we are assisting Nick's department on aspects of forensic evidence surrounding the Copeland homicides. Albert and Reg Copeland, both in their mid-thirties, gunned down at close range at KC's nightclub, near Exeter's central retail district.'

'Dr Margo Betteridge conducted the autopsies, deputising at the last minute for Derek Ingalls, head pathologist at the morgue. I've scheduled a catch-up with Margo for a full report and to find out what support, if any, she needs from MFC.'

'Nick has also been working with me on the death of a young lad in Ivybridge, which could be drug-related. The victim, a member of a bikie gang. Katie, I believe you've been spending time with the boy's parents and siblings, correct?'

Katie nodded. 'This lad came from a well-respected family who had no idea their son belonged to the local branch of the Comancheros. Well-liked within his peer group, it hit everyone hard.'

'Anything else? Matt?'

'I downloaded the hard drive data from the lad's desktop,' Matt responded. 'Trolled through messages, searches, etc. Some useful stuff, which I'll pass on to Will Parker for follow-up.'

James typed into his laptop, then addressed the team again, 'Just got word today, through the grapevine; Lana Gibbs and Tom Markham flew out to Sydney yesterday from Heathrow. For Javier's benefit, Tom's media company owns the local newspaper, the *Newton Abbot Star*.'

'Lana Gibbs is the Star's senior editor. The reason for their sudden departure: two Devon girls were brutally attacked in the Australian outback a few days ago, which I'm sure you're all aware of. It's been broadcast all over the MSM and social media.

These attacks occurred within months of three backpackers, all women, being murdered in Australia. Police task forces in New South Wales and the Federal Police are committing extra resources to the homicides. The media in Australia are really ramping the story up. Tom Markham is hoping to beat the other papers to the inside story, corner some world exclusive interviews, etc.

'I'm liaising with Fiona, who coincidentally happens to be working at the main forensic lab in Sydney and is heavily involved in the backpacker cases, which may be linked to the attack of the two Devon girls. It never hurts to keep abreast of what's going on in other parts of the world. Incidentally, I'm particularly interested in the new technology Fiona has been talking about.'

James retrieved documents from the photocopier tray, handing them around. 'It makes interesting reading and details the extent of these brutal crimes, plus a new DNA analysis algorithm the Aussies are trialling to speed up gene sequencing and hereditary tracing.'

'Well, that about wraps it up for tonight. Tuck in, guys; plenty of nosh. I envisage a very busy few months ahead. It's nice to have you all on board, and once again, Javier, welcome to Moorland Forensics.'

***

Advance Pharmaceuticals/Origan Pharma Inc., Research/Manufacturing Facility Macquarie Park, Sydney, Australia
12 Months Earlier

'Welcome back, Blake. How was the conference in Hawaii?' Janine was ecstatic, her face lighting up the moment the lift doors opened. The last three weeks without Blake around seemed like an eternity.

'Boring.' Blake leaned over the reception desk to give her a brief kiss.

Janine instantly scolded him, 'Not here. Some of the board and division executives from Geneva are around this week, conducting strategy meetings. If they get the slightest hint we're in a relationship, they'll go ballistic; one of us will have to go. Have you forgotten protocols in relation to employees dating? Remember our initial contracts?'

Blake pulled a face. 'Yep, and no questions asked when the managing director turns up pissed most days. Bunch of hypocrites.'

'Well, aren't we lucky he's in Melbourne for the rest of the week? Flew out late last night. Coffee?'

31

'Please.' Blake walked into his office, removing his suit jacket and throwing it over the back of a nearby chair. A few moments later, Janine came in with two coffees, taking a seat opposite Blake's desk.

'Aren't you meant to be manning reception, answering the phone?' He questioned.

Janine placed her mobile onto Blake's desk. 'All taken care of; I've diverted the reception phone to my mobile. We can enjoy a java together. No one else is in yet; they probably won't start arriving for another half hour.'

Blake visibly relaxed.

'So, what's your schedule like for today?' Janine enquired. 'Any chance we can have lunch together?'

'Sorry, I'll be working in the lab all morning. Upper management has scheduled a snap meeting. I'm guessing the preliminary evaluation drug results are back for Miracle Zee. Five years of hard slog, I hope there's positive news.'

'And if it isn't? Can't you still trial the drug, aspire for the best?'

'Too risky.'

Janine snorted. 'I wouldn't put it past Davey; that guy's a devious bastard. He wouldn't care how many lives he destroys in the end; it's all about the big bucks.'

'Nah, even Dodgy Dave has more common sense than to play Russian roulette with people's lives. Apologies, Jan, but I need to press on. Why don't you drop by the flat tonight, say around seven? We can pop to the local Korean BBQ place and grab a bite to eat.'

'Sounds like a plan.'

Janine took her latte back out to reception, quietly shutting Blake's door on her way out. She knew he liked to be by himself before starting work in the lab.

***

Cornwall, England

With the sun now just a faint orange glow in the western sky, Will and Mallory exited the army training facility to be greeted by a frigid force 7 gale and a wind chill factor of -5C, punching in off the Channel.

Tired and ravenously hungry, the two detectives had spent most of the day attending a hands-on, self-defence training refresher in Cornwall. Will hated these types of seminars; at his age, there was little desire or need to start physically taking on burly criminals. He would happily leave any confrontation to the younger recruits, the ones with the appropriate physical attributes.

'Waste of time learning that rubbish,' Will grumbled as the two detectives scanned the carpark for the Jag saloon. 'Since the "powers that be" at the Home Office threw the long-standing physical standards out the door, kowtowing to the destructive DEI woke agenda, the new recruits are going to need more than a band-aid judo course to survive on the street. If I were in charge, every cop would pack a 9mm automatic.'

He unlocked the doors, tossing their backpacks onto the back seat. 'How about a pit stop on our way home, Mal? There's a trendy little pub on the other side of the Tamar Bridge. What do you say we share a meal and a couple of beverages? Had a recent decor makeover; lively atmosphere and a new London chef, I'm told. Be nice to share your company in a setting away from work. What do you say?'

Mallory hesitated; it was almost as if Will was coming on to her, immediately dismissing the idea as ludicrous. She was engaged to Bruce; Will Parker was her boss. Surely sharing an evening meal with a male colleague was permitted.

'Sure, why not. It's been a taxing day. What is it, 5pm, I'm starving. I wouldn't feed that army swill they served up for lunch to my dog.'

'Right, let's go. A night away from the television, in the company of a beautiful woman, what a treat.'

Mallory was confused, a little embarrassed even, subconsciously fiddling with her engagement ring, pretending to consult her diary schedule, hoping the body language wasn't obvious. She liked Will, but she certainly wasn't looking for anything more. She hoped it didn't appear as if she was leading him on. Life was complicated enough without adding to the stress.

***

Sydney, Australia

Fiona dropped the boys off at school close to her apartment in the harbourside suburb of Mosman and then drove into the city, heading west on the M4 to the Forensic Medicine and Coroners Complex at NSW Government Pathology and Health in Lidcombe. She arrived shortly before nine, after battling the usual peak hour traffic snarls on the Harbour Bridge.

Naturally, with the pressure and uncertainty of adapting to a new environment, the creature comforts and relaxed atmosphere of the Moorland Forensic Office back in Bovey Tracey were an occasional source of nostalgic regret.

However, Fiona Sinclair was not about to admit that to anyone. She really wanted her new job and life in Australia to succeed, already settling nicely into the challenging role at the labs. Returning to the UK would signify weakness, a word that didn't exist in her vocabulary.

Fiona's original contract assigned her to work at a major Sydney teaching hospital, but at the last moment, an unexpected vacancy for a relief pathologist became available at the FMCC, securing Fiona a far more interesting position, better suited to her qualifications and experience.

Fiona was equally excited about the prospect of catching up with a few "ex-pats" currently domiciled in Sydney. Harvey Driscoll, for instance. An old friend she had already made contact with, having known Harvey a number of years, originally meeting at the Dart Valley Rifle Club. Fiona herself was an expert marksman, taking first place three years in a row for Practical Shooting and Lever Action, which included Classic Calibre and Open Calibre. She hardly ever missed a target, even out to 500 yards. James and Katie had privately nicknamed her *the Scarecrow*.

Bringing her thoughts back to the present, Fiona entered the cool lab environs, crossing the room to join her colleague, Jacinta Brayer, busy setting up an array of instruments on a stainless-steel trolley.

'What delightful surprises await us today?' Fiona asked, tongue in cheek, unpacking a fresh white lab coat from a sealed packet.

'Twenty-three-year-old German national found lying at the bottom of a canyon in the Blue Mountains. You probably heard about it on the news.' Jacinta continued to set up the trolley. 'Apparently, plenty of physical trauma is evident with this one. DCI Linton Ansley wants to drop by after lunch for a full report.'

'Right, well, time is of the essence; better get into it then,' Fiona advised, donning her coat and other protective gear, noting the time on the dissection room clock. 'Does our victim have a name?'

'Beatriz Bergmeister. Her Aussie friends called her Bea.'

Fiona flicked off a white sheet covering the body, shoving it to one side, glancing down at the young woman's face. 'She's very attractive. How could anyone do this to her?'

'Sick psychos are around every corner; I pray I never run into one,' Jaz acknowledged. 'Linton's a skilled cop; like a dog with a bone, he'll eventually catch the bastard or bastards and lock them away.'

'I hope so.'

'This is the third victim police believe may have been killed by the same person, being dubbed the *Aussie Thrill Killer*,' Jaz enlightened Fiona, adjusting the digital camera. 'Your predecessor, Ross Peterson, conducted the other two autopsies. I can have the files delivered to you this afternoon, if you like.'

'Sure, that would be useful. I've received a brief report from the coroner; ruling on the other victims was by heroin overdose, expect we'll come to a similar conclusion with Beatriz. Right, Jaz, let's get started.'

Fiona started a careful examination of the corpse, chatting as she made discoveries. 'Closely inspecting the ligature marks on her wrists and ankles, I'd conclude our victim was held captive for some time. My conjecture: thick twine or rope. You can see where pieces of fibre have embedded themselves in the skin. Synthetic for sure.'

'Hours, days?' Jaz probed, already impressed by her mentor's outward calm and professional demeanour. Jaz had no inkling that Fiona continually struggled mentally with confronting death, something she had to contend with from a young age. Every autopsy Fiona performed, and homicide attended, required a massive effort of her will.

'Possibly weeks,' Fiona eventually replied, focusing on the marks and indents around both wrists. 'Notice the extensive bruising to the upper body, Jaz; I bet X-rays reveal a few broken ribs. At first sight, you'd have to say the nose is broken in two places; throw into the mix a possible fracture of the left wrist.

Wow, this poor young woman would have suffered a great deal. I certainly hope Linton is as competent as you say he is, Jaz. The "bastard," as you referred to him, who's out there, could possibly strike again. The bloody rampage only ceases when they're caught.'

'Any idea yet what killed her? Are you correct with your overdose theory?'

'There's blunt force trauma to the side of the head,' Fiona stated, pulling back strands of hair from the victim's forehead to expose a deep cut. 'Yet, I'm leaning towards an overdose of some kind. Check out the telltale needle marks on the lower arms. We'll run full drug GC/Mass Spec screens for clarification.'

'I hate to ask, but was our victim raped?'

'From what one can see here now, I would say yes, but again, I need to conduct a thorough examination before I can make that conclusion. Anyway, the lab has scheduled acid phosphatase and DNA analyses for foreign sperm traces.'

Fiona paused to steel herself, taking a couple of deep breaths.

'Now, I'll get you to record all the observations and findings on the tablet, and we'll make this official, shall we? Once the autopsy is completed, there'll be a clearer picture of what happened to this unfortunate young woman, the prospect of bringing some semblance of closure for family and friends.'

Ruth tentatively opened the bathroom door, peering out into the blackened hallway. Immediate thoughts went to her children asleep upstairs, hoping they had not been harmed. Her whole body ached with pain from the recent beating he'd inflicted on her.

For the past hour, she lay curled up on the cold bathroom floor, unable to move. Even now, as she moved across the landing, her efforts to climb the stairs were thwarted with difficulty. It took her over ten minutes to reach the top of the staircase, something which normally took a matter of seconds.

Chapter Three

Sydney CBD, Australia

Harvey entered the air-conditioned corporate office on the penultimate floor, forehead glistening with beads of sweat, pale blue shirt clinging to his broad chest. 'Christ, it's hot outside; must be at least mid to high-thirties. I'm heading straight to the bathrooms to change before I duck out for lunch.'

Brenda stood at the reception desk, arms folded, determination on her face. 'What time do you call this, Harvey? Solomon's been on the phone from Lae since eight, demanding to talk to you. What's up with your mobile? Where have you been?'

Harvey brushed past the Company Secretary, almost nudging her out of the way. 'You're not my mother, nor my keeper, and certainly not my bit on the side anymore, Brenda, so lay off. Fetch us a mineral water, there's a love. I'm dying of thirst, and these temperatures aren't helping.'

Brenda, about to let fly with a cutting remark, quickly decided otherwise, resorting to a scathing look before marching off towards the tearoom. No use inflaming the situation right now; she needed to keep her job, what with the high cost of living and substantial mortgage repayments to find.

Sydney ranked number three on the scale of most expensive cities in the world, provoking Harvey would not earn any kudos, and Brenda didn't need further reminding it was her embarrassing "stuff up" with the quarterly financial updates that had caused Harvey to be curt. She only had herself to blame.

Showered and changed, Harvey retreated to the sanctuary of his office, proceeding to cursor through a new batch of private emails, most from his soon-to-be ex-wife, Rowena, demanding money.

'God, how I despise that woman,' Harvey spoke out loud, needing to vent. 'Well Row, my dearest, it's only a matter of time until you realise you're getting nothing, bitch.'

Brenda barged in with a drinks tray, banging it on the desktop.

'Watch it, stupid woman,' Harvey barked. 'By the way, did you manage to contact Fiona Sinclair and arrange dinner or something?'

'Not yet, maybe later today. Would you like me to contact Colin in the Perth office and find out what time his flight's due back into Sydney?'

'What. No. I spoke with Colin last night; he's staying a tad longer in the west to try and sort out those report headaches you caused with the Stock Exchange. Brenda, you don't need to bother the Chairman; remember, you report directly to me, not Colin.'

Brenda's cheeks coloured. 'At least Colin's civil to me, unlike you. I'd watch yourself, Harvey; when you climb to great heights, you have further to fall.'

'Are you threatening me?'

'No, just stating the obvious. Now, if there's nothing else, I'm taking an early lunch and won't be back until two. I'm owed the time.'

Watching an angry Brenda storm down the corridor, Harvey leaned back in his chair, starting to drift off. He wished someone would do everybody a favour: make Brenda disappear. On several levels, she was becoming more than annoying.

Forcing himself to wake up, Harvey retrieved his personal mobile, toying with it for several minutes before finally sending an SMS. After five minutes, the mobile vibrated with an incoming call. 'What's up, bro?'

'Ryder, hi, it's Harvey. Thanks for calling back on WhatsApp. Is everything sorted? Do you think we can pull this thing off?'

Ryder's deep guffaw resonated down the line. 'Sure, it's easy; relax, dude. Everything's going according to Hoyle; we're on our way to freedom.'

'Bloody hope so. I can't take much more of this stress. I've debts coming out of my arse.'

'Just stick it out for a few more weeks, man, and we'll be off.' Calm authority in Ryder's words. 'Chill, relish the Aussie sunshine.'

'We've gone through everything with a microscope, vetted all the possibilities, but what if something goes wrong?'

At the other end of the line, Ryder's bushy eyebrows rose. Feet up on a desk, he opened another can of beer. 'What is it with you Brit types, always flapping? Bunch of penguins. Thank God I'm from the good ol' Lone Star State. Not much fazes us, like it does you guys. I'm ex-Air Force remember? Every detail is planned with military precision; all you need to do is turn up on the day, and I'll take care of the rest. Now, go do some work or get back to whatever else is occupying your time down there in the office. Leave me in peace; we'll talk again soon.'

The line went dead. Harvey pocketed the phone and swivelled slowly around, taking in the magnificent panorama through the 15th level window. The iconic Art Deco Bridge and Opera House sails; the largest deep-water harbour in the world, sparkling blue, revelling in a traditional Sydney nor'easter.

Far to the west, ominous black cumulus thunderheads were building over the Blue Mountains. Within a matter of hours, a violent maelstrom of lightning and hail would bear down on Sydney suburbs, sweeping through the City and Harbour and out to sea, its fury finally spent. Par for the course on a sweltering Sydney summer's day.

Exiting the lift on the basement carpark level and walking to his car, stark reality started to sink in for Harvey. There could be no turning back; the dye was cast. Harvey and the team had no choice but to trust Ryder and his experience. If he allowed too many emotions to surface, it could jeopardise the entire operation.

***

Advance Pharmaceuticals/Origan Pharma Inc.,
Sydney, Australia
12 months earlier

Blake Carleton shut down the desktop, removed thick reading glasses, slowly massaging sore temples. Time to go home, but first, the long-awaited briefing for the new breakthrough cancer drug, code-named "Miracle Zee".

Blake's entire day had been spent in the lab, running through the latest pharmacological data spreadsheets with his technicians, including skipping lunch, leaving little opportunity to collar a Director and maybe get the inside on the latest trial feedback decision from the Pharmaceutical Board.

Slowly descending the staircase to the floor below, Blake dubiously entered the boardroom, clearly the first to arrive. Sitting down, he looked out across the featureless business park and beyond to the traffic streaming towards the city on the M2 Motorway, his vision momentarily distracted by the first raindrops, splashing against the window from a late afternoon thunderstorm. His expression was blank.

What if they had fallen at the last hurdle? What if all those years of hard work were down the drain, with no payday at the end, precipitating a bleak future for many people? For Blake, it wasn't about the money; it was about finding a cure for cancer.

Five minutes later, Danilo and Warren strolled in, both wearing huge grins, brandishing two Magnums of French champagne. Janine and several other employees followed with flutes and plates of snacks.

'We did it, Marvel Man.' Danilo slapped Blake firmly on the back. 'Miracle Zee is provisionally approved for initial administration trials to a select group of cancer patients, starting in two weeks. You should be immensely proud of yourself.'

Blake looked stunned. 'Wow, I was hoping this might be the outcome; admittedly, I had my doubts. Gee, and here was me thinking they would come back with a load of queries: breathing issues, other side effects. Our lab rat tests weren't always fully—'

'Relax, old boy, get yourself a glass of the good stuff. This is a top day for one and all, especially Origan Pharma. Now, drink up; it's time to celebrate.'

***

Devon, England

Dr Margo Betteridge, FRCP, looked up in surprise as James Sinclair and Will Parker entered her office, James wielding an assorted bunch of colourful roses.

'For you.' James handed over the flowers.

Margo's look of surprise continued. 'It's not my birthday. What are these for?'

'Friendship.' James removed a pile of laboratory reports off the only available chair, creating room to sit down. 'We've both been through a lot lately, and I feel it's important to remember those you hold dear.'

Margo burst out laughing, removing a large graduated cylinder from the shelf, filling it with water before adding the roses, and positioning the "vase" on her desk. 'Jim Sinclair, you're turning into an old softie. These flowers are magnificent. Now, I reckon this is no social call; are you wanting to rack my rusty neurones over something?'

'I never could completely pull the wool over your eyes.' James smiled. 'Firstly, it *is* a social call. I wanted to see how you're doing. And how *are* you doing?'

'Not bad. I miss Myles more than you can imagine, but what's the use locking oneself away, wallowing in self-pity? Life is meant to be enjoyed. As a result, I've decided to relocate out of Loddiswell; the house holds too many memories.'

I've found a lovely little cottage in a village on the other side of Kingsbridge that will do nicely; West something or other, on the estuary. I'm also tempted to purchase one of those high-end campervans and take myself off to see the British Isles before old age and senility set in.'

'That'll never happen.' James chortled. 'Old, you will be one day, but senile, never. You have one of the sharpest minds around. Now, what in blazes happened to the boat we inspected down at the Salcombe Marina? The 32-footer you put a holding deposit on, pending a marine survey.''

'Damn beautiful lines, if you ask me. Don't disappoint, Margo; I've been devouring YouTube sailing videos, practicing for the warmer weather. You promised we could take it over to Brittany next summer, even a few races along the coast thrown in.'

'Yes, I needed some time to think about that one. The owner's in no rush to sell. He's taken it off the market till I decide either way. However, if you're that committed, why not? I'll take another look at the boat next week.'

'Now you're talking.'

'You always were the ultimate charmer, Jim Sinclair.' Margo beamed. 'Now, before you gentlemen bombard me with a load of questions, which I believe you're about to do, how are Katie and Fiona? I want all the gossip. Myles was fond of those girls and would never forgive me if I didn't ask. I also want the latest on young Jason; bet he's growing up fast.'

James relayed the latest news on his sisters and son, genuinely pleased to be in Margo's company. He fondly recalled her steadfast mentoring during his early days as a biochemistry PhD student, later as a tyro forensic scientist and loyal friend.

'Well, it's about time Katie tied the knot,' Margo announced. 'Matthew Tyler's a decent young man. I'm not so keen on Fiona taking the plunge and relocating to Australia. It's a long way; you must all miss her terribly.'

'It's early days. We've been mega busy, to be truthful. Javier Quintana has taken her place on a temporary basis. Are you acquainted with Javier's background?'

Margo appeared deep in thought. 'Yes, I do believe we've met at the occasional virology seminar. Has an interest in vaccine syntheses, am I right? One of the leading whistle-blowers calling out the new, dangerous Messenger RNA "vaccines" proliferation and the worldwide harm resulting. They're not really vaccines; "gene therapies" would be a better description.'

'Spot on. See, there's nothing wrong with the old grey matter, Margo.'

Margo's infectious laughter filled the room once more. 'Having you drop by, James, is a breath of fresh air. Too often the loneliness gets to me; cooped up in this hospital science lab surrounded by colleagues, but not real friends. Also, that business with Gareth took the wind out of me. Can you believe it? Right under my nose and never in a thousand years would I have thought him to be a serial killer. My usual instincts about people must be slipping.'

Will Parker, who had been standing quietly for some time, casually taking in the scientific equipment spread around Margo's lab office, elected to speak, 'No one could have predicted that one, Margo. Gareth hid it well; most killers do.'

'Well, it still astounds me to think I quite liked the chap. In the future, I must choose my employees more carefully. Now, with all the news out of the way, how can I assist you fellas today?'

'Do you have anything more for us on the Copeland homicides going back a few months?' Will questioned Margo. 'We know the cause of death for both victims resulted from gunshot wounds. What sort of—?'

Margo stopped him mid-sentence, raising both hands in the air. 'Er, no, that was not the case, Will. How did you arrive at that conclusion?'

Will and James exchanged puzzled looks across the room. 'That's the message I received on my mobile from DCI Wallis,' Will enlightened Margo. 'I didn't get a proper handover from that clown, just a few cryptic messages; Wallis went off on extended sick leave shortly before I returned to work.'

'Well, what a surprise. That explains why no proper follow-up was initiated and the coroner shelved the inquiry.' Margo looked annoyed. 'I requested Wallis get in touch, but I never heard a dickie bird. Right then, let's get this straight, so you're aware of my conclusions: both victims were already dead when they were shot.'

Will Parker stared at Margo. 'I don't understand. Then, what *did* cause their deaths?'

'Plant toxins,' Margo proudly announced. 'No doubt about it. I ran the tests myself back here at the hospital with the help of my tech officers. Took a long time to find what I was looking for, but we got unequivocal confirmation in the end, thanks to Nick Shelby's Liquid Chromatograph/Mass Spectrometer screens over at the Forensic Centre.'

Margo stood up and marched triumphantly over to a tall, three-drawer, combination filing cabinet. Once unlocked, she pulled open the top drawer to retrieve a slim grey file, which she handed to Will, before regaining her seat.

With Will lost for words, Margo continued, 'That Wallis imposter was an absolute goose, Will. I have no idea why he was assigned the role during your absence. He cut corners, made spur-of-the-moment decisions, and never read through files or reports. Thank heavens he's retreated back to London and the bad joke known as the Met. They deserve each other, and thankfully, we've got you.'

'What plant toxins are we referring to?' James interrupted, looking over the DCI's shoulder, curious to check out the file contents for himself.

'Ah, this is where it gets interesting,' Margo answered. 'It's our old friend from the mists of antiquity, hemlock, scientific name Conium maculatum L. Significant amounts were detected in the victims' stomach contents, easily sufficient to kill them both in a horrible way. Doubtless they would have suffered agonising deaths.'

Margo paused for a few moments, savouring the stunned looks on her guests' faces.

'Crushing the leaves releases a distinctive repellent odour. My theory: the hemlock was blended into a quiche; this was the last meal they ate. It would not have been noticed, the presence probably disguised by parsley and other herbs in the meal,' Margo continued.

'You'd both be aware hemlock was the plant allegedly given to the Greek philosopher, Socrates, at his execution. The toxins in hemlock are alkaloids, including coniine and gamma-coniceine, a class of chemicals known as choline esterase inhibitors, which cause muscular paralysis, leading to respiratory failure and eventually, death.

'All these tie in nicely with my findings after conducting the autopsies. Only a tiny amount of hemlock can prove fatal to a human or livestock. We're talking blood concentrations as low as 1 microgram/ml. I envisage both the Copelands collapsing, immediately followed by death.'

'Jesus Christ, not what I was expecting to hear,' Will announced. 'Frankly, I was convinced they were just gunned down, execution style.'

'Oh, they were shot alright, but definitely not until after death. Of course, you'll want Roger Tudor's boys to run an expert eye over the ballistic evidence,' Margo acknowledged. 'Nevertheless, I think you'll find he'll be in agreement with me; the Copeland brothers didn't die from gunshot wounds.'

Usually, he lashed out with his fists, but last night was different; he opted for the leg of a wooden chair. From the three-minute beating, her entire body ached, the blows delivered with such force, she could barely walk.

She wanted to get away, but how? Where would she go? There were two young children to think about. Any attempt to escape would be fraught with danger. He would drag them back into his clutches; things would get so much worse.

Chapter Four

Advance Pharmaceuticals/Origan Pharma Inc.,
Sydney, Australia
12 months earlier

Danilo and Warren left the boardroom, striding purposefully down the corridor to enter a vacant lift, grateful to be free from the noisy group still celebrating the news and enjoying the last of the refreshments.

'That went well,' Danilo remarked, pushing the button for the basement carpark. 'Blake is none the wiser. He believes any "issues" with Miracle Zee are no longer a cause for concern.'

'Yeah, until people start getting seriously ill.' Warren sighed. 'What then?'

'Davey's covered all bases, including "fine-tuning" the test results data for the licence approvals; stop stressing, Dan. Advance has too much power and influence. The important thing is to finish off the pre-production program schedules, get the drug out there and start pulling in the big bucks. It's been a long day. Want a lift to the station?'

***

Devon, England

James lay back on the bed, idly watching a sensually slim, naked Sofia search for silk underwear discarded haphazardly around his Indio Road duplex bedroom. 'Come on, you don't have to leave; my watch says it's only seven.'

Throwing on a red jumper, Sofia threw back her hair, tying it in a ponytail, before reaching for black stretch jeans. 'I'll be back tonight. Besides, you've got work, and Jason will wake up soon.'

James, feeling himself harden, threw Sofia back down onto the bed, giving her a tender kiss. When their lips finally parted, he leaned on one elbow, studying her fine features. 'We're going to have to tell them eventually.'

'Yeah, but not now, James, please. I'm still adjusting to the idea myself. It's not the right time to share our news with anyone.'

***

Devon, England

Javier, dozing head down on the laboratory bench, woke with a start to the piercing alert emanating from the ICP/Atomic Emission Spectrograph, not sure where he was, momentarily disoriented. Stretching across, he switched off the sample run programmer.

Quickly checking the digital and hard copy chart recorders and satisfied with the elemental results, he initiated a systematic shutdown protocol of the instrumentation; a routine check on the heavy metal impurities in China clay samples for a local miner was not really his thing, but Javier accepted it as part and parcel of the role at Moorland Forensics. As long as there was forensic pathology work at MFC to indulge his passion, everything was right with the world.

The lab clock showing just after midnight, Javier rose slowly off the stool, calf muscles protesting, a hectic workday hitting home. One more job: set up a liquid chromatograph run for James; something to do with anabolic steroid checks on urine samples for a high-profile athlete defence submission, apparently.

Thankfully, it was agreed that for the time being, Javier would bunk down in the upstairs living quarters of the Moorland complex until suitable accommodation turned up, meaning he only needed to climb the stairs and collapse into bed.

He'd viewed a few places within the past week, either too small or in the wrong location. He needed somewhere with a garden for two Keeshonds to run around. Sam and Ella would not be impressed being stuck inside all day. Javier, having been lumbered with the dogs at the last moment, added complication. With the breakup imminent, he'd been forced to sell the Teignmouth property, allowing Wendy to temporarily relocate to Carlisle, attending an ailing mother.

Whilst exiting the laboratory through the airlock, Javier's mobile vibrated, and he was intrigued who could be ringing so late, then realising it was probably a midday call from Australia. Picking up, his heart sank. Whenever Blake phoned, in lieu of emailing, it usually meant something was wrong.

'Hey, slow down,' Javier instructed, hearing Blake's voice racing from the other end.

Once Blake seemed more composed, Javier was able to listen, then provide information and instructions.

'Once they are well enough, Lisa and Christina need to get out of the country,' Javier directed. 'It's vital they get right away from Sydney.'

'Naturally, but they're insisting on returning to the UK; isn't that just as dangerous?' Panic was rising in Blake's tone.

Javier gave a sigh. 'Blake, hear what I say: nowhere will be safe for those young women with Origan on to them. The main focus; to ensure you and I aren't implicated in any of this, or they'll be chasing us next, and in all honesty, we need more time to sort this out and obtain all the facts to bring matters out into the open. A few more weeks maximum and we'll be done.'

'Time we probably haven't got,' Blake concluded. 'I eavesdropped on a conversation today between the head honcho and his sister; they are edging closer to finding out the truth.'

'Then we need to ramp it up, hurry things along, and expose them for what they've done before they strike again, killing more innocent people,' Javier replied. 'Do whatever you can to retrieve that vital bit of information, Blake, but don't get caught. Whoever has that USB is in the driving seat; it's vital we take back control.'

'What if Lisa or Christina has the USB, then what?' Javier questioned.

'That's something you'd better find out, Blake. Sorry man, it's late; I'm tired. We'll talk again soon, I promise.'

***

Sydney, Australia

Fiona took the lift up to her seventh-floor Mosman apartment, shattered after a long day. Right on cue, her stomach protested, the delayed effects of working through lunch, her last "meal," a Mars Bar at 2pm, now a distant memory. The boys were staying the night with friends; thankfully, she could whip up something simple, run a hot bath, and collapse into bed.

Exiting the lift, she collided with a woman rushing along the corridor, carrying a large cardboard box.

'Sorry, my fault,' the woman apologised. 'Can't see much over this damn thing.'

'No problem,' Fiona answered, about to turn and head towards her apartment.

'Hayley Parsons.' The woman placed the box on the ground, extending her right arm. 'We're in apartment seven; by *we*, I'm referring to my better half, Jordan. I've caught glimpses of you from time to time; you've got the twin boys, am I right?'

'Fiona Sinclair.' Fiona shook Hayley's hand. 'Yes, for my sins, I have two teenage boys, who were very cute once.'

'We're trying for a family,' Hayley gushed. 'Jordan's forty-four, I'm thirty-one, so we need to get a wriggle on. The trouble is, both of us are so busy with work. Sorry, I'm harping on; Jordan complains I talk too much.'

Fiona forced a weak smile, only half listening, her mind on possible dinner options. 'It's the quiet ones you need to worry about.'

Hayley grinned. 'So, I've heard. And what do you do, Fiona? It can't be easy holding down a full-time job with two teenage boys. I often see you driving off most mornings, I assume to go to work.'

'I'm a forensic pathologist attached to the government Lidcombe laboratory.' Fiona, briefly studying Hayley in more detail, was captivated by her striking features. Endowed with dark brown eyes, high cheekbones, and long auburn hair, Fiona calculated Hayley could easily work as a model, doubly blessed with above-average height and a trim, athletic figure.

Hayley pulled a face. 'Ooh, dead bodies and that kind of stuff. You're a medico then. Don't think I'd have the stomach for that. I work part-time for a real estate agent in Darlinghurst; Jordan's a teacher. Do I detect an English accent, Fiona? You don't sound Aussie.'

'Yep, from the south of England. I've only been here a few months, but I'm loving it so far.'

'You must come over to dinner one night,' Hayley offered. 'Do you have a bloke? You can bring him too, if you like.'

Once more, Fiona smiled. Hayley's direct manner was a little unsettling. 'I have a boyfriend over in Japan at the moment, umm, I have a close male friend here in Sydney. Thanks for the invite; I'm sure Harvey would love to join us for dinner.'

'I'll check my diary and get back to you. Jordan and I tend to travel a lot, but I'm sure we can work something out.'

'Apologies, I've not eaten much all day. I need to fix myself a toasted sandwich.'

'Ah, the old toastie, can't go wrong with one of them. Nice to have met you, Fiona Sinclair, forensic pathologist.'

'Likewise.'

Watching Hayley disappear around a corner to the lift, providing access to the gym and ground-level swimming pool, Fiona swiftly unlocked the door to her apartment. Without delay, she retrieved the sandwich maker from a kitchen drawer, proceeding to whip up a toasted ham, cheese, and tomato sandwich. She then sank into the sofa with a large glass of chilled chardonnay, luxuriating in the peace and quiet.

After placing her dirty plate in the dishwasher, Fiona topped up her wine glass, then, on the spur of the moment, retrieved the laptop from her work bag, despite common sense telling her to head off to bed for an early night. Settling back into the lounge, Fiona logged into the server, bringing up the post-mortem reports on the two backpackers, which Jacinta had emailed across that afternoon, Fiona's curiosity getting the better of her.

The pathologist's conclusions read exactly as expected: Renata Fabrizio and Astrid Johansson met the same tragic ending as Beatriz Bergmeister. All three women were raped repeatedly, bashed, and tied up for lengthy periods of time, eventually having been administered lethal doses of heroin.

The backpacker homicides were now attracting attention from the international media, and Fiona found herself, by some bizarre twist of fate, suddenly thrown slap bang into the middle of it. Here was the golden opportunity not only to make her mark and cement the start of her new life down under but also, possibly, at the same time, help bring to account the perpetrators of these heinous acts.

Fiona reached for her mobile phone, putting a call through to her sister back in England. She tried a couple of times, but it always went through to Katie's voicemail. Eventually Fiona left a message:

Katie, it's me, your big sister. I'd like you to take a look at the autopsy results from all three backpacker victims. The ones in the news. I'll flick them over in an email marked highly confidential. Can you work up a profile for me on the killer?

These murders are particularly brutal. I could use your expertise to figure out what might be going through the killer's head. I'm in regular contact with the DCI working the case and am sure he'd be interested in your findings. Thanks, and chat soon.

Fiona eased out of her chair, about to head into the master bedroom when there was a firm knock at the door, a primeval adrenaline surge triggering.

'Who is it?' Fiona wasn't about to open the door to anyone.

'Hayley, your neighbour, sorry, won't stop. I have something for you.'

Fiona opened the door to be greeted by a smiling Hayley, producing a gift-wrapped box.

'Me again. A welcome present,' Hayley announced, hair still wet from a dip in the pool. 'You must get homesick from time to time; I find chocolates always fill a void.'

'Thanks, that's very sweet of you. Would you like to come in?'

'Nah, thanks all the same, but I'm about to serve up a casserole. Jordan just arrived home, delayed at work. I'll check my diary tonight; we can set a date for that dinner party. Night, Fiona, and welcome to Oz.'

Fiona closed the door, walking back into a spacious but uninviting lounge room, empty save for a small oak occasional table and second-hand settee, purchased at the local St Vincent's charity shop the day she moved in with the kids. No big deal.

She could handle it, knowing the container with her cherished furniture and collectables was due to arrive from England in a few days. Mostly, she missed her vintage hi-fi system and classic jazz LP collection. It wasn't the same listening to digitally encrypted music fed through a download streaming service.

So far, everyone Fiona had met in the apartment building appeared friendly. The older man in number nine seemed nice; the Greek woman in number three always waved a hello, making Hayley feel welcome. What a stroke of luck. Normal neighbours.

By contrast, Fiona's neighbours back in Devon had been odd: one side a couple in their seventies who often embarked on bizarre nighttime rituals, and across the street, a noisy couple with six screaming kids. Fiona was settling seamlessly into the Aussie way of life; memories as part of the Moorland Forensic team fading fast.

***

Devon, England

Will picked up the phone at the third ring, instantly recognising Shirley Copeland's grating Essex accent on the other end.

'Hemlock, of all the fucking ludicrous ideas. I want the mongrels found, Will. I won't stop nagging until the arseholes are locked away in Wormwood Scrubs.'

'You spoke with Margo then?' Will surmised correctly.

'Damn right I spoke with Margo; I needed facts. You lot take ages providing families with the information they need to grieve and move on; slow as a wet week, as my Queensland aunt would say. Anyway, those responsible for the death of my nephews need to be caught and punished. I won't rest, Will, until you get results.'

'Yep, I thought as much.' Will sighed softly, flashing coloured lights heralding the inevitable start of a migraine. 'I'm working on it, Shirley; these things take time.'

'*Time*, you don't need bloody *time*.' Shirley scoffed. 'What you need, my friend, is for you and your team to get off your fat backsides and track down the killer; that, or you'll all be feeling the heat down there at CID when I have a quiet word with Stu Manning next time he pops in to KC's. *Time, my arse*, that's just an excuse. Now, years ago, a proper detective worth his salt—'

Will hung up, heart rate elevated, massaging his neck, desperately scouring his desk drawers for codeine tablets. What he'd give to still be on leave, away from all the drama.

Ruth couldn't remember when the abuse first started; for so long, it seemed part of her very existence. If a few days went by without him either yelling abuse or lashing out, she began to think something was wrong. The only reason she didn't give up living was for her children, who were now at an age to understand what was happening.

Sometimes, Nick would try to ward off his father, but that only fuelled the man's temper. Ruth begged Nick not to get involved; she needed him to stay safe, out of harm's way.

Chapter Five

Lana hovered around in the hospital corridor, waiting for Trudie to finish her shift.

'I shouldn't be talking to you,' Trudie grumbled, swiftly ushering Lana towards a side exit and down a flight of fire stairs. 'If anyone finds out, I'll lose my job.'

'That won't happen,' Lana reassured, passing over a takeaway cappuccino. 'Now, come on, spill the beans.'

Trudie led them outside into blinding mid-afternoon sunshine, across the road towards a playing field attached to the nearby university colleges where a noisy, girls' softball game was in progress. Sitting down on a bench, out of earshot of passersby, Trudie briefed Lana on what she knew.

'Christina was discharged early this morning; I assisted her to the taxi. She sustained three rib fractures, a broken nose, and a superficial break to the left forearm. Heaps of bruises all over; anyway, she'll be fine. Lisa, on the other hand, ended up with four fractured ribs, a dislocated shoulder, a broken jaw, plus damage to her spleen. She's undergone surgery, doing well considering there was a lot of internal bleeding. I believe Lisa's due for discharge in a couple of days.'

'Very lucky girl. Thanks for this update; you're an angel. Look, I don't suppose you've heard what's going down with the police investigation?'

'Nope, nothing of actual substance,' Trudie confessed. 'There are two uniformed officers stationed outside the ward, but the cops aren't saying much, even among themselves. I've been listening to the news and speculation on social media; many believe these attacks are linked to the backpacker murders; I'm not so sure.'

'Really, why?'

'Oh, I dunno. The person who killed the backpackers has never simultaneously attacked two victims before; this is a first.'

'There must be a valid reason for the media to reach this conclusion,' Lana continued. 'The police must have more than they're admitting, perhaps not yet ready to make their findings public.'

Trudie shrugged. 'Maybe. Sorry, I must be off. Got to pick the kids up from school.'

Lana pulled a wad of dollar notes from her jacket pocket, handing them to Trudie. 'Here, this will help with your new car repayments; you don't earn enough as it is.'

'No, you're fine. Next time we catch up, you can shout drinks.'

Trudie disappeared across the oval, leaving Lana to repocket the money before heading back to the hospital. She located Tom in the main foyer, trying to work out how the coffee maker worked.

'Damn contraption doesn't want to cooperate,' Tom grumbled, frantically punching a few buttons.

Lana took coins from her jeans, programmed in a large latte, and watched the machine whirl smoothly into action, eventually producing a hot latte. She passed it to Tom. 'It's not what you do; it's the way that you do it. Have I taught you nothing over the years?'

***

Devon, England

'The trouble with you, Desmond, is you can't keep your bloody mouth shut.' Shirley fumed, pointing a bony forefinger at the pimple-faced youth busy stacking glasses in the dishwasher behind the bar. 'You're here to do a job, Des, not make friends with all and sundry, and don't for one moment think I'm in the dark about the drugs. Lucky for you, our buyer can hang off for a second batch. What do you take me for, an idiot?'

Desmond reeled back, dropping a glass on the tiled floor in momentary panic. He didn't bank on Shirley twigging he was the culprit who had helped himself to the secret fentanyl stash in the storeroom vault, hoping she'd partition blame to one of the security guards.

In the future, he needed to be more circumspect; he couldn't afford to be complacent. Shirley Copeland was dangerous; even her own family wasn't safe around her.

Shirley's features softened; the tone of her voice lightening. 'It's fine, Des, we need each other right now. We're mates, remember. Tell you what; flick the kettle on and we'll discuss an important job I've got for you, a nice little earner. Then, when that's done, you can piss off, and I never want to set eyes on you again.'

***

Police Media Press Conference
Rosehill Racecourse, Sydney, Australia
One Week Later

Lana Gibbs and Tom Markham arrived an hour before the scheduled press conference, securing chairs in the third row of the spacious convention room, affording an uninterrupted close-up view of the conference table, positioned on a raised platform.

Christina and Lisa arrived half an hour later, escorted to their seats by a senior police officer. Lisa sat next to her mother, who'd jetted in from the Costa del Sol only hours earlier. The woman was clearly stressed, clutching tightly to her daughter's hand. Christina's grandparents, sole guardians following the tragic plane crash claiming her parent's lives, were not due to arrive in Sydney for several days.

At precisely 11 am, DCI Linton Ansley, the lead detective in charge of the case, entered the large, noisy auditorium, now crammed to capacity with an eclectic mix of reporters, ghoulish members of the public, and other assorted types with a vested interest in proceedings.

Ansley, bearing the physique and craggy features of one you would say probably played representative rugby in his youth, led out an entourage, including the minister of police, clearing a way through the media scrum, mounting the temporary stairs, and settling in behind the podium table.

Following a quick sound check, with microphones alive, the DCI introduced himself to a sea of expectant faces and cameras. 'At the outset, can I say a quick thank you to everyone for coming today. We feel it necessary to hold this press conference in the hope it will assist us in tracking down those responsible for the brutal attacks on these two innocent women. The trauma they have suffered is unfathomable.'

'Both women arrived in Australia nearly a year ago, looking for new experiences, to travel through this beautiful land, and sample its unique diversity and rich culture. It saddens me, and I am sure all of you as well, by the way they have been treated and the message this crime must send to the rest of the world.'

Australia is normally a safe place to visit, a country to be proud of. Everyone should be allowed to live in a safe, happy environment, free from violence. At the conclusion of this conference, we'll allow time for general questions, but first, Lisa Marshall would like to read a victim statement.'

Lisa remained seated, behind the table, avoiding eye contact with everyone in the room, instead looking down at a carefully prepared monologue. She pulled in a mic and cleared her throat.

'Firstly, Christina and I would like to thank everyone for helping us, too many people to mention, but a special thank you to Conrad, the truck driver who came to our aid when we were lying injured in the remote Australian bush. A huge appreciation for the efforts of the doctors and nurses who cared for us while we were in the hospital, and to the dedicated police force who are working tirelessly to apprehend the persons responsible.'

She stopped to take a sip of water, her hand visibly shaking. Her speech slow and deliberate, breathing laboured; the effects of broken ribs, not fully healed, plain to see.

'What Chrissy and I endured, no one should ever go through. We came to Australia to have fun, experience a new way of life, and make friends. Instead, we found ourselves in a horrible situation, fearing for our lives.'

'We didn't realise what was happening to us until it was too late. When we saw the car broken down by the side of the road, our immediate thoughts were to stop and help. I was driving and got out to investigate. The next thing I remember was seeing Christina being dragged from the car, hearing her blood-curdling screams. The rest is a blur as we were both knocked unconscious.'

We urge anyone travelling along that particular stretch of highway, on the day of our attack, to please come forward if you noticed anything unusual that could assist the police with their investigation. Chrissy and I were the lucky ones; Astrid Johannson, Renata Fabrizio, and Beatriz Bergmeister were not so lucky.'

Lisa's voice began to falter as she continued reading from the prepared script, 'Somewhere, out there, is a monster who needs to be caught before he or she kills again. Thank you.'

Lisa sat back down, her mother leaning in, giving her daughter a gentle hug with a few quiet words of praise, before the journalists in the room erupted with an unscheduled barrage of questions.

The moderator pointed to a female journalist from the *Independent*, seated in the front row. 'Did you ever meet the other victims, Lisa?'

'No, but we were well acquainted with what happened to them. Travellers in Australia have strong connections; we try and look out for each other.'

A mature woman in the second row raised her hand to indicate she was about to speak. 'Anita Dorfman, *German National Paper*. Forgive me for being blunt, but Lisa, why do you think you and Christina were not sexually abused by your attackers? The three other victims were raped before being murdered; why do you believe your attack was different?'

Lisa took a deep breath, wincing from the stabbing pain of a strapped ribcage. 'As I said before, we were the lucky ones. Perhaps our attackers were scared off; who knows?'

'Huh, in the middle of nowhere in the Aussie bush, very unlikely,' Lana whispered to Tom, who responded with a sharp elbow in her side.

Getting the nod, a male reporter from a major New Zealand radio network stood up in the seventh row, announcing himself as Fergus McDonald. 'Did you see your attackers, Lisa? Are you able to say if they were definitely male? Did they say anything?'

'They didn't speak; they wore grey balaclavas. I'm positive of that. Everything took place in a split second; it was only moments before we were lying on the ground with those horrible injuries.'

'Any idea how many attackers?' McDonald probed.

'At least three, maybe as many as five.'

'Definitely lying,' Lana whispered to Tom. 'The body language and eye movement; obvious giveaways. I think she *knew* or recognised her attackers but isn't saying.'

Tom once more dug Lana sharply in the ribs, irritated by her ongoing commentary. He was intrigued by the press conference, eager to listen and form his own opinions, not be swayed by anything Lana had to say.

'Can you recall the type of car the assailants were driving?' McDonald asked.

Lisa looked flustered. 'Not really. We've already told the police it was a four-wheel drive of sorts, dark in colour.'

'That's enough questions,' DCI Linton Ansley announced, standing up. 'We urge you all to please respect Lisa and Christina's privacy during this difficult time. These brave young women have been through a tough ordeal; they need time to rest.'

'Do you have any plans to return to the UK, back to Devon?' Lana piped up, shouting above the throng to be heard.

Christina glanced in Lana's direction. 'Lisa and I anticipate being back in England by the end of the month.'

A plainclothes detective ushered Christina and Lisa through a back exit to a waiting car. The media conference continued for another thirty minutes with statements from Ansley and the minister providing an update on the police investigation.

Everyone seemed to disperse from the room at once, creating havoc. Lana stepped to one side, almost treading on the foot of a male journalist with a lanyard around his neck indicating an employee of *News Corp*.

'Sorry,' Lana muttered, glancing up into large pale blue eyes, the property of a young man with a mass of blonde curly hair, a tanned complexion, and the alluring physique of an "ironman." Lana blushed, taken aback by the surprise encounter.

'No need to apologise; I'm Spen Evans.' He held out his hand for Lana to shake.

'Lana Gibbs.' She accepted the handshake, still captivated by the blue eyes.

'English, one presumes. The accent's a dead giveaway.'

'Yes, my colleague and I are from the same area as Lisa and Christina, Devon, in the south.'

'Lovely, unspoiled piece of England. Been there a couple of times. So, tell me, Lana Gibbs, what do you make of these shenanigans?'

'Er, I don't quite follow.' Lana proceeded with Spen towards the exit doors, Tom fighting through the throng to keep up.

'Seems to me these women are drawing their own conclusions their attack is linked to the murders of those other women,' Spen explained, halting briefly to allow Lana to inch through the doors first.

'Oh my God, that's what I was thinking!' Lana exclaimed, excitement in her voice.

'Or it could simply be the police know there's a connection, but they're not ready to divulge that piece of information at this point in time,' Tom butted in, taking an instant dislike to Lana's new friend, with the fake smile and handsome features. 'Has that thought not crossed your mind, Lana? The police have already interrogated Lisa and Christina closely, discussing things the rest of us are not privy to.'

Lana deliberately turned her back on Tom, once more addressing Spen as they shifted out into the bright sunlight flooding the racecourse concourse. 'We could discuss this over a drink, Spen, if you have time, of course. I'd love to hear your take on things.'

'Sure, why not. You joining us, mate?' Spen glanced over at Tom standing nearby, wearing a moody, disinterested expression.

Inside, Tom seethed, trying to hide rising anger. 'No thanks. I'll grab a lift back to the hotel, rest for a while, and recover from jet lag, I reckon. Catch you later, Gibbs.'

Exiting their taxi at one end of George Street in the CBD, Spen led Lana to a popular bar and restaurant on the sidewalk in the Rocks. Once inside the air-conditioned space, patronised by a vibrant lunchtime mix of animated, excited tourists planning an exploration of Circular Quay and business clientele luxuriating in a brief break from the tedium of the office, Spen turned and smiled.

'What would you like to drink, Lana? I can recommend the Tasmanian pinot dry white, grown and bottled at a friend's vineyard near Hobart. Light, tonnes of flavour.'

'No kidding. Sounds awesome.'

'Right, well, you sit yourself down over there; I'll be back soon.'

Lana navigated through the crowd to the vacant booth Spen indicated, making herself comfortable on a soft leather bench, soaking up the atmosphere.

'How long have you worked with that idiot?' Spen queried, returning with a bottle, two glasses, and the lunchtime alfresco menu, placing them on the table, clearly anxious to discuss where Tom fitted into the picture.

'Oh, Tom's not too bad; he's quite laid back most of the time. He's my boss; he owns the *Newton Abbot Star*. I've been churning out copy for the paper for a number of years; the truth is, I'm hanging out for that lucky break, hoping to transfer to one of the big nationals if the opportunity arises.'

'Stick with me and I'll see what I can do. What you need, Lana, is an important exclusive, one you can reap lasting kudos from. This story we're currently covering might do it for you. Let me see what information I can obtain from this end and pep things up a bit. We can keep in touch once you return to the UK.'

Lana's face lit up. 'Really, you're willing to help me?'

'Sure, why not. You do realise Lisa Marshall worked as a hooker for a while, don't you?'

Lana's wine glass didn't quite reach her lips, absorbing this bombshell. 'Are you for real?'

'Yep, got it from a reliable source. A mate of mine is on the *Daily Mail* online media team in London. Had a word with him a few days ago, and he swears Lisa worked in a nightclub back in England, a strip joint by all accounts. Not sure where, I'm still waiting for confirmation on the details.

'Imagine how that'll go down once the right people get hold of it. My money's saying Lisa is a little bit of a prick tease. I'm confident she knew who her attackers were, going on her shady past and all; no way on earth is she going to let that one slip out.'

A wave of excitement swept through Lana. It certainly seemed as if Spen knew what he was on about.

Spen raised his glass. 'Here's to uncovering scandals. Cheers, Lana.'

Lana raised her own glass, letting it gently clink with Spen's. 'To scandals and lots of them, and my chance to finally shed the shackles of the *Newton Abbot Star*.'

***

CID, NSW Police,
Central Sydney, Australia

Linton, fighting the persistent physical withdrawal symptoms, counted slowly to ten, reluctantly glancing at his digital desk calendar, noting the last episode was five long months ago. He knew all too well; if he opened a bottle now, releasing the demon within, his whole world could come crashing down; the violent temper would surface, and he risked losing everything, including Marilyn, his new girlfriend.

Linton had deliberately thrown away the key to the bottom drawer of his desk, concealing an unopened single malt, cynically knowing it was more a symbolic gesture than an actual, viable deterrent.

Desperate to divert his mind from the gnawing cravings, Linton cleared a space on a cluttered desk, flipping open the weighty file on the three dead backpackers, scanning the lead page, revisiting the handwritten, cryptic summary he'd hastily scrawled the previous evening:

First victim, Astrid Johansson, twenty-four-year-old Swedish artist from Stockholm, in Australia only two months into an extended working holiday, prior to her murder. The corpse was discovered crudely dumped and concealed in a shallow grave in Heathcote National Park on the outskirts of Sydney. Found by two fishermen, the naked body half submerged in water, overflowing from a nearby flooded stream.

The second victim, an Italian national, Renata Fabrizio, twenty-five, originally from Siena. Renata had been in

Australia nearly ten months before her death. Prior to arriving in Sydney, Renata spent six months in Melbourne visiting distant relatives, etc. In this instance, her body was located at Port Stephens, roughly a two and a half hour drive north of Sydney.

The latest victim: Beatriz Bergmeister, a twenty-three-year-old German resident of Munich. Remains encountered on a rarely used hiking track in the Blue Mountains, west of Sydney. Beatriz was living in Sydney five months when the remains were found.

According to the autopsy reports, Astrid and Renata had been raped and then strangled by a thick rope, possibly the type used for sailing. The actual cause of death noted as a lethal dose of heroin.

Linton puzzled over the crimes and why these particular women had been targeted. So far, there was no indication they knew each other or had even been travelling the same routes. No obvious patterns stood out, except all were backpackers and had been killed using the same method.

As Linton's team began filtering into the office, he decided on an impromptu catch-up.

'Those last two leads I ran down were dead ends,' Detective Constable Pam Fratelli remarked, plonking down a takeaway breakfast meal on her desk and turning towards her boss in anticipation.

'Got something for us, Linton?' Lydia Chapman delved, slating the blinds and flooding the room with warm, early morning light.

'Nothing really.' Linton deftly caught a marker pen thrown by Chapman, moving towards the whiteboard in the centre of the room. 'Change of tack, people. I'd like us to take a closer look at our three victims, not their backgrounds or travel itinerary. I have a hunch there's something we're missing, a thread that connects all three women.'

'That's bloody obvious, unless we have three different killers with a connection,' Ty Conville whispered to Fratelli, unfortunately loud enough for Linton to hear.

'Ah, Mr C, you fancy yourself as a bit of a comedian, huh?' Linton was momentarily distracted by the aroma of Fratelli's bacon and egg muffin. 'Right, well, you can start the ball rolling and give us suggestions on how our three victims could have drawn the attention of our killer, and I don't mean in the sense they were all pretty. I want connections here; why were they targeted?'

Tyrone stood up, smiling, exuding bravado. 'Okay Inspector, I'll give it my best shot. Perhaps they frequented the same gym. From the photographs I've seen, all three women appeared to be fit and healthy, indicating they could have regularly worked out; it's easy to get temporary gym memberships. There are some places where you can work out 24/7. An easy opportunity for someone with no time restraints.'

'Right, check it out,' Linton instructed. 'Converse with friends of the deceased; see if any of these young women mentioned joining a gym. You're up next, Fratelli.'

'Maybe they stayed at the same hostel; perhaps they attracted the interest of a person who worked there,' Pam proposed.

'Already checked that out,' Linton explained. 'Astrid had a long-term room booking at a hostel in Bondi; Renata stayed at a backpackers' in the city, and as far as we know, Beatriz mostly bunked down with friends, spending only two nights in a hostel, which I think was in Paddington.'

'A sightseer minibus or taxi driver, I reckon,' Lydia interrupted. 'They could easily extract information from our victims, ask them seemingly harmless questions, especially a taxi driver. They may have picked them up or dropped them off at the place where they were staying.'

'That would be a hard one to narrow down,' Tyrone countered. 'How many bus and taxi drivers are there in Sydney? Too many to know where to begin looking. Then of course, you've got Uber drivers, mostly from Sub-Sahara Africa, the Middle East, or places unknown in India, some on highly suspect immigration work visas. There's no way we can explore that avenue.'

'Let's keep it simple,' Linton suggested, sketching the ideas provided onto the whiteboard with a black marker. 'Start with what the three women were interested in. What did they get up to after hours? We already know their employment didn't link them at all.'

Astrid worked in a Bondi bar, Renata held down a casual babysitting job for a reputable North Shore family, and Beatriz hadn't sought any employment; her bank account indicated sufficient funds to support her entire stay in Australia.'

'Lucky her,' Tyrone mumbled.

'Gee, fat lot of good that did her, uh duh, she's now dead,' Fratelli reminded her colleague.

'Luck of the draw.' Tyrone shrugged, lacking compassion.

'Focus team, let's not get sidetracked.' Linton needed their full attention, the unopened bottle of scotch looming larger than life. 'Our killer seems to be taking their time between each strangulation; any ideas, guys?'

'They're busy.' Detective Sergeant Lydia Chapman contributed.

Tyrone, adopting a mock voice, mimicked the killer, 'I've not been killing much lately, been too busy; moving house, going to work, playing tennis. With any luck, I'll get more free time over the coming months.'

'Cut the jokes,' Linton warned, his tone icy. 'These may be valid reasons why our killer has taken a hiatus. Highly unlikely our predator is a homeless down-and-out, humping around a couple of supermarket carrier bags, clogging up the sidewalks with nothing better to do than hunt down vulnerable females.'

Think outside the box; the killer could well be a business type, highly respected in the community. Now, one thing we've not touched on is does this person have an accomplice. We're certain the perpetrator is male, due to the fact the first two victims were raped, and traces of semen were found inside both victims.

By the way, I haven't received the autopsy results yet on Beatriz, but the forensic lab assures me I'll get them soon. So, what do we think about an accomplice? Thoughts, please.'

'Possibly,' Lydia piped up. 'In which case, we could be looking at a male or female aide-de-camp.'

'I definitely think another person is involved,' Pam responded. 'It would make things easier, especially trying to keep the women hidden and quiet.'

'I agree with Pam on this one,' Tyrone piped up. 'I can never get my women to shut up, even when we're trying out kinky sex...'

'Yep, we get the picture,' Pam interrupted, raising her eyebrows and shaking her head. 'The photographs of the deceased women show extensive bruising; in particular, I remember seeing a number of defence wounds on the palms of Astrid's hands, a clear indication she put up a fight.'

Linton sat back down, passing fingers through thick brown hair. 'It's a tough one. We don't have much to go on; the dearth of tangible physical evidence from the crime scenes is a real bummer. I'd like you all to read through the files once more and look for fresh evidence and leads.'

'What are your thoughts on the attacks of those two British girls? Are we searching for a connection?' Lydia asked, grabbing her file copy and heading back to her desk.

Linton shook his head. 'No, not at this stage. I really want our backpacker investigation kept separate. If there happens to be a connection, it'll eventually surface; for now, complications are the last thing I need. Let's treat the attack on the British girls as an individual case.'

When Ruth first presented at A&E, she told the medical staff she'd tripped, stumbled down the front steps; thankfully, they believed her. Her right arm was broken in two places, requiring a full cast, another thing that would annoy him; how was Ruth going to cook and clean for him with her impairment?

Of course, it was all her fault, this constant abuse;, that's what he told her. She wasn't good enough; she was lazy, and she disgusted him. He was not to be blamed for anything.

Chapter Six

Sydney, Australia

'Tom, it's me. Are you awake?' Noticing the door unlocked and not waiting for a reply, Lana barged into Tom's room, catching him half-asleep lying on the bed, the television on as background noise.

'Spen is an interesting bloke,' Lana announced, dropping her handbag on to the side table and removing her high heels. She plonked herself down on a chair, gently massaging aching feet. 'Now, this will interest you, Tom; according to Spen, Lisa Marshall worked as a stripper back in England. What do you make of that? Not the innocent young lady she led us all to believe, huh?'

Tom grunted, rolling onto his left side, facing away from Lana. 'I wouldn't believe a word that bronze larrikin tells you. Strikes me as the type to invent stories to boost a pathetic "wannabe" career.'

'Do I note a touch of jealousy?'

Tom forced himself into a sitting position, leaning on a pillow, eyes half-open. Disoriented, he checked the time on his vintage Constellation: six o'clock. It was obvious jet lag had set in. He'd slept the whole afternoon.

'I wouldn't want to be *him*.' Tom chortled. 'I'm satisfied with *my* life, thanks. Owning my own newspaper is quite an accomplishment. I'm just saying, be careful, Lana. Don't be tempted into reporting something you don't know to be true. It could land us in all sorts of trouble.'

'Oh, it's the real deal alright.' Lana sounded defiant. 'I can't wait to see the look on your face when everything comes out in the open. Watch this space. Now, if *you're* intent on spending half the trip holed up in this hotel room, see you later; I'm off for a swim.'

Tom bounded off the bed. 'Er, no, I've had plenty of shut-eye. It's morning back home. I could do with some exercise, then a drink, a very large one.'

***

England
Two Weeks Later

Clearing customs, Lisa and Christina were met by a private security team, who ushered them out of Heathrow Terminal 4 through a side entrance often used by celebrities, before being shepherded into a waiting car.

Quickly exiting the airport surroundings and out onto the M3, the saloon sped swiftly away from London and the Home Counties, heading southwest through thinning mid-morning traffic.

'Strange being home,' Lisa commented, her feelings mixed, gazing out of the window at the dark and brooding Wiltshire countryside sliding seamlessly past. Pockets of winter's first dusting of snow still evident, the landscape eerily aping her mood.

'What sort of reception do you think I'll receive from Jerome? He's been harassed by the media nearly every day since the attack; I've not heard from him in days. Perhaps he's planning on calling off the wedding.'

Christina placed an arm around her friend. 'Hey, that's not going to happen; Jerry's nuts about you. He'll be over the moon to have you home, safe and sound.'

'Let's pray you're right, Chrissy. Everybody's supposed to be attending a banquet tonight at the local Indian; let's hope Jerry turns up.'

Both girls slept for the remainder of the journey. Lisa awoke when the car pulled up on the edge of Dartmoor, outside her one-bedroom apartment in the centre of Bovey Tracey.

Tentatively, Lisa exited the vehicle to make her way along a narrow path to the front door. Fumbling slightly with the key, she finally managed to unlock the door to walk inside, grateful the heating had been switched on. Quickly checking that everything appeared normal, she turned and gave a cheery wave to Christina, who nodded to the driver, the car then driving away to drop Christina off at her home an hour's drive away, down on the coast.

Lisa, apprehensive at being alone, went directly to the kitchen, opened the blinds, filled the kettle, and switched it on. Confirming her sister had put fresh milk in the fridge, she located a packet of biscuits at the back of the pantry, then once the kettle had boiled, popped tea bags into the teapot, filling it with hot water, before sinking down into the green two-seater sofa, breathing deeply.

Waiting for the pot of tea to brew, Lisa reached inside her red leather handbag on the side table, extricating the pink

USB, twirling it lazily around in the air several times. Now, what could be the perfect hiding place? Somewhere they wouldn't think to look, if indeed they came looking. No, *when* they came looking. Lisa knew perfectly well the USB was the reason for the outback attack and why her life was still in danger.

***

Devon, England

It was now well over a week since Christina had touched down in the UK, making the decision to move back in with her grandparents, unwilling to return to her studio apartment on the outskirts of Kingsbridge; a wise decision under the circumstances.

Most nights, Chrissy would lie in a darkened bedroom staring at the ceiling for hours, delayed jetlag not the culprit, her brain in hyperdrive, wondering how long before those people came looking for the information they knew existed. Christina had begged Lisa incessantly to destroy the USB, but she wouldn't have a bar of it.

'This will put us on easy street,' Lisa reiterated, defiance in her tone.

'We've already been attacked once; maybe next time, they won't be so kind; they'll finish us off.'

'Not here, Chrissy. They won't bother with us now that we're on the other side of the world.' Lisa hoped her voice held an element of conviction. Deep down, she knew Christina was possibly right but was not about to admit it. The flash drive was their way to freedom, the path to a very comfortable life.

Christina gave a mock laugh. 'As if that's going to stop them. Lisa, these men are dangerous. They want that flash drive; they'll stop at nothing until they get it. You haven't thought this through logically. Things have gone past the point of no return. Even if we willingly surrendered it, they won't believe we haven't run off digital copies, the data already in the hands of a third party.'

'For God's sake, Chrissy, cut out the melodramatics; it's not going to happen. Try not to think about the past. Australia's best forgotten; we need to move on.'

Every time they had this conversation, Lisa insisted they were safe. How could anyone harm them now that they were back on British soil?

***

Sydney, Australia

Linton Ansley pushed open the double doors, exiting the Rushcutters Bay conference venue, noting the time. Happy to be out of the stifling, tepid aircon, he drank in the refreshing cooling nor'easter, piping in off the Sydney Harbour waters.

There was still plenty of time to get over the Bridge and down to the yacht club for the Thursday twilight race. Right about now, the usual crew would be rigging his pride and joy 10-metre racer, anxious to cast off.

Linton loved the approach up to Christmas, the best time of year. It was getting on for five but would remain light well after eight, courtesy of daylight saving and a rapidly approaching summer solstice.

Hurrying to the unmarked Falcon pool car, Linton's mobile vibrated; deducing it was the guys wondering where he was, he picked up.

'Linton, Dr Fiona Sinclair here, State Forensic Centre. Sorry, I realise it's getting late; I have the autopsy results pertaining to Beatriz Bergmeister. I'll stay back till six-thirty. I believe you're anxious to get the updates; if it's inconvenient, I'm in tomorrow after twelve.'

'Yeah, Fiona, thanks for prioritising the examination; tomorrow suits me better; unfortunately, I'm on my way to a prior—hold on, just a moment.'

Linton checked his watch again, calculating if he took the Toll Tunnels straight through to the M4, thus bypassing looming peak hour city traffic, he might just make the appointment with time to spare.

'Six-thirty, you say. Right, I'm on my way.'

Cursing the shit timing and undying devotion to his job, Linton hung up and reluctantly rang Hal, his long-time sailing buddy.

Fiona, pleased to know that Linton was on his way, returned to uploading a casework schedule, finishing with a couple of urgent phone calls. All done, she ducked into the bathrooms for a welcome freshen-up after a full-on afternoon attending a new grad's dissection, which had turned into a mini disaster; the overly obese corpse rolling off the trolley, crashing onto the floor, and taking down a high-end digital camera array in the process.

Linton strolled in, spotting Fiona in a deserted staff room, struggling to squeeze a large espresso from the last beans in a recalcitrant coffee machine.

'Hi there. You look nice and relaxed. Easy day, hey?'

'You're kidding me, right? This is my first one today. Oh, incidentally, my apologies; I didn't mean to put any pressure on you.'

Managing a weak smile, ceramic mug in both hands, Fiona escorted the DCI into a small office.

'This is what I have for you.' Fiona passed over a three-page document.

Linton sat in silence, quickly scanning the details, methodically absorbing the key points. After several minutes, he responded to the report, 'I'm getting the picture: all three backpacker murders were committed by the same person, wouldn't you agree?'

'I'm one hundred percent certain the person who killed Beatriz is the one you've nicknamed the Aussie Executor, responsible for the deaths of Renata and Astrid. Apart from conclusive DNA evidence, I've read through the other reports put together by Ross Paterson, and the matches across the board are uncanny.

'I'm also waiting on a forensic murder profile being emailed across from my sister in the UK. Katie's a forensic psychologist, one of the best in the business. It will be fascinating to hear what she makes of these murders and her take on the type of person we're looking for.'

'Excellent. We can do with all the help we can get. I held a briefing with my staff recently, and we basically agree the killer didn't act alone. What are your thoughts, Fiona?'

'I agree; most certainly another person's involved; too bad the modest amounts of foreign DNA captured on the swabs were heavily contaminated by environmental biological material or were severely degraded. Multiple replications gave inconclusive fragmentation patterns.'

'Our lab chemists can't determine whether this person is male or female. However, sperm DNA genetic chromatograms confirm the victims were raped by only one man; logic tells me the secondary person could well be female, indicated by no additional force used on the victims. Not conclusive evidence, I'm afraid, more of a hunch, which isn't much use to you.

'The heroin, technically diacetylmorphine, and its breakdown derivatives detected in multiple tissue samples of all three victims were way above recommended therapeutic dose levels, meaning death for all three victims was only minutes away.'

'The photos you see in the report show clear puncture wounds in the necks of all three women, indicating administration by syringe penetration, just below the left ear.'

'Excellent work, Fiona. I hope a fourth victim doesn't turn up. The authorities are already getting anxious; overseas travellers, particularly young females, are being cautioned not to travel to Australia. A bit over the top as usual from alarmist federal government information bureaucrats in Canberra, shooting off press releases without evaluating the consequences for the tourist industry; still, I guess not the ideal holiday destination at the moment.'

'Yep. Anyway, let's pray this sexual deviate psycho slips up, providing you with more concrete evidence. As soon as I receive the profile from my sister, I'll shoot it across; that might help.'

'Thanks. Speak soon.'

Linton headed to the lift, leaving Fiona tossing up if another caffeine fix was needed, finally deciding it was.

***

Bovey Tracey, Devon, England

'Chrissy, it's me. Been trying your phone for the past two hours. Please ring me back ASAP. I'm being followed. Holy crap, it didn't take long for them to figure out our location. The "media blackout" on our travel itinerary was utterly useless. I'll be hiking across Dartmoor to stay with a friend. Call me.'

Lisa, shoving the mobile into the back pocket of her jeans, grabbed a few items of clothing, throwing them haphazardly into a large backpack, before stealing out the back door, through the rear garden, and over the fence onto a track leading out of Bovey Tracey, towards the high moor.

Being run off the road earlier that afternoon, to avoid a head-on collision, was appearing less and less accidental. Without a doubt, Lisa was convinced their Australian pursuers were now in England, determined to finish the job.

***

Bovey Tracey, Devon, England

Blake sprang up the hotel steps, carrying a modest overnight bag, his thoughts elsewhere, solely focused on Christina and Lisa. It was now more imperative than ever that he track them down and retrieve the elusive USB stick.

'Staying just the one week, Sir?' The clean-cut young man, wearing an obligatory white shirt and crimson vest, confirmed, glancing up from the computer screen.

Blake nodded, placing a credit card on the desk.

'Let me guess, from New Zealand?'

Blake rolled his eyeballs in mock horror. 'Australia.'

'Nice. Let me see, we have you in room twenty-four, a lovely classic suite with views of our spectacular gardens. Sign here, please, and I will have someone take your luggage up to your room.'

'This is all I have; umm, I'm travelling light.'

The reception clerk expressed mild surprise. 'Wow, even those coming here from London have more luggage. Here's your key pass, Sir. There's an information folder book in your room with the times we serve meals and hotel services, along with a list of local attractions. If you need anything at all, you can call down to reception; someone will be on duty twenty-four seven.'

'Thank you, er—'

'Leo. Leo Flannigan.'

'Thanks, Leo. I was hoping to have dinner in my room tonight; is that alright?'

'Of course. I can have someone take your order a little later.'

'Great.'

Following directions, Blake mounted a convoluted, intricately carved, wooden staircase to room twenty-four on a mezzanine level. Flopping down on the king-size bed, Blake removed his trainers, simultaneously checking his watch, still on Sydney time, thankful to have reached his destination after a delayed, sleep-disturbed flight. Within minutes, Blake drifted off, dozing lightly for about an hour, free of anxiety for the first time since leaving Sydney.

After unpacking, he headed down to the ground floor foyer, venturing into the cathedral room, craving a coffee; a spectacular open space featuring lofty domed ceilings and wood-panelled walls, the late Arts & Crafts interior design features imparting a cosseted, castle-like feeling.

Blake, making himself comfortable in a wide lounge chair, casually observing guests indulging in afternoon tea or a port, soaking up the ambience from open fireplaces, picked up his cell phone.

'Hi, it's Blake. I've arrived safely. When can we catch up?'

A long pause ensued, after which Javier spoke, 'Is that wise, Blake? I mean, it could be dangerous. Did anyone follow you down from London? Have you seen anyone acting suspiciously?'

'No, all seems fine.' Blake, again quickly and methodically, surveyed the room where other guests sat quietly reading or deep in conversation. No one was paying attention to him, ensconced in the far corner. 'How about tomorrow at eleven? You could come to the hotel for a spot of lunch.'

'Alright, let's meet in the foyer, but if you start feeling uneasy, call me; we'll make other arrangements.'

'Sure.'

'What about the item? Do you have it?' Javier lowered his voice, aware of James hovering near the photocopier.

'No, not yet, but it's only a matter of time.'

***

Sydney, Australia

Fiona sat relaxed on a stool at the bar in Jackson's on George Street, waiting patiently for Harvey to arrive, who had sent a text indicating he was about fifteen minutes away; she'd already taken the liberty of ordering the first round and a few packets of crisps from the attendant behind the bar.

Harvey and Fiona's friendship stretched back several years, when they had both joined the Dart Valley Rifle Club as teenagers, fresh out of school. It had been a pleasant surprise when Fiona decided to relocate to Sydney, learning Harvey was close by.

Harvey waved a greeting as he entered the pub, meandering his way to the bar, where Fiona sat checking messages on her phone.

'How do you like living in Sydney?' Harvey asked, pulling out a stool, giving Fiona a hug and a peck on the cheek.

'The Mosman apartment is great,' Fiona gushed, brown eyes sparkling. 'A new build, with spectacular views across the harbour, so that's a bonus. Can you believe a communal swimming pool and a short drive to an array of fantastic beaches? The shops are within walking distance, and of course, the Sydney weather is an instant attraction.'

'Oh, don't be fooled.' Harvey chuckled. 'Wait until the La Nina arrives with weeks of monsoonal downpours. And, I haven't mentioned winter, when the temperature drops to single figures and the electric blanket comes out. You'll soon start complaining.'

Fiona laughed, reacquainting herself with Harvey's friendly, familiar features, practically unchanged since his send-off party five years ago. 'The colder months are a long way down the track, spoilsport. Let me appreciate all this heat for a while. Now, drink up. Looks like my glass is empty. Your shout.'

'You don't change, do you?' Harvey teased. 'Direct as usual. God, you're a sight for sore eyes, Fi. I was amazed to receive your email with news you were relocating to Oz. I imagined you forever wedded to Moorland Forensics.'

Fiona's face took on a more serious look. 'Not after everything that happened. The bomb explosions at Harrington Court rattled me more than I realised. I needed to get away, start afresh. I still experience unsettling hallucinations from those events. Can't seem to get the images out of my head. Therapy helps a bit, but even so.'

'Sorry, I forgot,' Harvey apologised, remembering Fiona had once confided in him regarding her difficulty confronting death. 'I've been caught up in my own world lately, work taking precedence.'

'Which reminds me, we've been invited to dinner by my new neighbours,' Fiona informed Harvey, lifting the topic of conversation. 'Please tell me you'll make it. I don't fancy going by myself.'

'What are they like, these neighbours?' Harvey probed. 'Typical Aussies?'

'They seem nice. Hayley's in real estate; her partner, Jordan, a teacher of English, I think.'

'No, I mean to look at.'

'That's right, it's all about appearance with you, isn't it?' Fiona teased.

Harvey gave her a gentle shove. 'Not at all; I just like to know how to dress; are they casual, easygoing or stuffy, formal, self-opinionated, that sort of thing?'

'Well. Hayley's thirty-something, quite attractive, with long auburn hair, brown eyes, and collagen enhanced lips for sure. Medium height, quite a slim build, actually; not a bad figure, now I come to think about it. When I met her, she was wearing gym gear; definitely a fitness junkie, one of the daily workout crowd.'

'And this Jordan guy?'

'Haven't met him. I get the impression he's away a fair bit. Anyway, dinner's next Saturday; what do you say?'

'I'll pop it into my diary. Now, what's happening with those two terrors? I expect they're growing by the minute.'

Fiona gave Harvey the latest on her boys, enjoying his company. Just what the doctor ordered: an evening to let her hair down, relax, and savour a meal and wholesome company, away from autopsies and the constant pall of death.

***

Devon, England

Wrapped in the complimentary monogrammed hotel bathrobe, a large white fluffy towel draped over one arm, Blake quietly opened his hotel room door, planning a swim before breakfast. He glanced up and down an empty corridor; eerily quiet, hardly surprising seeing it was a little before six, most guests still nestled into comfortable beds, the day staff yet to sign on.

Distracted, Blake's gaze averted downwards, noticing a brown parcel sitting outside the door, a stab of nausea creeping into the pit of his stomach, alarm bells ringing, wondering what the package contained and who had put it there. Apart from Javier, no one was supposed to know his whereabouts.

Bending down, Blake carefully picked up the parcel, surprised at how light it felt. He carried it back into his room, placing it on the bed, before ripping off the brown paper, bound with strips of adhesive tape. Inside, he found a white clockwork mouse, a typed note attached:

Thought I'd wind you up, Blake. Welcome to Devon; hope you have a pleasant stay. Enjoy this little gift, bro, and remember: treat each day as if it's your last, which it could well be.

Merry Xmas.

Blake sank down on the bed, throwing the toy mouse back in its wrapper. After a moment, he scooped up the parcel, pitching it into a nearby bin. With his fury building, it would be wise to put in some quick laps and consume excess anger and energy.

He pondered whether to tell Javier about the package, then decided against it. If Javier felt the walls were closing in, he would run a mile; Blake needed Javier Quintano; there was no way he could fight this battle single-handed.

Ruth often tried to disguise the bruises. She secretly bought cosmetic books and learnt the best concealers to apply, making her skin appear unblemished. If anyone suspected her husband of domestic violence, his temper would increase.

Nowadays, Ruth didn't venture out much. She made a quick dash to the supermarket once a week but stopped seeing friends or going out for coffee. Even the kids made their own way to and from school. Ruth was a prisoner, trapped in her own home.

Chapter Seven

Dartmoor, Devon, England

'This bloody hiking and bike riding business has to end once we get married,' Katie grumbled, stopping momentarily to dislodge an annoying stone from the inside of her Jodhpur boot, shaking it out onto the damp ground.

'I have a perfectly decent pony who loves galloping across the moors; all I have to do is sit back and admire the view, none of this hard slog up heathery slopes on a bike that's seen better days, peddling through dense woodland, resulting in scratches and bruises.'

'You need to exercise your lovely legs, my sweet.' Matt jested, helping Katie regain her balance as she forced her boot back on. 'Otherwise, you'll end up as fat as Polo Mint, and that *won't* be a pretty sight.'

Katie threw him a look of disgust. 'I happen to be exercising at the local pool twice a week. Actually, it's you who's putting on weight. That t-shirt's looking snug; you won't fit into your wedding suit if you keep piling on the kilos.'

'I could always turn up in my birthday suit. I'm sure—'

'What's that?' His words lost, Katie pointed out an object halfway down the gully.

'What's what?' Matt craned his neck in the direction she pointed. 'No idea, perhaps scrap metal.'

'It looks like a broken drone; I'm heading down to take a closer look.'

'Leave it; the car has to be moved before…' Reluctantly, Matt scrambled down the slope to where Katie stood, close to the shattered object.

'Bound to happen,' Matt concluded, picking up the drone and turning it over. 'Fragile. These things are made down to a price and can't cope with more than average abuse. Cheap, lightweight synthetics, easily damaged during heavy landings. Their shape dictates that if they land on an arm, undue force transfers to the joints.'

'I wonder who it belongs to.' Katie, not the least bit interested in the dome's architecture, was keen to find its owner. 'I hope they're not lying hurt somewhere.'

'Probably kids mucking around,' Matt surmised. 'Come on, let's head towards the reservoir. We'll have to wheel the bikes; this path is too dangerous to ride along.'

Matt led the way down a narrow path towards the reservoir, quickening his step, mindful to keep moving at a reasonable pace, aware of the looming clouds up ahead. Katie, on the other hand, preferred a more leisurely stroll, possessing an annoying habit of stopping every now and again to admire the view, fiddle with her backpack, or take photographs.

'Do you see that!' Katie exclaimed, glancing over at the embankment to her right.

'See what?' Matt was growing impatient. 'Are we going to keep this game going the entire morning, Katie; spotting anomalies on the moors?'

'Definitely a body,' Katie continued, edging closer, ignoring Matt's request.

Matt shielded his eyes from the glare. 'A young woman. Stay here.'

Katie, in hot pursuit, ignoring the instructions to stay put, followed Matt to the edge of the reservoir.

'Is she dead?' Katie probed tentatively, peering out from behind Matt, both hands securely holding on to his waist. 'Gee, I think so, not breathing. Her face is weird. Looks like she suffered a seizure or something; she might have choked on stomach contents.'

Matt, now kneeling beside the woman, looked up at Katie. 'Yep, gone. Hell, she's so young. Get onto the lab; James will know what to do. I'll contact Will at CID; they'll dispatch a team, most likely by chopper.'

Matt got to his feet. Katie put her arm around his waist, firmly ushering him away from the immediate surroundings.

'Come on, Tyler. It's important everything remains intact; the cause of death is unknown, and this could well be a crime scene. The wind is dropping; I sense snow coming. Let's make these calls.'

***

Bovey Tracey, England, Devon
Moorland Forensics Consultants Facility

Javier pushed aside the half-completed lab reports, removing reading glasses to ease up from his office desk, letting out an unexpected yawn, trying to remember when he'd last experienced a decent night's sleep.

On the whole, he was liking his role with Moorland Forensics, but with James away all week attending a seminar on the latest DNA diagnostics techniques, Javier's workload had intensified. Of course, Nick Shelby was on hand for emergencies, but from what Javier had observed, Nick displayed distraction elsewhere.

Checking the wall clock, Javier decided to stroll up Bovey High Street, intent on sampling a Cornish pasty from the main bakery. He'd only taken a few steps when his plans momentarily stalled; the reception phone buzzing incessantly.

Letting out a long sigh, Javier answered the call, immediately requesting the caller to slow down, unable to decipher what they were saying, the line cutting in and out. When everything finally made sense, he realised it was Katie he was speaking to.

'A deceased female, right? Where did you say again? On Dartmoor?'

'Up near Burrator Reservoir, a bit isolated, I'll text you the details. You might want to drive James' Land Rover. Will Parker's on his way, but it may take a while for police support to arrive. Will's been given the go-ahead for a preliminary in-situ attendance by MFC. Derek Ingalls is flying in later with a tech team. Try and get here as soon as you can; it's vital we preserve evidence.'

***

Devon, England

Javier Quintana bent down to take a closer look at the female victim. 'Young, possibly early twenties. From a

97

cursory initial observation, she hasn't been dead long. I'm thinking within the last four hours, but at this stage, I can't determine much else. Not a pleasant death, though.

I'd say she was in a lot of pain when she took her last breath, judging by the way she's lying and the look on her face. The regurgitated stomach contents may mean something didn't agree with her, perhaps an allergic reaction. I witnessed something similar when I was growing up in our village in Luzon. Never forgot it. Scares the hell out of you.'

Javier stood up, flexing fingers. Glancing across the embankment, he noticed a grey, unmarked Subaru SUV making a noisy entrance to the muddy carpark. 'Here comes the cavalry now. Who's that with Will?'

Katie grinned. 'Will's current offsider, "Jock Strap," aka Detective Sergeant Jock Fletcher.'

The two men, kitted out in dark blue fatigues, exited the police vehicle, pushing aside fallen branches and thick low bushes, clearing a path to where the others stood, several metres from the deceased.

'Nice day for it,' Will sarcastically remarked, joining the group, a long grey scarf secured around his neck to ward off the growing chill. 'Apologies for the delay in getting here; the damn sheep decided to park themselves in the middle of the road, completely oblivious to the sound of my car horn.'

'Maybe that piece of artillery might have worked.' Matt pointed to Will's special issue Heckler and Koch SOCOM Mk23 semi-automatic strapped around the DCI's waist. 'Expecting a bit of action, hey William.'

'What's that? Oh, no, sorry. Jock and I were over at the range in Ashburton doing some tactical training stuff.' Will turned to Javier. 'Well, what have we got?'

'One deceased female, most likely early twenties.'

'The cause of death?' Will probed.

'Odds are she suffered some sort of seizure, although it's best if I leave Dr Ingalls to investigate the bloodstain patches on the grass near the skull.' Javier removed his PPE mask, taking in a deep breath, once more casting an analytical eye over the scene. 'I'll start checking for evidence in the immediate vicinity and stake out the area for when Derek and the SCOs drop in. See what I come up with.'

Javier glanced up at a threatening bank of nimbostratus, building to the north. 'Bloody cold up here, guys; wouldn't be surprised if a flurry is on the cards.'

Will Parker smiled, amused by Javier's attire, more suitable for a tropical resort than a routine December day on the exposed high moor. 'A bit different from Cebu, huh. Tell me, Javier, do we have an ID on our victim?'

'Sorry, Chief Inspector, I haven't looked for any yet.'

'Morning, comrades.'

All attention fell upon Tom Markham, owner and self-appointed chief journalist of the *Newton Abbot Star*, meandering his way towards them, a photographer in tow, struggling with a camera bag and lighting equipment.

'That's all we need.' Will clenched his teeth. 'This is turning into a bloody jamboree.'

'What you got for me, Willy boy?' Tom jested, edging nearer to the body. 'Ooh, looks nasty.'

'Piss off, Markham,' Jock growled. 'We're not ready to broadcast to the rest of the world. We don't even know what we're dealing with yet.'

'People *are* "breaking news" addicts,' Tom stated, easing a duffle bag off his shoulder and placing it on the ground.

Opening the front pocket, he pulled out a mini recording device.

'How come you're here so quickly?' Katie directed her question at the insufferable journalist. 'We've only recently stumbled across this lass.'

'Ah, a female victim?' Tom grinned, speaking clearly into his portable tape recorder. 'Thanks, Katie, my dear. At first glance, and with the way the body is positioned, I had trouble determining the sex.'

Katie could have kicked herself, offering Will Parker an apologetic look and mouthing *sorry*.

'It's okay, Katie,' Will reassured her. 'This ruthless rat and his sidekick, Penfold, would have turned up sooner or later.'

'Dead right, pardon the pun.' Tom smirked. 'Coincidentally, we were just down the road, scouting locations for a lovely full-colour holiday supplement coming up in next month's edition, and lo and behold, I hear from a local farmer something's occurring up here on the high ground. Well, you know me; always willing to lend the authorities a hand where I can.'

'Nosey, you mean,' Katie fumed. 'Kick you out of Oz, did they? Shame. We were elated in the peace and quiet. Mind you, I'm not surprised; they shut their doors to convicts a long time ago. You're 150 years too late.'

'Always ready with the wit, Ms Sinclair. Perhaps Olly here could get a picture of those who discovered the body. From where I'm standing, it looks like it was you, Katie, and perhaps Mr Tyler. The light's better over this way if you could shift a bit and look pensive and upset. My reader's like the authentic photos.'

Matt went to lunge at Tom, but Jock pulled him back. 'Not worth it, laddie. Markham knows not to print anything before he gets permission from the superintendent; otherwise, his tatty little rag might land him in strife.'

'Always the dutiful copper, Jock,' Tom retorted in thick, mocking Scottish brogue, helping Oliver detach the camera from its bag before adjusting the lens. 'Don't mind us; we'll fire off a few snaps, but I promise to converse with your boss before anything goes to print. Toodles, I can see you're all very busy.'

With that, Tom and Oliver stepped to one side, camera at the ready.

***

Devon, England
Midday News Bulletin

'In breaking news:'

'Earlier today, the body of an adult female was discovered near Burrator Reservoir on Dartmoor. In a statement to the media, issued twenty minutes ago, the victim has not yet been formally identified. A forensic team is currently at the scene, working to determine a probable cause of death.'

'Sergeant Dianne Quirk, Public Relations, Devon and Cornwall Police, is urging any member of the public with relevant information, which may assist authorities with their enquiries, or anyone who might have been in the reservoir area on or around the day in question, to please come forward.'

***

Devon, England
Three Days Later

'We finally have a confirmed identity for the female found on Dartmoor, and it may come as a bit of a shock,' Detective Jock Fletcher informed the group, hastily assembled in the conference room at Exeter police headquarters. 'We now know the body to be that of twenty-three-year-old Lisa Marshall, the young woman who was attacked in the Australian outback back in early October.'

Acting DI, Mallory Wakefield, let out a gasp. 'Wow, can you imagine the headlines? Social, media and the internet will be in meltdown. The international press will descend on Devon in droves. What in God's name did that young woman do to get herself killed? Talk about rotten, stinking luck.'

'No, not bad luck. We're working on the premise that both Lisa and Christina were deliberately targeted, for whatever reason,' Jock announced.

'The little tart probably deserved to be done in,' Charlie muttered, loud enough for Mallory to hear. 'From what I've heard...'

'What *have* you heard?' Mallory interrupted, shooting Charlie a scathing stare. Mallory had a loathing for Charlie Haig, a lazy, ineffectual copper who flirted with anything in a skirt.

'She gave it about a bit, by all accounts,' Charlie explained, momentarily emboldened, happy to voice his opinion. 'One of my mates at the...'

'Your mate would do well to keep his mouth shut,' Mallory retorted. 'And you need to learn more respect for women, in general.'

'Yeah, like you never flirted with a bloke before, "Ms Mallory." You women are all the same, acting like you're all pure and innocent, when really, you're desperate for it.'

'Just because you're boring and dateless doesn't mean you can view all women as sex objects,' Mallory fired back, her temper rising.

Will Parker, standing at the rear, nursing a persistent headache, stepped forward to take control before the meeting descended into a full-blown slanging match. 'Okay, okay. Listen up, ladies and gents; please keep comments relevant to this investigation. Jock, what have we got to go on so far?'

'I spoke with Javier Quintana earlier, the consultant pathologist first on the scene. The doc believes Lisa Marshall was poisoned, although blood stains on the grass are most likely from where her skull impacted a rock. A full autopsy is scheduled, but that's about all for the time being.'

'Have next of kin been informed?' Will asked.

'Lisa's mother has been notified, naturally in a deep state of shock, not able to be interviewed at this stage. She's already sighted photos, confirming the deceased *is* her daughter, but she doesn't want to view the body. Not that I believe she'll be able to add anything of value.'

'Vicki Marshall did tell one of our officers; the immediate family had minimal contact with Lisa since returning from Australia. They were all trying to get on with their lives after recent events, and who could blame them?'

Will turned to Mallory. 'Dig around; try and establish what Lisa has been doing since her return from Australia. Chat with friends, neighbours—you know the drill.'

' Yes, boss.'

As the meeting came to an end, Charlie leaned in closer to Mallory. 'Boss, huh? I see the looks you and "the boss" give each other, Wakefield. He practically drools all over you. Yuck.'

Mallory turned red, digging Charlie hard in the ribs. 'Stick it, Charlie. You'll end up demoted, doing the school patrols, if you don't keep your foul mouth shut.'

'Nah, it's not me that needs to mind my Ps and Qs. If word gets around that you and "boss man" are an item, the shit will hit the fan. How does he like it, Mal, hard up against the wall, or is he the romantic type?'

Mallory gathered up a few scattered sheets of paper on her desk, stuffing them into her portfolio case, before marching out the door, heading for the lift down to the carpark. She hadn't twigged that people were noticing her close rapport with DCI Parker. Perhaps she needed to distance herself from Will for a while. She was up for promotion; she couldn't allow anything or anyone to jeopardise that.

***

Teignmouth, Devon, England

On hearing the news of Lisa's murder, Christina knew the walls were closing in. Considering the sudden turn of events, it was inevitable, without any doubt; she would be the next victim, the logic undeniable. She had to get away, but how?

The idea came to her gradually, soaking in a hot bath at 2am as the music streaming service flicked randomly through her favourites. Not a solution one would deem ethical, but in her mind, it was called self-preservation.

***

Bovey Tracey, Devon, England

Katie unlocked the door to James' duplex. Placing the keys on the side table in the hall, she strolled into the lounge. After a cursory look around, she went straight to the built-in bookcase located under the stairs, unlocking the doors, remembering that James' prized antiquarian copy of "The Renaissance and Origins of the Enlightenment" she intended to borrow was inside.

Glancing along the eclectic row of volumes, Katie finally pounced on the maroon leather-bound edition, pulling it out. Idly walking back into the hallway, distracted, inspecting the book, she almost collided with a petite brunette hurrying down the stairs, carrying a basket of washing, the unexpected encounter making her heart skip a beat, leaving her momentarily gasping for breath.

'What are you doing here?' The woman fired first, her tone cool; it was immediately clear to Katie the brunette was not European, possibly Asian, the accent, however, not immediately evident. There was no denying she was beautiful, undoubtedly one of James' many female "conquests."

'Funny, I was about to ask you the same thing,' Katie rebuffed, finding her voice. 'This is my brother's place.'

'And this is my boyfriend's place,' came the curt reply. 'If you don't mind, I'd like you to leave.'

Katie was disturbed by the woman's icy tone and defensive body language. 'Hey, I didn't mean to upset you. Usually, James is fine with his family dropping by when he's at work. Not that we do this on a regular basis.'

'Yeah, well, best you change that practice.'

'By the way, I'm Katie, the youngest sister.'

'Sofia. I'm sure we'll see each other again, preferably at another location.'

Sofia wasn't creating a sound impression on Katie. She stood defiantly, arms folded, motioning to the doorway, waiting for Katie to leave.

One night, lying in bed, listening to his heavy snoring, the sound resembling a road train, Ruth thought back to when they'd first met, both in their early twenties. He'd not always been like this. When they initially married, he was charming, a company sales executive with high prospects. Then, he was involved in an accident at work; part of a ceiling collapsed, leaving him with chronic pain. That's when he turned to drink. Perhaps he wasn't to blame after all.

Chapter Eight

Sydney, Australia

'Hi, guys. Right on time. Welcome, please come in.' Hayley, beaming, stepped aside to allow her guests entry into a subtly mood-lit, carpeted hallway. 'Jordan's in the kitchen, finishing the starter. Let's head into the lounge. Champagne?'

'Your place is the mirror image of mine, definitely more homely,' Fiona announced, taking in her surroundings, the décor, furnishings, and overall effect carefully copied straight from the pages of an upmarket Australian casual living lifestyle magazine.

'We'll have been here five years next month.' Hayley passed Fiona a chilled glass of vintage brut. 'You've been in your apartment, what is it; only a matter of weeks, Fi? It takes time to convert a place into a proper home, girl; plus, we don't have any children, so we can go with the light colours without issues.'

Fiona agreed, rolling her eyes, 'I'm forever reminding the boys about dirty shoes, grubby hands, and clearing up after themselves.'

Harvey sat next to Fiona, accepting the drink Hayley offered him. 'You've a lovely place, Hayley. Thanks for inviting us over for dinner. Fi informs me you lead a very hectic life.'

'No busier than most.' Hayley sat down opposite her guests. 'Ah, here's Jordan now.'

A tall, handsome male walked in, a blue checkered tea towel slung over one arm. 'I see our guests have arrived.' He extended a hand in welcome. 'Delighted you could make it. I notice my dutiful wife has provided you with refreshments. That's a super bubbly from a winery near Orange, up on the Great Dividing Range, the ideal area for cool climate wines.'

'We always drop in and pick up a case or two when up that way. Our starter will be ready in a few moments. I hope you both like oysters—South Australian, fresh, and delicious.'

The evening was most entertaining. The food exceptional, the company cheerful, the alcohol flowing. Fiona felt the most relaxed in a long time. The relocation to Australia had not been an easy one; a busy work schedule left little time to meet new friends.

'You're both from Devon?' This was more a rhetorical question from Jordan. 'Nice part of the world. I did six months on exchange with the Royal Navy in Southampton a few years back, attached to the RAN as a defence contractor. Spent a couple of weekends at the Britannia Royal Naval College in Dartmouth, hosting anti-submarine warfare technical seminars. Loved every minute of it.'

'Good to hear,' Harvey replied. 'Fiona and I belonged—'

Fiona dug Harvey in the ribs, stopping him mid-sentence. Luckily, their hosts didn't notice. Fiona didn't want people learning of her shooting expertise, which she knew Harvey was about to mention, a subject she preferred to be kept under wraps.

Harvey took the *not too subtle* hint, feigning a coughing fit, continuing along a different line, 'Sorry, I was about to say Fiona and I belonged to a local outdoor club, hiking, bike riding, that sort of thing.'

'No kidding, we're outdoor fanatics,' Hayley joined in. 'Jordan and I travel a fair bit around Australia. It's valuable for the soul. We invested in one of those state-of-the-art campervans with all the latest mod cons. The only state we've not yet explored is Tasmania. We're looking at getting there next year.'

'Something you and I should consider, Fi,' Harvey commented. 'Hire a van and see the country; get away from the city for a few weeks.'

'It's a bit crazy here at the moment, though, with the backpacker murders,' Hayley confessed. 'Tourism is suffering. I feel for the small operators. After the events of the last few years with the draconian lockdowns and vaccine mandates, I'm amazed we have any industry left.'

'Yep, it sure is,' Jordan agreed. 'Surely, the police will run the bastard down soon. Been dragging on well over a year now; people are feeling uneasy.'

'I know the lead detective working on the case,' Fiona proudly proclaimed. 'Top-notch, one of their best. He'll get them eventually; it's just a matter of time.'

'One can only hope.' Jordan was busy searching the wine rack for a port. 'Social media is in meltdown; convinced the backpacker murders are linked to the attack on those two British girls.'

'Wasn't one of those young women found dead only a few days ago, in a place called Dartmoor?' Hayley broke in. 'I expect you'd know all about that, Fiona.'

'I heard it on the news. However, I'm not convinced the two cases are related; they seem poles apart to me.'

'In your line of work, you'd know a fair bit about the state of the investigations,' Jordan declared, winking at the others. 'Inside knowledge and the like. I'm sure you're in regular contact with your counterparts overseas; find out what's happening in different parts of the world, stay ahead of the curve, that sort of stuff.'

'Er, on occasion,' Fiona reached for the last bread roll, discreetly avoiding eye contact. She wasn't keen for Hayley and Jordan to know any details about the case; her line of work required total professionalism, which included confidentiality.

'Anyway, the person or persons responsible must be fucked in the head, coupled with a long psychiatric history,' Hayley stated. 'That's where I'd start the search: profiles recently locked up for rape, aggravated assault, and attempted murder.'

'Well, I know DCI Ansley isn't leaving any stone unturned,' Fiona responded. 'Now tell me, where do you guys mostly travel to when you escape from "the big smoke"?'

'Wherever the mood takes us,' Hayley replied. 'Once I get pregnant, life will become too hectic to hit the road; we're trying to see a bit of "the wide, brown land" whilst the window is there.'

'And where did you two meet?' Harvey asked, swirling the red slowly, watching the alcoholic film form in the glass.

'Brindabella National Park,' Hayley proudly announced. 'I was camping there with an old flame when we met Jordan. There was instant chemistry between Jordan and myself, so I ditched my boyfriend; the rest is history.'

'I expect your ex was devastated, being dumped like that,' Fiona remarked.

'We still keep in touch,' Hayley informed her guests. 'He was best man at our wedding, no hard feelings. I think he realised we weren't really suited.'

Fiona glanced at her watch. 'I didn't realise it was this late. We'd better get going.'

'Not before coffee and dessert,' Hayley pleaded. 'Jordan whipped up a pavlova. The story goes, it originated either in Australia or New Zealand in the early twentieth century, named after Anna Pavlova, principal dancer with the Russian Ballet. However, other claims have also come forward, so who knows, but it's a yummy dessert. Definitely sounds more appetising than a "Nijinsky," hey.'

After devouring a large slice of pavlova, washed down with coffee, Fiona and Harvey stood up to leave. They thanked their hosts for a wonderful evening, with hugs all round, and headed across the foyer to Fiona's apartment.

'You can crash here tonight,' Fiona informed Harvey, giving him a gentle shove towards the guest bedroom. 'It's late; we've drunk a fair bit; best to leave the car keys on the table.'

'No complaints from me. Funny, pleasant night and all, lovely people, but did you notice something unusual about their flat? Modern, functional, and all, but lacking soul, cold? I didn't spot any artworks, pictures on a wall, or a nice standout individual period piece anywhere, not even flowers in a vase. Stark. Maybe it's just been a long, exhausting week. Anyway, night, Fi, see you tomorrow.'

***

Streete, Devon, England
Natividad Restaurant and Bar

'Always lovely to catch up with you two.' Roger Tudor grimaced facetiously, half-heartedly raising a Guinness in mock salute. 'Especially when it's your shout, Parker. Mind you, sheer insanity to be out when it's cold enough to freeze the whatsits off a brass monkey.'

'Why didn't you just read my report? Would have been better for all of us. As a last resort, there's always Zoom, for Christ's sake. Hope you blokes didn't park your worthless junk within fifty feet of the Aston. The Deputy Chief Constable will be hearing from me if there's the slightest scratch. Don't you worry; I'll be giving her the once-over when we leave.'

'What report?' Will Parker grumbled, ignoring Tudor's concerns about his special 80th-Year Anniversary Edition Vanquish. 'John Wallis spilt so much liquid on the damn thing, it was barely legible.'

'There *are* such things as emails; they've been around for a while.' Tudor made a tutting sound, adjusting his large, bulky frame on the bench whilst undoing the button on an ill-fitting double-breasted jacket. 'Could have shot across another copy in two minutes. Would have saved a lot of time and trouble. Instead, you force me out of my home on an

112

evening when snow is predicted. Shit, it's bloody cold in here. Can you see the waitress about the heating, Jim?'

'What, and miss out on seeing your friendly face?' James interjected with a smirk, signalling a nearby waitress. 'We're anxious to learn what you've got on ballistics for the Copeland lads, if you're willing to share. Old Shirley's keen for a conviction.'

'I bet she is,' Tudor retorted. 'That woman's grotesque; I must confess I have never been a fan. Shirl Copeland is slippery as a snake and twice as toxic. On the subject of snakes, did you know Wistman's Wood on Dartmoor is home to the odd Adder, reclusive and non-aggressive, but their bite is venomous if provoked?'

'The "Wood" is an oak wood, home to the incredibly rare horsehair lichen (Bryoria Smithii), amazingly found at only two sites in Britain. Fascinating, don't you think?'

Neither James nor Will looked impressed, patiently waiting for "The Scarlet Pimpernel" to divulge the information they were after. Unfazed by the unenthusiastic response, Roger leaned back in his chair, his attention momentarily diverted by a duo of mature, attractive women who fronted up to the bar.

'Right lads, enough with the botanical lecture. What do you want to know?'

'Everything,' Will responded. 'To start with, Margo Betteridge tells us the Copeland brothers were poisoned first, then shot. Would you agree with that?'

'Yep, looks that way.'

'The gunshot wounds didn't actually cause their deaths?' James probed.

'Nope. Although I'm speculating they were shot shortly after death from reading through Margo's report. What I do find interesting is the type of firearm used; it is very peculiar. Bloody unfortunate we don't have more available evidence.'

Will sighed, shaking his head. 'Nothing, according to the notes Wallis left us, along with the physical evidence log. The Copeland brothers were found deceased in a disused section of the club.'

Tudor shrugged. 'Shame no weapon was found, but leave it with me. Like I say, these things take time. I'll run more tests, contact some firearm manufacturers, get the boys to research the internet, and that sort of stuff; see what we come up with.'

'At this stage, I *can* confirm entrance and exit wounds match pretty well with a dud .303 calibre, fully intact unfired round we found in the basement storeroom at KC's under the freezer.'

'What? You're telling us the brothers were shot with a rifle?'

'I'm 99% certain. The firing pin indentation on the base of the discarded round indicates a Short Magazine Lee Enfield Mk 3. The standard main battle rifle in service with Commonwealth forces for over sixty years; designed by James Paris Lee near the end of Victoria's reign at the Royal Ordnance Factory.

In action from the Boer War right up to the Northern Ireland troubles. But I'm leaning towards a more refined, updated version of the standard SMLE production rifle. Might be a special limited production model; I don't know.'

'Crazy. I've shot off a few rounds with a 303 at the local gun club. Deadly accurate,' James informed his colleagues.

'Spot on, James, my man. It tops the Mauser 98K as the best all-time bolt-action rifle, of course; that's my opinion.'

Tudor glanced down at his empty glass. 'Another one for the road, thank you; better make it a very large bitters and lemonade.'

***

Aveton Gifford, Devon, England

Christina walked into Dr Finch's office, the Japanese filleting knife concealed under her black leather jacket.

'Hi.' Neil Finch removed reading glasses, indicating for Christina to take a seat. 'We're going to be joined by Katie Sinclair shortly, a leading forensic psychologist. I hope you don't mind. Katie would be the ideal person for you to build a rapport with, to assist in putting the recent traumatic events behind you, and help move on with your life.'

Christina tried to hide the unexpected shock; she *had* hoped Dr Finch would be by himself; she wasn't sure how her idea would pan out with a third person present. Time was against her; she needed to execute her plan; opting out now was not a viable option.

'Er, sure,' she mumbled, taking up residence in one of the chairs forming a semicircle.

Moments later, there was a brief knock at the door, and Katie Sinclair entered the consulting room, extending a hand to Christina. 'Lovely to meet you, Christina. Dr Finch tells me you're doing really well, considering what you've been through.'

'Er, likewise. I don't really need you here, you know; I'm happy to speak with Dr Finch on my own.'

'I actually requested to be here,' Katie explained. 'I thought you would appreciate someone you can chat to on a regular basis. Dr Finch's role is very different from mine, but if you'd rather I left—'

'No, you're here now; you might as well stay.'

Katie took out her notebook and pen, positioning them on her lap. 'I'd like to ask you a few questions, Christina, if that's okay. We're keen to make sure the treatment you're receiving meets your needs.'

'Fine.'

Neil Finch nodded for Katie to proceed.

'Christina, I know the past few months have not been easy for you. Would you say your anxiety levels have increased of late?'

Christina began playing with strands of auburn hair, twirling the fibres around her long fingers. 'Maybe. Lisa's death hit me hard. I keep thinking I'll be next.'

'It's understandable to have these thoughts,' Katie reassured her. 'Do you believe Lisa's murder is linked to the attacks that took place in Australia?'

'Of course. They wanted the—'

'Wanted what, Christina?' Katie probed, scribbling in her notebook.

'Nothing. It's obvious I'll be next, and there's nothing anyone can do to stop them.'

'Who's "them"?' Katie grilled. 'If you have crucial information that could lead to an arrest, we urge you to talk to the police.'

'Too risky,' Christina mumbled. 'These men are ruthless.'

'Do you know who attacked you in Australia? Is it the same person or persons you suspect murdered Lisa?'

Christina let out a long sigh. 'Look, I don't know anything; I'm tired, and these sessions are a waste of time. I'm ready to leave now. Can I go?'

'We're only trying to help you, Christina.' Neil Finch broke in. 'Ms Sinclair and I are concerned for your welfare. You're suffering from post-traumatic stress disorder. Discussing what took place in Australia and your feelings will help you cope better in the future.'

Christina let out a shallow laugh. 'Surely you don't believe that for one moment; *I* don't. Lisa and I were beaten up by three men, who wanted us dead. They killed Lisa, and it's only a matter of time before they come after me.'

Katie and Neil exchanged brief glances; it sounded as if Christina knew the identity of her Australian assailants, clearly keeping this information from authorities.

Christina suddenly stood up. 'Thanks for your time; I'll be off now.'

Neil also got to his feet, gently touching Christina on the forearm; it was then she produced the knife.

'Back away or I'll make sure you never walk again,' Christina hissed, waving the knife in the air.

Neil eased a few feet back, holding up his hands. 'Hey, no one's going to harm you, Christina. I can tell you're frightened. Sit back down. Let's talk. We're here to help you.'

Katie, who'd sat quietly as Christina brandished the knife around, gradually rose to her feet. 'Christina, look at me. You're safe now.' Katie urged Christina to face her, hoping to redirect her thoughts.

'Safe? No one's safe.' Christina spat back. 'These people are dangerous.'

Neil advanced another step towards Christina, hoping she would calm down. 'We won't let anything happen to you, I promise.'

Christina lunged at Neil before he could dodge out of the way. The knife effortlessly pierced his white coat, slicing into his left side, causing him to cry out in pain. He stumbled backwards, clutching his lower abdomen with one hand and a chair with the other, crashing helplessly against the desk and onto the floor.

Katie gently shoved Christina out of the way, rushing to assist Neil, now doubled over in agony, the grey carpet rapidly turning red. Applying pressure on the wound, Katie reached for the desk phone, calmly dialling 999. Christina dropped the knife, staring incredulously at Finch. She had never really believed she would carry out her plan, but what other choice did she have?

***

Bovey Tracey, England, Devon
Moorland Forensics Consultants Facility

Nick entered the Moorland office through the emergency rear exit, his mobile pressed hard against his right ear. Appearing deep in conversation, he brushed past James, heading to the kitchenette, intent on a double-strength cappuccino. 'He's harmless, Mum, elderly like you. Try and be nice.'

Deciding against a ceramic mug from the wash-up rack, Nick opted for a paper cup from a fresh pack, placing it in position on the machine and proceeding to top up the dispenser with fresh beans.

James, flicking through a file at a nearby storage cabinet, had little trouble catching snippets of the animated conversation emanating from the kitchenette. He knew how hard it was for Nick with his mother in New Zealand, her memory loss becoming worse.

Silence prevailed whilst Nick listened to his mother on the other end of the phone. Eventually, he took over the conversation once more. 'No, he's not out to get you, Mum. Mr Spinner likes to keep to himself; you must respect his privacy. Stop checking up on him all the time. No, I'm not being unreasonable, Mum; his daughter has put in a complaint, which I need to deal with.'

Hot drink in hand, Nick walked slowly over to reception, pulling out a swivel chair, pale, gaunt features mirroring built-up stress and concern.

'Look, Mum, I'm at work. Got to go. Call you later, hey.'

'Trouble?' James enquired, watching Nick end the phone call, leaning back to stare into space.

'Mum's becoming overly fixated on one of her neighbours,' Nick explained. 'She thinks he needs looking after. Her fixation borders on harassment.'

'Probably just a phase she's going through,' James stated. 'They say dementia progresses through different stages.'

'I'm not so sure. This has been going on for several months now, and the way things are going, I might need to make a quick dash back to New Zealand to sort stuff out.'

'We can manage here,' James reassured his friend. 'Now Javier's on board, we can easily catch up on our case load and the commercial customers.'

'Thanks, I'll keep you posted. I'm hoping affairs will settle down. I really don't have time to go overseas right now. How did we go with the Sean Joyce case?'

James' smiling features said it all. 'Rudy Jenks rang me this morning. The Crown Prosecutor has enough evidence to take it to trial. Police forensics lifted Sean's prints off the cricket bat. We got corroborating confirmed DNA and rug fibre matches from the crime scene.'

'Sean smothered the old lady before hitting her over the head, smashing in her skull. I'll be happy to see that prick rot in maximum security for the rest of his days.'

'Well, in relation to the Copeland murders, here's what *I* know. Parker wants top priority given to the Copeland matter; word is that London's putting pressure directly on Izzy Bax, poor bastard. The Home Office is desperate for any positive news to divert attention from the appalling mess the force is in after the disastrous immigration riots. Social media and independent news outlets are creating hell for Westminster and the Met.'

'I've diverted two of my technicians to work full-time on artefacts from the scene, plus anything else related—not that we have much to go on. Margo's lab is running screens on biological swabs from the nightclub to help me out, but I can't understand why the lads were initially poisoned, then shot. Not much physical evidence to really go on. Finding the rifle would be handy.'

***

'How's Neil doing?' Fiona asked, scouring the depths of her freezer for frozen berries. Deftly switching her phone to speaker, she continued concocting her favourite smoothie.

'He'll be fine,' Katie replied. 'The knife didn't go in too far; luckily, no organs were impacted, and blood loss was kept to a minimum. I think it was the shock more than anything. Neither of us was expecting Christina to produce a knife; we never saw it coming.'

'What about Christina? I take it the boys in white coats have hauled her off to a psychiatric unit? She sounds dangerous.'

'Christina's been admitted to a private facility in Plymouth, but you know, Fi, I can't help thinking that little madam hatched this plan to get herself put away, out of reach of the people she believes are after her and whatever it is she possibly possesses.'

'You could be right. From what you've already told me, it sounds as if Christina and Lisa definitely knew their outback attackers. Will Parker must be channelling his enquiries in a completely different direction with this latest bit of news. I know from chatting with Linton; he's keen to work closely with Will to try and solve this crime.'

'If Christina refuses to talk, it won't be easy for Will and his team to trace those responsible,' Katie continued. 'No one has come forward with any information; they seem to be hitting that proverbial brick wall.'

'Have you had a chance to speak with Christina yet?' Fiona positioned herself on a kitchen stool, leisurely sipping her drink.

'No, she's undergoing psychiatric assessments. If my theory's correct, she won't be talking anytime soon. She'll want to stay in solitary confinement, out of harm's way.'

'Poor thing, but if anyone can get her to open up, it'll be you, Katie.'

'Um, not sure about that one; we'll see. I plan to wait a while before making contact, giving her time to think about what happened and generating some guilt. Neil certainly didn't deserve to be stabbed. His fiancée was beside herself when she went to visit him in the hospital. I must admit; he didn't look all that flash when first admitted.'

There was a moment's silence down the line before Katie opted for a change of subject. 'Tell me, what is happening on the male front, Fi? You chat a lot about Linton and Harvey on our weekly phone calls. Is there romance in the air?'

'Er, yes, but not with either of them. I'm still seeing Haruto, who's trying to make time to fly over from Tokyo. I'm really missing him; so are the boys. He makes me laugh, and laughter is definitely something my life craves right now.'

'You can't go far wrong with laughter,' Katie agreed. 'Now, before I hang up, you *are* coming back in April to help with my wedding preparations, aren't you?'

'Of course. Now, are you going to disclose the venue to me? I've been racking my brains as to where this amazing wedding will take place; it's even starting to keep me awake at night.'

Now, it was Katie's turn to laugh. 'Not yet; you'll find out soon enough. Must be off. Got to start working on those profiles I pledged; speak soon.'

Nick sat at his bedroom desk, listening to his mother's pleas for mercy, finding it impossible to concentrate on homework. He heard her apologising for the burnt dinner, for forgetting to purchase beer; the list was endless, but in reality, such trivia.

If he were older and stronger, Nick would put an end to his father's abuse, but he wasn't. Instead, he lay down on the bed, feeling helpless, trying to work out what to do.

Chapter Nine

Devon, England
Science Department, Torbay Hospital

'Lo and behold. The Light Brigade no less. Do come in, gentlemen. Grab a pew.' Dr Margo Betteridge, FP, seated at her desk, polishing off the remains of a cheese and pickle sandwich, waved the trio of visitors into her office. 'Make yourselves comfortable. I suspect you're anxious to hear my autopsy findings pertaining to one Lisa Marshall.'

Will, James, and Javier took up residence on three chairs, waiting in anticipation.

'Ah, this is an interesting one.' Margo smiled, throwing her sandwich wrapper into a nearby bin, sweeping the crumbs off the desk with the sleeve of her lab coat. 'Not seen many of these in my time, but when I do, wow.'

'And?' Will pressed.

'Our victim was poisoned by the Death Cap mushroom, scientific name Amanita phalloides, which happens to be responsible for most of the fatal mushroom poisonings around the world. This is what it looks like.'

Margo pulled up a photograph on her laptop.

'Looks similar to a normal mushroom you'd see in the shops,' Will commented, glancing at the screen.

'Very similar,' Margo replied. 'What tends to give it away is the tinted green cap. However, a person is less likely to touch Fool's Conecap and Panther Cap, which you'd know to stay well clear of by their unique appearance. If someone had failing sight, they could easily mistake the Death Cap for an edible mushroom. It's a lethal cretin.'

Margo paused to bring up the chemical structure of an alkaloid on the overhead monitor. 'The Death Cap holds the unenviable title of the world's most toxic mushroom as it contains alpha-amanitin, which causes liver and kidney failure. Ingestion of just half a cap can lead to death.'

'How common is it?' This question came from Will.

'I can answer that one for you,' James stepped in. 'It's very common in England. You'll find it growing on the ground in broadleaved woods from August through November.'

'Did Lisa ingest it in its natural form?' Will cross-examined. 'I mean, it seems odd why a young woman would randomly pick a deadly mushroom and eat it.'

'Ah, that's where I can provide you with more detail.' Margo beamed. 'Our young victim consumed the mushrooms in a quiche. There are distinct similarities to Lisa's death and that of Albert and Reg Copeland. This MO doesn't occur too often, and suddenly, out of the blue, we get similar homicides within a matter of weeks, which I don't believe is a coincidence.'

'Murphy's Law,' Will remarked.

Margo nodded. 'Whoever killed the Copeland brothers also murdered Lisa. However, in Lisa's case, they didn't shoot her; perhaps the environment was too exposed for them, fear of being seen or heard possibly. Loss of blood from lacerations at the base of the skull, in my opinion, was the result of her falling backwards, impacting a large rock.'

Will Parker almost jumped out of his chair. 'No way. What the heck. How can this be possible? Surely there has to be some mistake. I don't get how Lisa and the Copeland murders are linked.'

'Scientific observations don't lie.' Margo continued, amused at the surprise still visible on the DCI's face. 'Also, I can confirm Lisa definitely died at the reservoir, having consumed the quiche only a matter of hours prior, but the exact time of ingestion, I can't be certain, like I said; it's a lethal cretin.'

'I agree with your estimate, Doctor.' Javier broke in. 'I routinely checked the victim's physiological parameters on arrival at the scene, which indicated death only a couple of hours earlier, little doubt.'

'The cause of death is what we initially thought at the scene: choking on her own stomach contents, the result of a seizure, activated by the mushroom poisoning, and of course, her vital organs would have shut down. I'm not up on mushrooms in England, but from James' early remark, this Death Cap isn't available at the moment, right, Doctor?'

Margo inwardly smiled. She liked Javier; he was knowledgeable yet happy to hear expert opinions. Margo provided him with an answer: 'Whoever got hold of the Death Cap and utilised it to kill Lisa Marshall would most likely have kept the fungi in their freezer until they found use for it.'

'So, definitely the cause of death?' Will probed. 'No doubt in your mind, Margo?'

Margo shot Will a barbed stare. 'Detective Inspector, I've been doing my job for a number of years. I found traces of the deadly mushroom in the victim's stomach and had it properly analysed. Surely, you're not doubting my years of experience as a forensic scientist.'

Will blushed. 'Er, no, of course not, Margo, sorry.'

Margo continued with her findings, 'From the autopsy results, I found extensive kidney and liver failure, to be expected. Our victim would have experienced initial symptoms from the poisoning anywhere six to twenty-four hours after ingestion.'

'Those symptoms would include vomiting, diarrhoea, severe abdominal pain, followed by jaundice, seizures, coma, and eventually death. Not a pleasant way to go. Now gentlemen, your job is to determine if this was murder or accidental homicide.'

'Whoever made the tasty quiche, did they know the mushrooms were poisonous, or was it a grave error on their behalf? Did our victim die by mistake, a tragic accident?'

'Given what we know about Lisa Marshall, I very much doubt it.' Will concluded. 'Thanks for your time, Margo.'

'Ah, one more thing before you go, chaps. Jan Stafford's lab technicians at the mortuary are looking at evidence Javier and your SOCOs gathered from the immediate crime scene at the reservoir. Nothing noteworthy; essentially fibres, pieces of clothing, an empty beer bottle, sweet wrappers, etc. When they come up with anything of interest, I'll be sure to get in touch.'

***

Totnes, Devon, England

The DCI turned off the B Road and swung the Jaguar saloon into the carpark at the White Rook Public House.

'Whose idea was it to meet up with Lana Gibbs, anyway?' Mallory probed, hoping the meeting wouldn't take too long.

'Hers. Claims she picked up some juicy titbits from her trip down under, keen to share. I'd stay, but I have another meeting to go to.'

Mallory pulled a face. 'I don't trust her.'

Will pointed to a vehicle near a clump of trees. 'Lana's already here. That's her car.'

Mallory glanced in the direction of the trees. 'By the way, does seven o'clock suit you? No need to bring anything; it'll be a simple meal, spaghetti of some sort I'm thinking, and don't worry, I can handle Gibbs.'

'Sounds good.'

'Hi there,' Lana called out, her valiant attempts to exit a canary yellow Lotus Elise coupe parked nearby, attracting the stares of beer garden males, feasting their gaze on her shapely legs and body-hugging white leather leotard. Donning a stylish, full-length woollen coat, Lana waved her keys, locking the flashy, low-slung sports car with the deft press of a button.

Will and Mallory waved in acknowledgement as Lana approached, Will winding down his window. 'Back from your travels, I see; got yourself a bit of a tan.'

'Four long weeks, living out of a suitcase,' Lana grumbled. 'I'm working on articles now. Will, that's partly why I suggested a catch-up with Mallory.'

'No publishing anything until it's cleared by me first, right?' Will instructed. 'I don't want hassles with my Super for any of the *Star's* libellous misinformation.'

'Why would I do that, Chief Inspector? The *Star* always prints the truth and the facts,' Lana shot back, waiting for Mallory to exit the vehicle. 'Always on the defensive,' Lana remarked, watching Will drive off. 'By the way, Wakefield, what's going on between you and Parker?'

Mallory blushed, looking away. 'What do you mean?'

Lana threw her head back laughing, a mischievous look in her flashing, aqua blue eyes. 'Oh, come on. I can tell when two people are bonking; it's all in the body language. I thought you were engaged to that radio chap, Bruce.'

Mallory tried to hide her left hand, which sported a large diamond ring. 'It's complicated.'

'I bet it is. I take it Bruce is none the wiser to this; what shall we call it, *affair*?'

Mallory sighed. 'It's hardly an affair; I'm still single, remember.'

'Yeah, with a bloody big stone plonked on your engagement finger that you've just tried to hide.' Lana sounded amused. 'How long have you and Will been canoodling?'

'Lower your voice,' Mallory warned, wary of patrons in the vicinity, as they entered the restaurant, settling in a booth near the bar, instantly ordering cappuccinos.

'Is it a casual fling or more serious?' Lana probed, not letting the subject go.

'Lana, please don't say anything,' Mallory begged. 'My feelings are all over the place. I'm still fond of Bruce, but I'm not sure I want to get married again just yet; another divorce would kill me.'

Lana held her hands up. 'Hey, I'm not about to blab. I've slept with more men in my time than you've probably had roast dinners; most of them were married or in a "relationship." I'm the last person to preach. Just curious, that's all. Isn't Parker married?'

'Divorced, two grown-up kids.'

'That's the complicated part,' Lana cautioned. 'I sincerely hope you're up to handling all the extra baggage.'

A group of noisy, middle-aged women entered the bar, occupying the adjacent booth, rendering the two women silent for a moment.

'What did you want to see me about?' Mallory finally grasping the chance to transition from affairs of the heart.

'Lisa Marshall,' Lana dutifully replied. 'I've been liaising with an Aussie journalist I met in Sydney; Spen is working his UK media contacts to find out more about Lisa and Christina in an attempt to join the dots on who may have wanted to harm them, and so far, he's come up with a few interesting facts that might assist you in finding Lisa Marshall's killer.'

'Fancy yourself as a bit of a detective, do you? You certainly seem to be interested in what's going on in everyone's lives.' A touch of irony was evident in Mallory's tone. 'Perhaps you should apply for a job at CID.'

'Right, I deserved that, but you really must heed what I've got to say,' Lana persisted. 'What you do with the information is entirely up to you. Just remember me when the time comes.'

'Go on.'

'According to Spen, before heading out to Australia, Lisa worked as a stripper at an Exeter nightclub; he doesn't know the name of the place, but I'm sure you can find out.'

'What's the relevance of this?' Mallory's tone was sharp.

'I would have thought that to be obvious,' Lana retorted. 'Lisa and Christina were brutally attacked in the Aussie outback, and not for one moment do I believe the attacks to be random; they were targeted. Nor do I think the attacks are linked in any way to the other three women raped and murdered in Australia.'

'Therefore, you need to start digging into Lisa and Christina's pasts. If Lisa *was* working in a strip joint or bar, she probably mixed with some unsavoury characters; perhaps she owed them money or was witness to something. Isn't that a suitable place to start?'

'And I suppose this Spen guy is 100% legit, with impeccable credentials?'

'Swear to God. Checked him out thoroughly.'

Mallory lounged back in her seat. 'Yeah, you could be right. So far, I've not been able to come up with much information on either of the girls. As you'll be aware, Christina has been admitted to a psychiatric facility for ongoing treatment. Her grandparents refuse to allow us anywhere near her. Lisa's mother is too distraught to talk to anyone; we're coming up against brick walls.'

'One other thing, Lisa had a fiancé, a bloke called Jerome Flint,' Lana informed Mallory. 'A bit of a rough diamond, been in and out of prison over the years; theft, armed robbery, attempted rape. Might be worth following up.'

'Thanks.'

Lana gently touched Mallory's arm. 'Hey, your secret's safe with me. Be careful, though. Someone's bound to get hurt eventually.'

***

Exeter, Devon, England
CID

Will Parker ambled into the noisy squad room, armed with his daily comfort food: takeaway coffee and iced doughnuts. 'Settle down, boys and girls. I can't hear myself think over your din.'

The room fell silent.

'Now, as if we haven't got enough to be going on with, the manager of the Bovey Castle Hotel just phoned for assistance; a guest has been found dead in one of the bedrooms; we're not sure if it's foul play; a male in his late fifties, name of Blake Carleton. A forensic team is on their way to the scene; Jock and I will head up there shortly.'

A barrage of loud groans erupted in the room, mostly complaints from the team already under deadline pressure, forced to share overtime hours with other nonrelated cases. A sad reflection of the current state of the UK police force. Static wages, abysmal recruiting standards, mass resignations, entrenched identity politics, plummeting morale, and embarrassing leadership—not to mention a UK government completely out of touch with the British people.

Once more, Will put up his hand for silence. 'Yep, I hear you, but there's not a damn thing I can do about it. If you want a better work-life balance, then maybe the CID task force is not for you; the Super's office is along the corridor, the third door on the left.'

'Now, everybody, please listen up, starting with Jock; what have we got on the research you were conducting on Lisa and Christina, going back to the time they spent in

Australia? Did you find out where they were staying and if they had any employment?'

Jock remained positioned at his desk, clearing his throat. A booming, grating Highland brogue rang out, commanding attention: 'According to friends and family, the girls had part-time jobs at a wine bar cum eatery down the business end of Sydney in the tourist strip near the Opera House. Circular Quay, the ferry terminal, I believe. Hold it, got the name here somewhere.'

Jock rummaged for his notebook, finding it buried under a stack of papers. He opened it, reciting aloud, 'The Aussie Battler, owned by a guy called Vernon Peebles. They worked there about seven weeks before handing in their notice.'

'And after that?' Will probed.

'Still working on it, boss, but it seems they struck it lucky; all of a sudden, they were depositing healthy amounts of cash into their Aussie bank accounts on a weekly basis.'

'That's interesting,' Will acknowledged. 'Keep it up, Jock; splendid work so far. Now, Mallory, I understand you've been digging closer to home?'

'According to a Sydney journalist, before heading out to Australia, Lisa worked as a stripper at an Exeter nightclub; it may have some relevance to her attack, especially if she was involved in drugs or prostitution.'

'Do you have the name of this club?' Will explored. 'Can't be that many in operation.'

Mallory shook her head. 'No, but I'm looking at a couple of likely candidates.'

'Excellent. Anything else?'

'Lisa was due to be married next year in May,' Mallory continued. 'Her fiancé is a Jerome Flint, a bit of a spiv by all accounts. I've compiled some background on Jerome, who could be a person of interest; he beat up his last girlfriend with a hockey stick. Broken nose, depressed fracture of the cheekbone—get the picture?'

'Charming fella,' Jock remarked. 'What the hell women see in these blokes, I have no idea.'

'Alpha males, Jock,' someone mumbled.

'Was Jerome living with Lisa before she set off on her travels?' Jock probed.

'No, Jerome lives with his younger brother in Tavistock,' Mallory enlightened the team. 'I'm trying to arrange a time to go and speak with him. I also found out that Lisa and Jerome signed up with a wedding planner, Ariadne Defoe; her business is based out of a residential address over the border in Liskeard.

'I attempted to contact Ariadne, but she was busy with last-minute wedding preparations for a couple getting married this weekend. I'll keep trying. I'm hoping to nip across to Cornwall on Thursday.'

'Superb work,' Will commended. 'Right, anyone else with important information?'

The room remained silent. Will checked his watch. 'We'll reconvene in a few hours for a quick recap. Jock and I are driving up to Bovey Castle Hotel now. Nonsuspicious by the sound of it. Hopefully, the scientific boys will put this one to bed quickly. Back by four-thirty, if the snow stays away. Then, we can all go home.'

Ruth lay awake, listening to the clock ticking on the wall: three, four, five—nearly time to get up.

Her mind started racing; what if she slipped something into his tea to help him sleep? He always loved a cup of tea before going to bed. That way, he wouldn't wake in the night, feeling the need to fight.

Ruth had to try something; the violence was getting worse. Her left wrist was covered in fresh bruises, the pain at times excruciating.

Chapter Ten

Dartmoor, Devon, England Bovey Castle Hotel

James Sinclair and Javier Quintana greeted the manager of the Bovey Castle Hotel shortly before 10am and were taken up to room twenty-four, where the body of a half-naked man lay face-down on a double bed, a pool of rancid stomach contents spilling out onto the pale blue carpet.

'Yeah, definitely deceased,' Javier proclaimed, after quickly checking pulse and eye movement.

'Who discovered the body?' James asked, baulking at the smell, his mask doing little to prevent his nostrils from reacting. Without hesitation, he pushed open the double windows, allowing a cold blast of welcome fresh air into the space.

'One of our room attendants,' Mr Crabtree explained, averting his focus away from the body. 'Adele was bringing up breakfast at our guest's request; he'd phoned reception last night asking for a 7am room-service continental breakfast.'

'Any idea who the victim is?' This question from Javier, already engaged, systematically shooting off photographs of the corpse.

'An Australian gentleman, Blake Carleton,' Manager Crabtree replied.

Javier tried not to look surprised. He knew the man lying on the bed was not Blake Carleton, but to state this fact would implicate him in all sorts of problems. For now, he had to remain silent.

'Right, well, the police will be here shortly,' James announced. 'I'm sure they'll have a lot more questions for you and your colleagues, Mr Crabtree; these things tend to…'

At that moment, a young lad burst excitedly into the room, out of breath, his round face flushed. He caught hold of the manager's shirt sleeve, trying to pull him away.

'Mr Crabtree, sir, there seems to be some confusion at reception. A Blake Carleton is down there speaking to Janice, demanding to know why everyone thinks he's dead. You have to come down and sort this out; he's furious.'

'What are you on about, Freddy? Haven't you got something you need to be doing? You can't waltz in here; this room is off limits, a potential crime scene. Now go, please.'

'Perhaps you *should* check it out,' Javier advised, beginning to heat up under the plastic PPE gear, despite the cold outside air now circulating the room. 'We need to secure this area of the hotel. The less people around, the better, no offence.'

The manager reluctantly turned to follow his young colleague back to the hotel foyer, where a tall man stood at reception, demanding answers.

'How can I possibly be dead when I'm speaking with you now?' His tone went up a notch, emphasising his broad Australian accent. 'Go on, answer the question. I'm here, breathing. Hello, can you hear me, or am I some figment of your stupid imagination? Arseholes, the lot of you, incompetent galahs. What I would describe as a shrimp short of a Barbie.'

The middle-aged woman on reception kept her cool, remaining polite, even though enduring a tirade of abuse. 'I understand what you're saying, Sir, but a body has been found, and we believe…'

'Can I help you, sir?' Brody Crabtree interrupted, stepping forward. 'I'm Brody Crabtree, manager of the Bovey Castle Hotel.'

The man turned to face him. 'I hope you bloody well can. Name's Blake Carleton. I arrived two days ago and checked in for a four-night stay. Now, I'm hearing from all and sundry; I'm allegedly deceased. I tried to get breakfast, only to be told I must be an imposter hoping for a free feed, as according to your staff, I'm dead. Please tell me I'm not on Mars.'

Brody managed a faint smile. 'Not sounding good, is it, Sir? Follow me; we'll go somewhere more private.'

Blake shot everyone a riveting glare before being led by Brody into a back office, where he took up residence in a black swivel chair. Crabtree pulled out a chair behind his desk, opposite Blake, trying to remember when he shot a Chinaman.

'Can I get you something to drink, Mr, er?' Brody offered, frantically trying to recall the hospitality seminar titled "Handling the Guest from Hell.".

'Carleton, for Christ's sake. The name's Blake Carleton. Yes, a strong black coffee.'

Once the order had been placed, Brody tried to fathom what was going on. He listened whilst Blake updated him on a few facts.

'Two days ago, 10:15am it was, I checked into room twenty-four. Yesterday afternoon, I complained my room's air-conditioning wasn't working properly, so I got transferred into room eleven. I was assured it would be fixed by the end of the day, but I opted to stay in the slightly bigger room, number eleven, with a much nicer view. Couldn't see the sense in a continual room swap, having to pack and unpack yet again.'

Brody nodded. 'That would be rather tiresome.'

There was a brief knock at the door, and a mug of percolated coffee was brought in. Blake visibly relaxed, stretching forward to retrieve the drink, before continuing his explanation, 'When I went down for a late breakfast this morning, around ten, I provided the supervisor with my name, and that's when all the fuss started. Now, I don't know who fucked up, but I'm very much alive and wish people would stop gawking at me as if they've seen a ghost.'

Brody stared at Blake. After listening to this long-winded explanation, he politely excused himself, strolling back to reception. He waited a few minutes for a couple of guests to disperse, then asked a much-needed question of the receptionist.

'Janice, did Mr Carleton switch rooms recently?'

'Yes, sir. I believe he did. The report from Grace yesterday mentioned a faulty air conditioner. Oh, shit. That means—'

'What?' Brody sensed the worst.

'We had a gentleman arrive around seven yesterday evening, sir, after the air-conditioning was fixed,' Janice explained. 'He was a drop-in, with no prior booking. Grace put him in room twenty-four, which was, of course, vacant, as Mr Carleton had switched to room eleven.'

Brody turned white. 'Do you recall this gentleman's name?'

Janice turned to her computer, opening a database, scanning the information that flashed up on the screen. 'Here it is, Mr Crabtree; Leonard Everett, a fifty-seven-year-old accountant from Southampton, staying five nights to attend the CPA conference in Exeter. He wanted to stay somewhere more convivial, away from the activity, happy to commute into Exeter each day.'

Brody, still looking pale, put in a request for Blake Carleton to be shown into the restaurant for breakfast. He then headed back upstairs to chat with the forensic team, almost colliding with DCI Parker and DS Fletcher exiting the lift. Within a matter of seconds, Brody blurted out what he knew, how it was now feasible the victim was a Leonard Everett, from Southampton.

Will took charge immediately, dispatching Jock Fletcher on a low-key reconnoitre around the hotel and grounds. 'Right, let's go somewhere more private. I'll need details on both these men, Mr Crabtree, and then I'll want to interview Mr Carleton, along with your entire crew.'

'I suggest you cancel any future bookings for the foreseeable future. My team will work swiftly, but it won't give your hotel much credence if your guests learn of this unfortunate event.'

Brody Crabtree, his visage now tinged sickly green, led Will back downstairs to reception and into an adjacent room containing filing cabinets, document archive boxes, and a desktop computer monitor.

Bringing up the relevant files on the computer screen, he accessed the current guest database, pressing print. Collecting the copies from the reception printer, he passed them across to Will, who promptly returned to room twenty-four, anxious for a forensic update.

'A medical episode?' Will quizzed, entering the room, and addressing Javier.

'Yes, of sorts,' Javier enlightened him. 'Not sure, though, if that's what actually killed this man. It appears he was alone at the time of death; there is no indication of another person present in the room. The large amount of stomach contents concerns me; we'll take samples for testing.'

'This may interest you, Will.' James handed Will a brown cardboard box containing remains of a meal. 'Looks like the hotel staff left a complimentary snack pack for our guest, containing a bottle of red wine, what appears to be the remains of a quiche, cherry tomatoes, and a piece of chocolate cake. I'll take this with me and run a few tests.'

'Can you tell when he died?' Will probed once more, maintaining a healthy distance from the corpse.

'We both agree probably sometime early this morning.' James placed the snack pack into a clear plastic bag. 'Details will be clearer after the autopsy. Now, here's the rub, Will: signs are this guy most probably endured an extremely painful death.'

'Most likely a seizure, but it's more complicated than that. I hate to speculate, Will, but this is showing all the markings of the other three murders currently on your plate: Lisa Marshall and the Copeland brothers.'

Now, it was Will's turn to pale. He let out a long sigh. 'Not my day, is it?'

James managed a faint smile. 'Leave it with us, Will; we'll get you the forensic results as soon as we can.'

'Right, thanks. I'd better go and chat with this Blake Carleton chap and see what he can tell us.'

***

Dartmoor, Devon, England
Bovey Castle Hotel

Blake Carleton was just finishing breakfast when Will spotted him at a corner table in the restaurant, struggling with a coffee plunger. 'A word, please, Mr Carleton, if you don't mind.'

'I don't suppose I have much choice,' Blake grumbled, studying Will's credentials, before getting up and walking into the vast living room, where he made himself comfortable in a recliner next to the fire.

'In light of finding a body this morning, one we initially thought was you, we'll need to ask you a series of questions and try to establish what's going on here. Firstly, Mr Carleton, I'd like to ask, what brings you to the West Country?' Will took a seat across from Carleton, whose body language indicated hostility.

'A mini break.'

'Do you have friends here, family?'

Blake shook his head, keeping his eyes averted.

'Why Devon?' Will pressed. 'I mean, it's beautiful, but most people head to the Lake District, or somewhere a little less remote.'

'I like remote,' Blake replied.

'You're from Sydney, right? What line of business are you in?'

'I recently resigned from my role as senior biochemist for a large pharmaceutical company.'

'Why did you quit?'

'Let's just say the board and I didn't always see eye to eye. Excuse me, Chief Inspector, why would that have any relevance to events here?'

'Look, Mr Carleton, Blake. I'll be honest with you; there's a high probability *you* were the intended target, and because of the unexpected room swap, the other gentleman was mistakenly killed instead of you,' Will volunteered.

Blake shook his head. 'No, not possible. I'm no one special; I don't have any enemies, well, none I'm aware of. Why would I be a target? I think you're reading too much into this, Detective. Now, if it can be cleared with the Devon and Cornwall Constabulary, I'd like to continue with my short vacation.

You have my details, should you need to contact me again. I hear there are lots of nice walks around here; I might pop across to reception and make enquiries.'

Blake shifted in his chair, looking as if he was about to stand up. Will tried to keep his cool, amazed at Blake's casual response.

'Staying here at Bovey Castle will no longer be an option for you, Mr Carleton,' Will advised. 'Until we know for sure you were not the intended victim, you'll have to find alternative accommodation, somewhere more secure.'

'Nonsense,' Blake scoffed. 'You're not my keeper, Detective. I like this hotel; the staff are friendly, the room is comfortable, and I'm keen to continue dining in the restaurant, where they have a superb menu and a first-class chef. I *want* to stay *here.*'

Will rose to his feet. 'I can't force you to seek alternative accommodation, Mr Carleton, but please be careful. One dead body at the hotel is enough to be going on with.'

***

Exeter, Devon, England
CID

'I think the intended victim was definitely Blake Carleton,' Will stated at the hastily convened team meeting, a few hours after ending his conversation with Carleton. 'Because of the room swap, the killer targeted the wrong man. This leaves us with two problems: one, a man who shouldn't be dead, and second, a man who should be dead and may still be in the crosshairs.'

'A stubborn individual by all accounts,' Mallory concluded. 'He seems very blasé about the whole bizarre event. A total disregard for authority and the probable fact that an innocent person has been murdered.'

Will nodded. 'Yep, a mystery man who won't provide us with much information. We need to find out more about Blake Carleton; let's start with the name of the Sydney pharmaceutical company he worked for, why he left, that sort of thing.'

'And what about the actual victim? Has his family been informed?' Mallory asked.

'We've someone in Southampton undertaking that task as we speak,' Will announced. 'A very sad set of circumstances.

144

We've already managed to glean Leonard Everett was recovering from treatment for a rare form of leukaemia. Doctors only recently deemed him well enough to attend these accounting seminars in Exeter.'

'Leonard was to be joined by his wife and two teenage daughters next week, where they planned to hike across Dartmoor. According to family and colleagues, Len was a lovely chap, well-liked by everyone. Apparently, he volunteered at the local children's hospital twice a week and gave a lot back to his community. A rare individual.'

'Even more reason for catching the bastard who did this.' Evidence of anger filtering into Jock's voice, who himself had been a cancer sufferer, currently in remission.

'And what do we know about the food box you found in the room?' Mallory enquired, recording the updates on her smartphone. 'Did that shed light on anything?'

'Jim Sinclair at Moorlands and Nick's lab chemists are scheduling a full physical and biological analysis program. With current backlogs and staff shortages, don't expect anything for a few weeks.' Will responded.

'According to the duty manager, Brody Crabtree, the hotel does not supply these sorts of boxes; it had to come from an external source. It appears someone left it outside room twenty-four with a note attached: *Compliments from the staff at Bovey Castle Hotel.'*

'No one saw or heard anyone dropping the box off, most probably deposited at a time when fewer people were about. Maybe late at night. There's no corridor security footage.'

'What about hotel security in general? Has that been taken away for analysis?' Mallory probed. 'Whoever killed the unfortunate Mr Everett entered and exited the hotel at some point.'

'Ahead of you.' Jock waved a flash drive in the air. 'The relevant CCTV data files have been downloaded. I've allocated WPC Norma Lacey the task of scrolling through all the footage.'

'The hotel staff must be in a state of disbelief and anxiety,' Mallory remarked, unconsciously fidgeting with a shirt button.

'True, I have to do something, I suppose. Check if Public Relations has anything left in the budget to nab Katie Sinclair from MFC for a short group counselling session at the hotel,' Will replied.

'Right, well, that's about it for today. Chas, I want you to check into Blake Carleton's background; Jock, you have the task of completing interviews with the hotel staff, and Mallory and I will chase up forensics. The rest of you can continue working on Lisa Marshall's case. Thanks, everyone, and have a pleasant evening.'

Will paused outside the conference room, waiting for Mallory to emerge, pretending to check phone message updates. Everyone else had cleared out a few minutes earlier.

'Fancy going for a curry?' Will petitioned Mallory, as she strolled out into the corridor, weighed down with a pile of papers, her handbag flung loosely over her right shoulder.

'Yeah, why not. It's been a crap day. Let's venture further afield to a nice place I know in Crediton, my shout.'

Once in the car, Mallory flicked a quick text to Bruce: *Apologies, I'm working late. Don't wait up; I'm not sure what time I'll be home.*

***

Lae, Papua New Guinea
Two Weeks Before Christmas

Solomon Leahy lit up another cigar, oblivious to the stares of an expat couple sunbathing under a nearby cabana. Stretching short, skinny legs out on the sun lounge, he signalled to the local attending the kiosk for an iced tea. 'Are you ready for this little escapade, Ryder?'

Thirty-nine-year-old Ryder let out a loud belch, sculling the rest of his lager. He hadn't bothered showering for a few days, the body odour intense, not that Solomon seemed to care.

Solomon himself looked like he'd only just woken up, long matted Rastafarian strands of grey-flecked hair hanging down over brooding green eyes, the dark facial features betraying mixed-race Highland Province origins. Leahy was desperately in need of a haircut.

'As ready as I'll ever be,' Ryder replied in a thick, languid Texan drawl. 'God, this heat is getting to me today; think I'll jump in and cool off.'

The swimming pool presented an idyllic setting; enticing crystal-clear water glistening under a blue tropical sky, a limpid sou'easter breeze filtered in off the sea, rippling through the coconut palms, the peaceful picture only disturbed by the occasional low-flying light plane skimming the treetops across the harbour on final approach to Lae iInternational aAirport.

Solomon watched Ryder stroll across the travertine. He stood for a few seconds near the edge, hesitating before raising his arms to dive in at the deep end, emerging a short while later to float on his back.

After twenty minutes in the pool, Ryder eased himself out over the side, grabbing a towel. He headed back towards the lounges, dripping water in his wake.

He was under the impression Solomon was dozing until his eyes slowly opened, and he lobbed a question, 'Perhaps we should go through the itinerary one more time. We can't afford any stuff-ups.'

'No, I know what to do.' Ryder was on the defensive, flopping back down under the umbrella. 'Five years at Bagram has seen me deal with plenty of dangerous situations. If anyone gets in my way, bam, the bastard will be blown to smithereens.'

'Keep that foul temper of yours in check,' Solomon warned, adjusting the sunglasses perched on the end of his nose. 'We can't afford any unnecessary attention drawn to us. Got it?'

'Yeah, yeah, whatever. You need to chill, Sol; leave safety to me. After all, isn't that why I'm your number one security guy?'

Solomon muttered a candid response, 'You're too gung-ho, Ryder; remember, you're not in Afghanistan anymore fighting a bunch of medieval, sandal-wearing, goat herders.'

'That's the way I like it, my friend. Have you spoken with Terry Coates? Has he agreed to be our pilot for the trip?'

'You bet, Terry's on board. Three of you will accompany the shipment from the mine site to Port Moresby: yourself, Terry, and Harvey Driscoll. Harvey will be here by the end of the week; make him welcome and don't put the guy off. His temper can flare as much as yours. This needs to be a hassle-free operation. Too much is at stake; I can't afford any repercussions back in the House.'

Cornwall, England

'Ariadne Defoe? Detective Mallory Wakefield, we recently spoke on the phone.'

'Ah, yes, of course. Do come in; it's bitter outside. How I hate December. My clientele drops off dramatically during winter; everyone wants a nice warm wedding. You got here nice and early; excellent. I don't start work for another hour.'

Ariadne ushered Mallory into an expansive, bright, open-plan kitchen, the centrepiece of which was a wood burner running full blast.

'Nice place you've got here; love the Brueghel,' Mallory remarked, sitting down at the kitchen table, taking in the matrimonial-themed surrounds and decoration, particularly the reproductions of classic paintings and Victorian prints of traditional old English bridal flower headbands.

'I inherited this house from the parents. My office and studio are at the front of the building. With today's rental prices, I couldn't afford an office in town. Forgive me my manners; can I offer you some refreshments?'

'No, I'm fine, thanks all the same. I won't keep you long. I'd just like to establish more information about Lisa Marshall: how well you knew her.'

'Oh, not well at all. She won a competition I ran in my magazine, *Modern Bride Quarterly*. Basically, most of her wedding expenses would have been covered. Within a budget, of course. You know how it works; various companies provide certain items, be it alcohol, wedding gowns, bridesmaid dresses, flowers, chocolates, photographers and, most importantly, the wedding venue. In return, these companies receive free advertising, which enhances product sales.'

'I guess weddings are a big business. What did Lisa have to do to enter the competition?'

Ariadne beamed. 'List her top ten romantic holiday destinations. The entries were then sorted, and the ones I liked best were popped into a hat. Lisa's name was pulled out first. That's how she won.'

'Did you ever meet her fiancé?'

'Only once; he's a builder; Jerry, Jerome, something like that. Lisa was stoked to have won the competition. At first, she was reluctant to accept the prize; she wasn't keen on publicity; she told me she would prefer a low-key wedding, followed by a two-week honeymoon in Cornwall, nothing fancy. According to Lisa, she entered the competition for a hoot, never expecting to win.'

'When did you last speak with Lisa?' Mallory continued, switching on a mini tape recorder and placing it on the table.

'Shortly before she returned to the UK. She wanted to know if another couple could claim the prize instead of her.'

Mallory paused the recorder, looking up in surprise. 'Why would she do that?'

Ariadne shrugged. 'Well, one assumes it can't have been easy for Lisa, having been attacked like that. I imagine she was suffering from some form of stress. I have to admit, she sounded nervous, not the bubbly person I once met.'

'Would that have been possible, I mean, to give the prize to someone else?' Mallory quizzed.

'It could have been done, but I felt Lisa needed a boost; why let those bastards ruin her life? In the end, she reluctantly decided to go ahead with everything on the understanding that she vetted articles and photographs before they went to print. Of course, I agreed.'

'Do you know why Lisa's fiancé didn't accompany her to Australia?' Mallory explored.

'Er, I think he had work commitments,' Ariadne offered. 'Originally, Lisa only intended to be overseas about six to nine months.' Silence prevailed. Ariadne drew a deep breath, slowly shaking her head. 'Now, friends will be attending her funeral, instead of an elaborate wedding. Unbelievable how life can change so dramatically in such a short space of time.'

'Yes, it is.'

'Now, let's focus on a more cheerful topic; I notice you're flashing a beautiful cut diamond on your engagement finger. Have you set a date?'

'Er, no, not yet.'

'Well, don't leave it too long,' Ariadne warned. 'Men eventually crave that honest woman business. Can't have him casting his gaze elsewhere, leaving you on that lonesome shelf.'

Mallory shrugged. 'Bruce is just as career-minded as I am. He's a radio host for BBC Radio Bristol, and in the throes of signing a new contract for his own breakfast show. I think marriage is possibly the furthest thing from his mind right now.'

'Ah, you'd be surprised; men can be just as focused as women, maybe more so. Financial security and power earn the respect of their peers and make them more confident and emboldened.'

After a momentary pause, Mallory fired another question at Ariadne, keen to take the focus away from herself, 'You're not married, Ariadne?'

Laughter filled the room. 'No, I'm not, thankfully. Call me a hypocrite, but marriage and children are not my thing, but please don't repeat that. My image alone goes on the *happily ever after.*'

Mallory checked her watch. 'I'd best be off. Er, one more thing: when you last spoke with Lisa, did she say anything about her attack in Australia? I mean, actual specifics?'

'Not really. I got the impression she didn't want to talk about it, and I didn't feel it was my place to pry.'

'No problem. Well, thanks for your time. If anything springs to mind that might help with our investigation into Lisa's death, please give me a call.'

'Certainly. Oh, before you go, why don't you fill out a form to enter our next competition? If you were to win, it might jolt you into making that final commitment. The first prize you know about; the second prize is a dozen bottles of very expensive vintage méthode champenoise from the Vallée de la Marne region of France, and the third prize is dinner for two at a Michelin Star restaurant in London. What have you got to lose?'

Mallory reached for the form Ariadne was holding out to her. 'Go on, why not. I'm certain Bruce wouldn't mind some nice bottles of French bubbly or even dinner in London. He might cringe at first prize, although having said that, he can be quite vain at times and loves a bit of publicity, especially with his line of work.'

Once the form had been completed and Mallory had written down her top ten favourite romantic movies of all time, she passed it back to Ariadne.

Ariadne paused before taking the form. 'I hope you find the culprit. That young woman had her whole life ahead of her. No one feels safe around the southwest at the moment, with a killer at large.'

Opening the plastic bottle, Ruth carefully read the label before dropping two small white tablets into the ceramic mug.

'Tea.' She placed it in front of him before heading upstairs to bed.

Chapter Eleven

KC's Nightclub

Shirley Copeland bustled around, moving a pile of last week's newspapers off a chair, clearing room for Will Parker to sit down. It was seven in the morning; Will was making an early start. For once, Shirley was without her usual heavy make-up, wrapped in a quilted dressing gown and slippers.

Two large Alsatians lay in one corner of the room, attentive, keeping a close eye on Will. He glanced over at them, their size and appearance unsettling.

'Come on, Scotch and Soda won't hurt you. Well, not unless I ask them to. Mind you, the boys are known to nip on odd occasions, probably out of boredom. You a dog person, Will?'

Will looked away from the dogs. 'Nope, I don't have time for pets, not in my line of work. Well, not anymore. The missus had one for a while; before we split, I was relieved it went with her, in retrospect.'

'Shame. They can be great companions. Now, you wanted to drop around to see me, something to do with that Lisa Marshall, I believe, the backpacker girl in the news. You didn't give much away when you rang on the way over. Keen to keep me guessing.'

Will shuffled slightly in his chair. 'It's come to our attention Lisa worked in a local nightclub before going out to Australia. We're thinking there was a high probability it was here, at KC's?'

Shirley admired her polished nails before answering Will's question, 'I've nothing to hide. Lisa was employed at the club for around six months prior to going out to Australia. Also got me out of a fix for a few weeks at my lap dancer restaurant up in Barnstaple.'

Shirley paused, drawing slowly on a cigarette, simultaneously reaching for her cup of Earl Grey. 'Lisa needed extra cash for the trip. It's no big deal, Will; lots of women work here over a period of time. You'd be surprised who I hire: nurses, doctors, policewomen, and wives of businessmen who spend a lot of time in London or overseas. Never judge anyone, William Parker; everyone has the right to make their own choices in life.'

'Now, the club's clientele?' Will probed. 'What can you tell me about them?'

'A lot of business types, old and young, but mostly men, of course.' Shirley grinned. 'We don't tend to cater to the gay, lesbian, and transvestite communities, they're well looked after elsewhere, although live and let live, is my motto.'

'Was Lisa popular with the punters?' Will explored.

Shirley raised both eyebrows, offering Will a cynical look. 'I honestly don't know why you're bothering to ask me these questions, Will. Lisa's death cannot be linked to KC's in any way. And before you ask, no, there wa no other employee she had a barney with, no client who harassed her; she got on well with my security team, and at the end of the day, I quite liked her; she kept her nose clean. There you go, done and dusted; you need to channel your investigation elsewhere.'

'Yeah, well, I must admit it does look that way. However, I wouldn't be doing my job properly if I didn't ask,' Will reacted, keeping his voice moderate and even, mindful of the Alsatians close by, sitting up alert and watchful.

Shirley looked earnestly at Will, reaching over the table to pat his knee. 'You're a decent copper, Will, one of the best I know. I thank you for not treating me like a leper, as some tend to do. I'm well aware my line of work isn't exactly orthodox, but at the end of the day, I see it as bringing a little pleasure into people's lives and probably keeping a few rapists off the streets.

'You can't deny there are a lot of lonely men out there, cast aside by vindictive, narcissistic women. See yourself out, will you, pet? All this interrogation has brought on a migraine; I need to go and lie down.'

Will stood up. 'Thanks for your time, Shirley. Let's pray our paths don't cross again this week. People will start gossiping.'

Shirley waved her cigarette in the air, a twinkle in her eye. 'You're welcome at KC's anytime, Will. I've some lovely young women; happy to oblige if you're feeling that way inclined. I'll even offer you a discount.'

'I'll keep that in mind.'

***

156

Mallory walked alongside Will, making their way to the Jaguar saloon parked at the rear of police headquarters. Neither noticed Bruce in the shadows, arriving back a day early from a trip to London, on the spur of the moment, electing to surprise Mallory, hoping she would join him in a drink at the local on the way home.

He held back, hovering near a police van in the dank, semi-darkness of the December evening, watching his fiancée pause as she allowed Will Parker to open the car door. Bruce's short temper exploded; consumed by a wave of anger, he kicked a nearby rubbish bin out of his way, the clatter causing Will and Mallory to turn around.

'Just the wind picking up,' Will announced. 'I don't know about you, Mal, but I could go for a nice, chilled glass of bubbly.'

'Just what I'm thinking; thought the day would never end.'

Will reached across Mallory, helping to fasten her seatbelt, and both conversed intimately, joking, relishing each other's company.

'Bruce won't mind if you get home late?' The wind blew in the direction for Bruce to hear the gist of what Will was saying. He conjectured Mallory's reply by Will's next comment.

'I love that expression, *when the cat's away*; that's a daring sentence from you, Mal, perhaps your relationship is starting to stale.'

Bruce caught the familiar lilting sound of Mallory's laugh, his anger increasing.

'Been meaning to try the new Mongolian BBQ down near the river; let's head there,' Will informed Mallory, checking his watch and hopping into the driver's seat. A few minutes later, Will eased the unmarked Jaguar out of the carpark, slotting seamlessly into the crawling peak hour chaos, heading towards Exeter city centre.

Panicking, Bruce sprinted back to his modest Citroën estate, recklessly charging out into the traffic, stalling several times in an attempt to keep pace with the rapid XF saloon. Once he had them back in sight, he slowed down, hoping not to be seen.

Within fifteen minutes, Will pulled up outside the restaurant, helping Mallory out of the car. She looked relaxed and happy. Will placed his hand in the small of her back, guiding her towards the restaurant entrance.

Bruce secured a parking spot across the road, planning his next move. He hadn't banked on confronting Will, likely drawing attention to himself, which might result in bad publicity. BBC Radio Bristol had recently promoted him with a brand-new contract and an increase in pay. A deeply embarrassing public spat with a well-known detective, surfacing on social media, would most certainly end his career.

Bruce entered the Asian bar and grill, raising the fur-lined collar on his flak jacket. Deliberately keeping his head down, he shuffled in closer to Will's table, pretending to peruse the takeaway menu, with no intention of staying long. He merely wanted to observe what was going on.

Mallory's infectious laugh rang through the restaurant. Will could be seen pouring champagne into two slender flutes, passing one to Mallory. His hand stretched across the table until he was caressing the fingers on her left hand. With one swift movement, Mallory removed her engagement ring, dropping it into her purse.

'Let's not spoil the evening,' Bruce heard her say. 'The ring is a distraction for us both.'

'Only if you're sure,' Will responded.

'Quite sure.'

Bruce nearly sent a diminutive Korean waiter flying in his haste to exit the crowded restaurant.

'You are not dining with us tonight,' the waiter remarked, regaining composure, beaming at Bruce.

'Fuck off, shit food anyway.' Bruce slammed the door in his wake, a few diners looking up in surprise.

Once back in the Citroën Estate, Bruce crashed both fists down hard on the dashboard, rage boiling over; Mallory and Will would pay for her infidelity; he'd make sure of that.

***

Newton Abbot, Devon, England

'What's this?' Tom threw the newspaper down on Lana's desk, opened to highlight a recent inside page editorial. He started to recite the article out loud:

Death of Innocence
Local Woman Attacked Down Under

The Newton Abbot Star was upset to learn a young female, recently attacked during a working holiday in Australia, has been found dead on the banks of a Dartmoor reservoir. Reliable sources close to the Star are claiming the demise of local Bovey Tracey woman Lisa Marshall is linked to a series of murders that recently took place in New South Wales.

Police are yet to determine the motives behind all four homicides; however, it's apparent there's a serial killer on the loose in Australia, now choosing to strike on British soil.

With more victims a definite possibility, the police are warning women to be vigilant and take extra care, particularly in Devon, where the murderer could possibly strike again.

In a sensational turn of events, a second woman, also viciously attacked alongside Ms Marshall in the Australian outback, has been admitted to a secure psychiatric clinic in Plymouth for ongoing treatment, following her unprovoked physical assault on a local high-profile psychiatrist. Reasons behind the assault remain unclear.

The backgrounds of all victims are being investigated by police, new evidence coming to light that Lisa Marshall worked at a Devon strip club. Vital questions remain unanswered: Is there a link to Lisa's murder with prostitution and drugs?

With all homicide enquiries, time is of the essence to prevent more deaths. Anyone with information should contact police immediately.

'Seems fine to me.' Lana sounded pleased with herself. 'Quite well written and certainly to the point. The public has a right to know what's going on, to stay safe.'

'Yes, and with little in the way of hard facts backing up what you've written, you'll precipitate unnecessary panic in the community,' Tom seethed. 'How many times have I stressed, Lana, cut out the speculative reporting; you'll land us *all* in shit.'

'Nonsense, take a chill pill, Tom. It's only an "Op Ed.". Seriously, do you want sales or not?' Lana let out an exaggerated yawn, feigning boredom. 'People have a right to know what's going on. Factual or not, it's my job; all respectable journalists are obliged to keep their readers abreast of the conversations happening on the street. There's your factual information.'

'I suppose you fancy yourself as some big-shot journo now that you've been mixing with that mob in Australia, capable of reporting for a national paper,' Tom leered. 'By the way, did you not stop to think about proofreading the article you penned last week titled *Living in Devon*? Since when has climate been spelt "climite," and as for country, well, that was practically disgusting, missing out the all-important "O."'

Lana chuckled. 'Yes, that was a *beauty*. I certainly received a few phone calls about that one, plus dinner invites.'

Tom snatched the paper back off Lana's desk. 'Do us all a favour and start focusing on work. Otherwise, you can look for another job.'

Lana childishly poked her tongue out, deliberately turning her back on Tom. She was sick of being told how to do her job. Spen had convinced her there were other options out there, and Lana was determined to prove her worth. Tom was welcome to his snotty rag, down a side street, with a smattering of readers. Lana envisaged a bright future, one that didn't consist of Tom Markham breathing down her neck.

***

Sydney, Australia
Pacific Rim Mining NL, Head Office

As the scheduled Zoom meeting approached, Brenda paced manically up and down the spacious conference room overlooking Sydney Harbour, making sure everything was in its place, particularly the computer screen backdrops, deliberately focusing on a selection of the company's large contemporary paintings by well-known artists depicting the Australian landscape.

Hair and make-up professionally attended to, a Bulgari watch and matching pearl clasp over a high-neck black designer top completing the picture, the Company Secretary was out to impress.

'Two minutes,' Brenda announced to Harvey, taking her place at the conference table, making a few minor adjustments to the computer screen to counteract a slight reflection. 'Such a shame Colin isn't able to join us on the call today. Stomach bug, you say?'

'Er, yeah, something like that.'

'I would have thought being the Chairman and CEO of Pacific Rim Mining NL, it was vital Col be informed the shipment has been brought forward a week.'

Harvey shot Brenda an unpleasant stare. 'Your role is not to question my authority or attempt to undermine me, Brenda. When Colin needs to know something, I, as head of operations, will be the one to tell him, not you. Do you understand?'

Disregarding Harvey's hostile rebuke, Brenda turned back to the laptop positioned in the middle of the table. 'Yes, of course, Harvey. Right, here are the others logging on now.'

Harvey glanced at the screen as Terry Coates came into view. Then the two Port Moresby based men appeared, grinning and waving.

'Welcome everyone.' Brenda pushed a loose strand of hair behind her ears. 'Shall we do a quick introduction? I don't think everyone has met before.'

'Come on, is that necessary!' Harvey exclaimed. 'I'm sure we all know everybody's roles within the company.'

Brenda ignored his comment, asking everyone on the Zoom call to introduce themselves. One by one, they obliged:

Solomon Leahy—'Hello all. I am the Deputy Minister responsible for all PNG Government mining, including the country's 30% share in the New Britain Mining Joint Venture.'

'Ryder Albero, ex-US military. Head of Security, Pacific Rim Mining Operations, and I'll be on the flights shipping the gold from the mine site to Japan.'

Harvey Driscoll—'Operations Manager of Pacific Rim Mining NL here in Sydney. I will also be on the helicopter accompanying the cargo from the mine site to Moresby, then charter all the way through to Japan.'

'Hi everyone, Terry Coates, originally from Brisbane. I'll be your chopper pilot on the first leg of the transfer from the New Britain mine site to Port Moresby.'

'And me, of course, Brenda Carr—Company Secretary, based here in beautiful Sydney.'

'Just to recap; Terry and I will be arriving in Port Moresby late Tuesday afternoon,' Harvey announced. 'Schedule lift-off from the mine site airstrip is 1100 hours Friday morning, weather permitting, of course.'

'According to the Bureau of Meteorology, we should be fine,' Terry confirmed. 'Bad weather isn't materialising in the Bismark Sea environs until the following week; with a forecast early arrival of the monsoon. I envisage a quick refuel at Lae, maybe thirty minutes, then straight to Moresby.'

'Right, now let's go over the shipment of the gold and the schedules in full,' Harvey continued. 'I've been in touch with our Japanese joint venture partners, and we will be met at Narita Airport once our flight from Moresby clears customs. I've negotiated an excellent deal on the charter, a Cessna Citation executive jet, custom converted for freight operations. I understand all signed off and ready to go.'

'The gold will be transferred to a Japanese, London-accredited refiner. After melt and assay, the resulting fine gold content on outturn will be allocated to each of the venture partners metal accounts at the refiner, as per the JV agreements.'

'Naturally, the partners are excited and hoping things proceed smoothly. Being the first delivery after a yearlong mine shutdown, I don't need to tell you this is not your normal shipment. Approximately 20,000 ozs of high-quality ore, 93% pure.'

'Naturally, the JV partners and especially the PNG Government, I'm sure Solomon will agree, are keen to receive their proceeds of the gold without delay. What's gold today; USD 2300/oz? I make the shipment value USD 40 million, give or take.'

'Bloody correct, mate. Treasury are hanging out for it,' Solomon confirmed. 'The government needs the funds injection to cover the next interest instalment on an IMF loan deadline in two weeks. A default is not an option; we're talking about a major national embarrassment, especially for my department.'

As soon as the Zoom call came to an end, Brenda finished typing the minutes, printing out a hard copy, before filing it away in an A4 binder.

'I'll email those off for you, making sure everyone in the meeting gets a copy,' Harvey suggested, reaching for the binder.

Brenda held it firmly to her chest. 'No problem, Harvey, you've enough to do. I can email them late this afternoon. I need to make sure Colin gets his copy. Your mind is on overload; you might forget Col in the process.'

'No, I won't forget him,' Harvey insisted, reaching once more for the file Brenda was holding on to.

'No, I'll send them.' Brenda had a look of defiance on her face. 'I'm more than capable of flicking off a few emails, Harvey.'

'Yes, I know. Look, at least wait until next week. Colin's not well. He won't thank you for reminding him of work when he's trying to recover. The medicos don't want any complications after Col's recent triple bypass.'

Brenda hesitated. 'Yes, well, you may be right. I'll leave the file on my desk, reminding me to email the minutes first thing Monday morning.'

Harvey physically relaxed. It was critical Colin Wheatley, the CEO of Pacific Rim Mining NL, knew nothing about the large shipment of gold being transferred ahead of schedule from PNG to Japan, not yet anyway. Harvey had convinced Colin to take a couple of weeks off and spend quality time with the family. To his work colleagues, Harvey announced Colin was away on sick leave with a stomach virus.

'What have you got planned over the weekend?' Harvey asked Brenda, throwing a few files into his briefcase, keen to change the subject. 'Warm and sunny, they're saying.'

Brenda turned, surprised by Harvey's unexpected kindness. Why the sudden change from the sullen and moody behaviour he'd been inflicting on office staff most of the week?

'Nothing planned for tonight,' Brenda responded. 'An early night catching the final episode of a Welsh crime show I'm watching. Such a lovely-sounding language, don't you think?'

'Er, yes, funny you mention it; not that I've heard much in my time, but my mum was born in Wales. I remember growing up; she would occasionally launch into some favourite Cymric tune from her childhood.'

Brenda smiled. 'Tomorrow, I'm heading over to Manly on the ferry for some sun and surf. In the evening, I'm meeting a friend at Watson's Bay for seafood. Afterwards, ah, I don't know, maybe I'll take a stroll along the waterfront before heading home.'

'Sounds idyllic.'

'And you, what do you have planned?'

'Vegging out. Sunday night Fiona Sinclair's joining me for dinner, but it won't be a late one.'

'Great, well, I'd best be off. Enjoy your weekend. See you Monday.'

'Night, Brenda.'

The pills worked for a while; then, he decided he was drinking too much tea, and he would no longer have a cup before going upstairs to bed.

Nick pleaded with his mother to leave; they could go and stay with relatives, but Ruth was adamant: leaving wasn't an option; she had to think of another plan.

Chapter Twelve

Sydney, Australia

Linton peered down from the rear of the Sydney Water Police launch idling near the seawall, mesmerised by the grotesque scene of three police divers in a dark grey RIB, struggling to untangle a body from the triple outboards hanging off the stern of a tourist "joy ride" fast cruiser.

Although the legendary Sydney nor'easter had sprung up, pumping in at a steady, refreshing 15 knots, the senior detective, despite being clothed appropriately in a polo shirt and jeans, was wilting in the heat of the Sydney summer and gesticulated towards a carton of mineral water.

'A bit of a mess, Ansley,' the launch commander proclaimed, joining DCI Linton on the transom to hand over the bottled water.

'Yeah, I can see. Male, female?'

'Female, for sure.'

'Do we know who she is?'

'Not yet, Linton.'

The DCI squinted from the dazzling late afternoon light bouncing off the water. He needed to invest in a decent pair of Polaroid lenses; these cheapies were bloody useless against the glare, initiating headaches.

'Who discovered the body?'

'That middle-aged guy on the walkway, leaning against the highway patrol car, chatting to uniform; short and stocky, wide-rimmed glasses. Strolls along the waterfront every afternoon between three and four for a daily constitutional. I believe he works for some large finance company, as a consultant or something, lucky enough to work from home. Raised the alarm, spotted the body lodged between the triple Mercurys of the "Harbour Thrills" charter powerboat. Contacted the authorities immediately.'

'Home being where?' Linton probed.

'Over there.' The commander pointed to the modernist, low-slung apartment complex lining the opposite foreshore of Sydney Cove, close to where streams of animated tourists made their way on the mandatory pilgrimage to the Sydney Opera House.

'Name?'

'Maxwell Sutton.'

'Right, I'll go have a word with him.'

Jumping onto the public pontoon as the police launch manoeuvred in close, Linton bounded up the steps and approached the eyewitness.

'At first, I thought it was rubbish washed up from yesterday's thunderstorm,' Maxwell explained. 'But edging closer, I saw the face; it was a big shock, all chopped up from the boat's outboard motors.'

'Yes, not a sight one encounters every day. Tell me, Mr Sutton, were there other people about when you discovered the body?'

'Close by, you mean. No; not that I recall. A lot of people, mostly tourists, were lounging on the grass in the sun or heading to the Contemporary Art Gallery and the Rocks. When it hit me, I rang emergency services immediately and tried to attract the attention of the Harbour Thrills people at the booking kiosk on the walkway.'

'Thanks, Mr Sutton, I'll have a constable take your details, and at some point, we'll get you to provide us with an official statement.'

'No problems. Glad to be of assistance. Hell, what a way to go.'

Linton headed back to the body, now being examined by a forensic team concealed under an erected white pop-up tent on the pontoon.

'Just when I was hoping to get in some Christmas shopping,' the government duty pathologist grumbled, removing seaweed from around the victim's neck. 'My shift finishes shortly, and I'm not hanging around. You'll need to contact the FMCCC to book the autopsy; can't guarantee who you'll cop.'

'Any idea of the cause of death?' Linton pushed.

'Christ Almighty, give me a break, Linton. My name's not Houdini.'

'Yeah, okay, Morris, but at this point in time, I've got bodies lined up in the mortuary, waiting for me to decipher how their lives were so brutally snuffed out. Any help I can be given with this victim would be much appreciated.'

'What I can tell you is the outboard motors didn't do this woman any favours; however, I'm not sure if that was the actual cause of death. These things take time, Linton. Plus, I very much doubt our victim died here, just thinking aloud.

'The abnormally high Christmas tide this morning, definitely a factor. Take your pick. One might automatically assume, on the surface of it, sorry about the pun, she was thrown or fell in near Milsons Point, but an intelligent guess might point to further down the harbour, maybe Mosman or Rose Bay.'

'The turbulence created by the Manly Ferry washed the body over towards the seawall in this direction, and hey presto, here she is, run over by "The Harbour Thrills," the driver unsighted by dirty water and floating debris.'

'Right, that's a start; thank you.'

'Let's get the body transferred to Lidcombe without delay,' the overworked medico announced, eyeing an ever-growing throng of curious onlookers on the seawall. 'You can request priority, Linton, just don't hold your breath. They might be able to slot in an early examination. All I can say is good luck. The dissection schedule is a disaster with Christmas around the corner.'

Linton watched the intricate procedure of lifting the body from the pontoon and up to the ambulance before handing back proceedings to the senior forensic officer. Scientific could deal with scouting the immediate locale for further physical evidence. He'd had enough for one day.

***

Sydney, Australia

'Thank God I caught you.' Jacinta sounded breathless from running. 'Any chance you can head back to the lab, Fi? A body's being fished out of the harbour; Campbell Street is requesting an immediate autopsy.'

Fiona turned to face her flustered colleague, who was bent double, hands on hips, attempting to bring her breathing under control.

'I was hoping for a quiet night, relaxing with a movie in bed,' Fiona protested loudly. 'The boys are staying with friends. It's bad enough working one weekend a month without having to put in extra hours over the festive season.'

'Please,' Jacinta begged, straightening up, letting out a long sigh.

'Are there no other medicos around?' Fiona complained, tension building in her neck and shoulders. 'Can't they call someone in on emergency overtime? Truthfully; I'm running on empty.'

'Trinni's already halfway home, on a plane to Perth for the Christmas holidays. Dr Gerry Wake, the new guy, left the lab over an hour ago with a bout of suspected food poisoning,' Jacinta explained.

'And the on-call pathologist?' Fiona probed once more. 'What the devil is so important that it can't wait for a day or two? Admin has to stop bending over backwards, saying yes to every law enforcement request just to score political points with the Police Minister. Perhaps then Pathology might get more respect and a bigger budget.'

'Morris Stutz attended the probable crime scene down at Circular Quay. Signed off early an hour ago and is not due back on the roster till after the break. I don't think they could coerce him to come in anyway.'

Fiona began to waver.

'Morris is thorough, but not easy to work alongside, and he detests doing autopsies. I'd rather have you on board with this one.' Jacinta's face mirrored a look of desperation.

Fiona reluctantly dropped the car keys back in her handbag. 'Fine, but you owe me big time, Jaz.'

Jacinta blew her friend a kiss. 'Of course. Thank you so much, Fi. I really appreciate this.'

The women headed back to the lab, entering by a side door, making a bee line for the canteen to grab refreshments, then to one of the locker rooms to don protective gear. They didn't have to wait long before DCI Linton arrived, updating them on the situation.

'Do we have an ID on this woman?' Jacinta probed.

'Forty-year-old. Brenda Carr,' Linton replied. 'Divorced, no kids, lives on the North Shore, works for Pacific Rim Mining NL, a company with its main office on George Street. Looks like she was stabbed twice in the back before being thrown into the harbour, then got tangled up in an outboard motor. We're not sure of the exact location where she was thrown or fell into the water. We're trying to trace her movements before the attack.'

Fiona took a moment to digest this information. 'Pacific Rim Mining? Can't be? A close friend of mine is one of the head honchos at Pacific Rim. This news will be a shock to Harvey.'

'We'll be informing the company shortly,' Linton replied. 'Family first, then work colleagues.'

'Any idea how long our body was in the water?' This question came from Jaz.

'The team who attended the crime scene are estimating twenty-four to forty-eight hours, but I expect you'll be able to determine more after the autopsy.' Linton concluded, observing a junior male lab assistant wheeling the body of

Brenda Carr through a clear plastic doorway into the centre of the room.

Fiona steeled herself and edged nearer, checking the contents of her instrument trolley. Jacinta hovered nervously on the other side, throwing anxious looks at Fiona, ready to take notes. Immediately apparent, large, deep lacerations on both legs and one running diagonally across Brenda's face; most certainly consistent with contact from rotating outboard propellers.

After photographing and recording bruises on Brenda's neck and torso, she was carefully repositioned onto her front. At this point, Fiona excused herself to the washrooms, returning five minutes later, face white, concealed behind the mask.

'Two deep stab wounds at the centre of the back,' Fiona noted. 'Penetration of the spinal cord around the 5th and 6th thoracic vertebrae. I'd say this was the cause of death, but we won't know for sure until the chemists get toxicology results and look at stomach contents, etc.

'The knife was at least five inches in length, with a straight edge, very sharp. Possibly a kitchen knife, not a large hunting or combat-type blade; nothing fancy.'

'Time in the water?' Linton pushed again, observing with interest from a healthy distance, hoping for some answers.

'I'd agree with your timeframe, certainly no longer,' Fiona answered. 'Leave this one with me, Linton. I believe the victim was already dead when she entered the harbour water, but I want to perform a full autopsy before confirmation; check the lungs for water and run other tests. I'll type up a report and email it across when done.'

Linton took this as his cue to leave. 'Thanks, Doctor Sinclair, always a pleasure doing business with you. Enjoy your evening, ladies. I'm heading out for a bite to eat. Steak and kidney pie, with mash and peas. I fathom you'll be here for a while; shame.'

***

Bovey Tracey, Devon, England

Katie rose from her desk, smiling as Sofia entered the reception area, Jason warmly dressed in a blue beanie and red woollen duffel jacket, holding tightly to Sofia's right hand.

'Hey little man.' Katie bent down for Jason to run into her arms. 'Want some chocolate?'

'I'd rather he not snack between meals,' Sofia remarked, taking up residence on the reception lounge. 'Is James about?'

Katie felt the verbal slap, initially wondering if she'd heard correctly. 'Er, yes, he's out in the lab preparing some important mineral samples for an AES analysis; I mean, does he know you're coming around with Jason? He requested no interruptions.'

'Would you kindly let him know I'm here?' Sofia's voice was devoid of warmth, only cold directions.

Deciding not to ring through on the lab phone, Katie walked down the corridor, entering the laboratory through the airlock, locating her brother at the far end of the instrument room, busily preparing, crushing, and sorting evidence samples in the fume cupboard for a full metal analysis on the Inductively Coupled Plasma/Atomic Emission Spectrograph.

He didn't turn around when Katie approached. 'Javier, can you finish up these last three acid extractions, filter and concentrate the eluents, and dry the residues? Here, take my safety glasses; you'll have to increase the sensitivity on the spectra readouts.'

'Thanks. I think the match of these metallic residues from the crash scene, coupled with the red paint fragments, will seal the deal for the defence on the Cotter hit-and-run manslaughter appeals. Made my day.'

'That's what we love about the job.' Javier offered Katie a broad smile.

Katie returned the smile before addressing James, 'Sofia's here to see you. You didn't mention she might drop in.'

James stared at Katie. 'Who, Sofia? Shit, I completely forgot our lunchtime appointment in Exeter with the solicitor.'

Katie returned to reception, where Sofia, a bored expression on her face, sat fiddling with a makeup purse. Jason was playing with one of his toy trains on the floor. James appeared a few minutes later from the bathroom, ditching his soiled lab coat into the laundry pick-up.

'James, what time do you want me to come over on Friday night to babysit?' Katie asked.

Sofia jumped in before James could reply, 'You won't be needed, thanks. I'll be around Friday night.'

'Oh, right. You sure, James? No problem really.'

'Seen my phone, sis?'

Sofia turned to James. 'We'd better get going. Don't want to be late.'

Katie went to give Jason a hug, but he was picked up by Sofia and carried to the door.

James turned to Katie, offering an apologetic smile. 'I won't be back today. Javier's off soon to a seminar. Before you lock up tonight, be a sweetie, punch out pot bromide discs on the Donnelly drugs samples in the desiccator, and run them through the Infra-Red Spectrophotometer.'

'I think that's it. Oh, if you get a few spare minutes, better make a start on the Cotter invoices for Levin and Gold Lawyers. Make it thirty hours, at £120 an hour.'

'That all?' Katie's sarcasm was lost on James, as he hunted for the keys to Fiona's TVR.

Left alone in the office, quiet save for the sound of the ticking of the office railway clock, Katie quietly seethed. She'd only met Sofia a couple of times, but what was the woman's problem, and more importantly, what the blazes did James see in her?

***

Exeter, Devon, England
KC's Nightclub

Club security stood to one side, acknowledging Will with a brief nod, ushering him inside the foyer, then through into the main part of the club. Jock, in tow, was amazed at how popular KC's was.

There was no need for ID to be shown; the large Samoan positioned at the front door had been alerted to the detective's arrival; in any case, they were well aware the club would not want its clientele alerted to cops entering the premises.

Once inside the seductively lit venue, Will and Jock forced their way through the throng to a crowded bar. KC's was jammed to the rafters; patrons milled around ordering drinks or lounging on scattered recliners; others strutted their stuff on the dance floor. A jazz trio, in a far corner, battled valiantly against the background cacophony.

'Busy place,' Jock commented, breathing in the heady mix of perfume, cheap aftershave, body smells, and cigarette smoke, his vision distracted by a scantily clad waitress loading a drinks tray at the bar.

'Par for the course on a Friday night,' Will replied, following another Samoan to the back of the nightclub, where they were directed up a steep flight of stairs, Jock reluctantly bringing up the rear, eyes transfixed on an almost naked blonde running through her pole dancing routine.

The door to Shirley's office was ajar. Will knocked twice and stuck his head around the door, announcing their arrival.

'Now, this time, you can surely have a drink. Beer, champagne?' Shirley unlocked a two-tier bar fridge with a silver key fixed to a tiny chain around her wrist.

'Technically no, we're still on duty, but a small one won't hurt,' Will responded.

'What can I do for you this time, Will?' Shirley directed her guests to a pleated red leather settee, passing both police officers a cold beer.

'Why didn't you mention the money last time I was here?' Will quizzed, sounding slightly annoyed. 'Quite a large sum from what I gather, around a hundred grand.'

'I thought you knew about that,' Shirley answered, conviction in her voice. 'I reported it to that Wallis chap, in your absence. Also, the theft of my gun, the one I keep locked away in the cellar under the house at home, did Wallis happen to mention that?'

Will blew out his cheeks. 'Nope, I don't recall hearing about a stolen firearm. What type of gun was it?'

'I'm not sure what you would call it, William, luv; they scare the living daylights out of me. My brother bought it in Australia, forked out a pretty penny, and shipped it over a couple of years ago, believing it had great investment potential.

'Asked me to look after it for him; I completely forgot it was there, to be honest. Someone broke in through the downstairs window and got away with some expensive sound equipment and other stuff as well. Knew what they were looking for. By the way, how was your vacation? I never asked.'

'Not bad, relaxing. I quite like the Algarve. Not stinking hot like the Costa del Sol. The cuisine I can take or leave, but apart from that—'

'Give me the south of France any day, darl,' Shirley announced. 'Not that I get to go away much. KC's is getting to be a millstone around my neck.'

'One hundred grand in cash is a bucket load of money,' Will stated, desperate to stay on track. 'I'm assuming you keep a safe; when did you realise the money was missing?'

'Next day. My safe was the best money can buy, set in concrete in the floor, under the rug.'

Jock and Will smiled at the unintended irony.

'What's funny?'

'Eh, nothing, Shirl.'

'I'm not joking. You're sitting on it. And before you ask, apart from myself, of course, only my nephews were privy to the combination. The money and the gun both went missing around the same time, shortly before Albert and Reg were done in.'

'A possible link to their murders,' Jock suggested, annoyed they were only learning now about the break-in.

'Gee, he's sharp, Will; best keep hold of this one,' Shirley jibed.

Jock went red, Shirley's sarcasm striking home.

'Any idea who might have helped themselves to the cash?' Will questioned.

'I would have thought that was bloody obvious,' Shirley snapped. 'Albert and Reg must have taken it, for what reason, I have no bloody idea, and now we will never know. I am surmising they were caught up in something not strictly "kosher," shall we say, and whoever killed them took off with the dosh.'

'Follow the cash trail and you'll find the killers; simple. The gun, who knows; that went missing a few days before the money was nicked. Now, drink up; let's head down to the bar. Follow me, and I'll introduce you to two young, delightful Russian ladies performing tonight. Busty Babushka and Titillating Tara. You both look like you could do with letting your hair down. Come on, we'll give you a night to remember.'

Jock practically rocketed out of his seat, quickening his step to keep up with Shirley, who was already halfway down the stairs. Will held back, not in the mood to watch naked women perform on stage. His headache intensifying, he fumbled in his pockets for two spare analgesics. Another exhausting day loaded with stress, the warm Algarve sun a distant memory.

***

Sydney, Australia

Fiona walked expectantly into Campbell Street Police, Central Command, shortly before eleven, hoping Linton received her SMS. She waited approximately twenty minutes, relieved to finally see his smiling face appear in the reception area.

'Sorry,' he apologised. 'Morning's been a killer. One meeting after another. Fancy lunch? We can nip across the road to a hip new alfresco brasserie, all the rage with the locals and tourists, if you believe the videos on social media. That's if you've time.'

'I'm game if you are,' Fiona replied. 'I've actually signed off for the day and stayed at home finishing off urgent reports. I was owed a few hours of overtime; I'm cashing it in.'

Fiona glanced around the reception area, surprised at how quiet it appeared.

'Calm before the storm, this is probably the busiest station in Sydney. It's not normally this quiet,' Linton spoke up, as if reading her mind. 'It *will* get busier later, Friday evening and all that. I'm confident bedlam will prevail. Right, well, shall we?'

Linton opened a side door with his swipe pass, holding it open for Fiona to walk through, leading the way down a flight of stone steps, emerging onto the street. Opting for an outdoor table, under a full-length street awning, adjacent to a noisy group of Swedish backpackers attacking gourmet burgers, conversation turned to how long Linton had been with the force.

He screwed up his face, thinking. 'Coming up for twenty-two years now. After uni, I didn't have any idea what I wanted to do. Drifted around doing casual jobs, mostly hospitality. I mean, a BA in History—what use is that?'

'I applied as a laugh one day and got accepted. Can't say I cared much for my first few years in uniform; pretty boring, but switching to investigation started it for me. Like most things, once you work your way up the ranks, life becomes more interesting. What about you? How long have you been a forensic pathologist?'

'About twelve years,' Fiona answered, busy scrutinising the specials board. 'Granddad was a research chemist in the war, worked on a team with Barnes Wallis developing the bouncing bomb, you know the "Dambusters", and other lethal stuff like the "tallboy" bunker busting bombs used against U-boat pens, all of which intrigued myself and my siblings, resulting in all three of us pursuing a scientific career. The stories my grandfather told us when we were kids growing up, you wouldn't believe.'

'Yes, I'm familiar with the Dambusters and the mighty Lancaster. What a coincidence. Mum's uncle, Denis, was a bomb aimer in an Aussie squadron and survived twenty nighttime missions over Germany. On their last, 110s were waiting for the bombers on their way back from Dresden. Shot up so bad, almost had to ditch in the North Sea. Crashed landed but made it home on two engines.'

'God flew with them,' Fiona remarked.

'You mentioned you were partners with your brother and sister in a forensic consultancy back home in the south of England; did I hear right? Dorset or somewhere?'

'Devon.'

'I've been to England a few times. Do you miss it?' Linton remarked. 'Sounds like the dream job; your own boss, picking and choosing the work, nobody telling you what to do.'

Fiona spoke at length about Moorland Forensic Consultants, the uncertainty in the early years, and the ups and downs of running a small family-owned scientific consultancy and laboratory. She then told Linton about the Devon bombings and the friends lost, having to confront head-on trauma and the inevitable long-term psychological effects.

Linton glanced up at Fiona, making eye contact. 'I've been fortunate; I've never been on the front line for anything like that. Had a relative, a police officer in Melbourne at the time of the Russell Street bombings. Very bad.'

'Yes, the incident rings a bell. I was surprised to learn how much criminal activity has taken place here in Australia, yet why it surprises me, I don't really know, especially with these backpacker murders.'

'There's always been a well-organised underground criminal network in Australia, Melbourne much more so than Sydney; it grew out of the so-called "Razor Gangs" of the twenties and elements of the trade union movement. Always involved around control: the nightclubs, strip joints, prostitution, illegal booze, and drugs. The usual stuff.'

'Got worse in the sixties and later with the unfettered immigration of Muslim gang elements from the Middle East, particularly Lebanon. Then we had the explosion of illegal drug use here and worldwide. The Unions are heavily involved to this day in major illegal business activity, like stand-over tactics and political corruption, funds misappropriation, you name it.'

'Sounds like back home in the Thatcher years,' Fiona added. 'You know, Linton, there'll always be murders, violence, and the usual physical dark side present in any society. The thing that truly scares me is the illegal stuff that goes on unpunished and accepted.'

'The high-level corruption and fraud are a result of Postmodern Marxism and activist socialist policies adopted without question or consultation, destroying western society; happily implemented by authoritarian governments and elitist corporations in collusion. And no one does a bloody thing about it.'

A young waiter came over to take their order. Fiona chose Balmain bugs in a creamy sauce; Linton opted for traditional fish and chips.

'Add a bottle of Rosé to the order,' Linton requested, pointing to the wine he'd chosen from the drinks list. 'Oh, and a serving of bruschetta to start.'

'I absolutely agree with you,' Linton continued, pouring two glasses of water from the coloured flask in front of him. 'I see this in the force every day, but at least I can get on with it, knowing experts like you have the technology these days to make our job easier.'

'Which reminds me.' Fiona reached into her bag, passing Linton a stapled A4 report in a plastic slip. 'The forensic profiling we spoke about. Katie has compiled two profiles after I provided her with a detailed brief; she strongly believes you are looking at two individuals for these backpacker murders. They make for an interesting read. My sister apologises for the delay in getting these across to you; her workload is crazy at the moment.'

Linton put down his drink, removed his sunglasses, and began reading the information Katie had put together:

The male perpetrator is most likely a professional of sorts. He comes across as charming, but not overly extroverted. His line of work enables him to blend in, never drawing much attention to himself, perhaps a financial institution, school, hospital, or medium-sized corporate company, possibly in the CBD area of Sydney.

In his mind, these killings are necessary;, he was an outsider, not particularly liked at school, and doesn't spend much time around family. I do not see him as a person who was previously abused. Having experienced a normal upbringing, the parents, probably professionals, conservative, encouraged their son to take a career path that would give him a reasonable income and secure future.

His initial murder was probably based on opportunity, with an underlying need for excitement, to take himself away from an everyday, boring, run-of-the-mill existence. His anger may have boiled over, desiring something his victim had, or at odds with something the victim said.

This person constantly needs to be in control. His "career" leaves little prospect for promotion; he sees himself stuck in a rut for the foreseeable future. The subject exhibits a temper but has learnt to keep it under control. To the outside world, everything is about the smiles, being liked, and not allowing people to glimpse a darker side.

His method of killing is about power, taking away a life because he can, again that need for control. I pick him to be in his forties, with the mind-set of someone years younger.

This man will keep killing until he gets bored or gets caught. He is careful in choosing his victims, but it also comes down to the fact that they are within easy reach. He can connect with them, strike up a normal rapport, perhaps in his line of work. No one would suspect him of harbouring evil intentions.

The female, on the other hand, is more of an extrovert, the life and soul of the party. She is possibly younger than the male but only marginally so.

Her connection with the killer was by chance; she got herself tangled up with the murders and now sees this as a way of life. I imagine she looks up to the killer, wants to impress him; she will undertake most directives he gives her without objection.

Her childhood was probably unhappy, her parents never having much time for her, hence the reason to be loved by someone, no matter what they do. In her mind, the killer is "King.".

She'd be someone who perhaps works in the fashion industry, as a corporate receptionist, or even in PR. Definitely has a lot to do with people, a role where she can impress. Without a doubt a follower, not a leader, but will go to extreme lengths to protect the killer.

In summary, these people merge seamlessly into the background, do not stand out in a crowd, you would greet them with a wave, enjoy a meal with them, listen to their banter, and accept every word they utter as gospel. Both are pathological liars; this is what makes them so dangerous.

Linton finished the report, leaning back in his chair, taking a few moments to reflect on the content, nonchalantly observing the passersby. 'I think your sister is spot on, exactly how I would describe them. These profiles clearly indicate people who blend easily into the mainstream, not easy to spot and certainly not easy to catch.'

'Until they slip up,' Fiona remarked. 'And they will; they always do.'

The idea came to Ruth in a flash after she'd been watching daytime television. The female presenter was discussing domestic violence and how women should learn to defend themselves and take back control. Ruth realised the presenter meant taking classes in self-defence, seeking help, but in Ruth's mind, all she needed to do was eliminate the problem.

Chapter Thirteen

Lustleigh, Devon, England

'You're lucky you caught me.' Katie opened the door of the two-storey thatched cottage, clad in a light grey tracksuit, hair tied up in a loose ponytail, secured by a headband. 'I was on my way to Bovey pool for a swim, but no big deal; I can go this afternoon. Come on in; I'll fix us a drink.'

'Looks like you've been busy in the garden,' Mallory commented, turning back to take in the front rose garden, littered with bags of fertiliser, potting mix, and garden utensils.

'Not me; Dad comes over every Sunday to potter about and get away from the pressure of the stables. He says it's a relaxing change having somewhere to plant a few flowers, unlike the farm where he and Mum live, with all that acreage; moorland and plenty of it, beautiful, but not the same as an iconic little cottage garden.'

Mallory, dressed casually in jeans and a blue puffer jacket, followed Katie inside to a cosy kitchen, watching her deftly throw a log into the roaring wood burner.

'I'd like one of those; I have a boring electric wall heater. Hardly fashionable. Will your parents ever consider a move?'

'I very much doubt it. The farm has been in our family for centuries, going back to the Civil War. Some of the stone buildings are heritage listed. It's recorded that Cavaliers loyal to Charles took refuge there after their rout at the battle of Bovey Heath. I wouldn't be surprised if James takes over the farm one day, not that he'll ever admit to that proposition.'

'Really, Jim Sinclair doesn't strike me as being the farming type.'

'You'd be surprised. Well, we all grew up on the farm, so we know more than a bit about the running of the place. Each fortnight, we take it in turns to spend a day up there, helping out. Next week's my turn. English Breakfast or Earl Grey?'

'Earl Grey, thanks.' Mallory slid into the breakfast nook behind a recycled rustic pine table, ditching her jacket whilst Katie clattered about, retrieving cups and other items.

'How are the wedding plans coming along?' Mallory ventured.

'Slowly.' Katie set down a vintage Torquay Ware teapot full to the brim with piping hot Earl Grey and a plate of freshly made scones. 'The venue is thankfully sorted. I'm about to start on the wedding invitations. The cake's an entirely different matter. Matt loathes sponge cake, and fruitcake's not an option; we need to find a compromise.'

'What about a croquembouche?' Mallory suggested. 'You know, a tower of profiteroles. They look amazing and taste fantastic.'

Katie slapped a hand on the table. 'What a great idea, Mal. I'll suggest it to Matt. You really are a genius.'

Mallory looked smug. 'Yep, I can't argue with you on that one.'

'So, what brings you all the way out here?' Katie asked, undecided whether to leave jam off her scone. 'Not that I'm complaining; it's lovely to see you.'

'I dropped in at the lab first,' Mallory confessed. 'The new guy, Javier, understood you were having the day off.'

'Yes, it's been rather hectic of late; you lot are keeping me busy with profiling, although I shouldn't whinge; it's the part of being a forensic psychologist I adore most. Then Will decides to load me up with group counselling sessions. Did you see Matt when you were there? He was meant to stop by and take a look at Javier's computer screen.'

'Yep, chatty as ever, had the desktop in pieces on the reception counter, James and Javier were in mild conflict, discussing whose turn it was to buy lunch. I must say, Katie, it's a relaxed place to work. I can't fathom why Fiona gave it all up to relocate halfway across the world to work in a busy city. Mad, if you ask me.'

'My sister had reached a critical point in her life; I believe she made the right decision. Javier's a suitable replacement; he fits in well. It's refreshing having him around. God bless her, my mother has taken a shine to him, often dropping into the lab with freshly baked biscuits and cakes.'

Mallory reached for the teapot. 'That's what I like about your parents: always doing stuff for others.'

They fell silent for a few moments before Katie took up the conversation once more. 'And you, Mal, how are you doing? Apologies for this; I must say you look tired.'

Mallory offered a wistful smile, pretending to inspect the hand-painted motif decoration on the teapot. 'The cold weather doesn't agree with me. Well, in truth, the new responsibility is frightening, coupled with the thought of an increased workload. I'm not sure putting in for promotion was the best idea, not that it's a given. I worry if I do take a step up that corporate ladder, I won't be able to cope.'

'You're a natural, DI Wakefield,' Katie reassured, refilling the teapot. 'Parker must be a sound mentor; I rarely see Will let anything get the better of him.'

'Oh, Will's cool.' Mallory sounded detached, playing with a coaster. 'Confidentially, we've become quite pally of late, having been out for a few drinks after work. He's well, you know.'

Katie raised her eyebrows. 'Go on, it sounds as if you have more to tell me.'

'Let's just say we'd never engage in pillow talk.'

Katie stared at Mallory. 'Surely you're not cheating on Bruce by indulging in secret after-hour flings with your boss, Mal?'

'No one's cheating on anyone, Katie.' Mallory sounded indignant, placing the coaster back on the table. 'Bruce and I have not yet tied the knot, so technically, I'm still a free agent. As for the relationship—'

'This won't end well, Mal. Please be careful. There's a lot at stake for you right now: your career and possible promotion. Don't let your heart rule your head, not now.'

***

Darling Harbour, Sydney, Australia

'Lovely we could catch up before you went away, Japan, you say?'

Fiona and Harvey settled into an outdoor table at an Italian restaurant in the flashy Barangaroo development, overlooking Darling Harbour, pulsating with activity, painted golden with the last dazzling rays of an early evening sunset. Ferries and assorted watercraft darted about, dispersing commuters home to suburbs, bringing in holiday crowds to the vibrant waterside restaurant scene, or embarking partygoers on a Christmas party cruise.

'The first shipment of unrefined bullion from our Papua New Guinea mine site after twelve months of shutdown. Kind of a big deal for the Joint Venture. Everyone's on edge.' Harvey reached across, taking hold of Fiona's hand. 'Should be gone a few weeks. A change of scenery will do me the world of good.'

'Yes, you'll be glad to get away from Sydney after Brenda Carr's death,' Fiona acknowledged. 'Guess things are crazy in the office right now; losing a work colleague like that.'

Harvey shrugged. 'Sort of, but I didn't know Brenda all that well. Shit happens.'

Fiona studied Harvey's rugged features. 'You don't seem too upset or overly concerned.'

'Sad for sure, I'll grant you that, especially for the family, but like I said, we weren't particularly close.'

'The autopsy clearly points to Brenda having been murdered.' Fiona lowered her voice a notch. 'This investigation could have quite an impact on all those working at Pacific Rim Mining: interviews, perhaps even interrogation if the police suspect someone working with Brenda committed the crime. Life won't be easy for any of you.'

'One reason for me to be out of the country.' Harvey flicked open the menu. 'Look, it's not that I don't care; you know me. I'm not heartless. To be honest, I've got so many other issues on my mind at present; I can't afford to take on board anything else right now. Thanks for the heads-up anyway. Let's order. What do you fancy?'

The tall, dark-skinned maitre'd approached their table, topping up their water, introducing himself as Angelo in a thick, regional southern Italian accent, displaying the whitest teeth Fiona had ever seen.

'You like the garlic bread.' He smiled, winking at Fiona. 'Buono, si? I helped to make it. My brother Tony owns this restaurant; he learnt to cook from our grandmother. Homemade authentic cuisine, a superb view, and the best Australian and Italian wine. I tell you, beautiful lady, you pick a magnificent place to eat. A lovely couple; here for romance. Bellissimo. A perfect evening.'

Fiona blushed. 'It's a very nice place. Perhaps we could order the main courses, Angelo, if you don't mind.'

'Sure. Why not go with the tasting menu?' Angelo flipped the menu to a certain page, passing it back to Harvey. 'It's very tasty; you get to try different dishes from Sicily, my home. If Angelo says it's good, it's magnifico.'

Angelo put two fingers to his lips and blew a kiss.

Fiona smiled. 'You're on.'

'And a bottle of your best Italian Brut.' Harvey beamed.

'You celebrate marriage?' Angelo pressed.

'No,' Fiona replied. 'Just friends.'

Angelo hurried back to the kitchen, gesticulating to the wine waiter.

'No more marriages for me.' Harvey pulled a face. 'That's one disaster I'd rather forget.'

'I gauged from your emails that things weren't going well,' Fiona speculated. 'Divorce invariably impacts kids the most. Do you get to see them much?'

'Eh, not really. Rowena prevents me from having regular contact with them. I manage to phone Pippa once a month, when she stays with her grandmother in Somerset. Glenn's not too fussed I'm no longer around; there's a lot going on in his life: school, friends—it's the age.

'Rowena can't help herself, showers the kids with expensive gifts, money, Caribbean holidays, electronic stuff, whatever they want really. She's currently organising for Glenn to go snowboarding in Austria, paying for everything: a five-star hotel, chauffeured transport—blimey, the lad's only fifteen.'

'Certainly seems extravagant for a fifteen-year-old lad to be travelling and staying in such luxury,' Fiona agreed.

'Well, look at the Devon house we were living in when I first got married,' Harvey scoffed. 'You dropped by on occasions, remember? It was a pathetic residence.'

'I recall a very impressive dwelling; I'll grant you that. How many bedrooms was it, eight?'

'Ten,' Harvey corrected. 'Indoor lap pool, outdoor swimming pool, four tennis courts. For crying out loud, Rowena couldn't even hit a ball over the net. And why the extravagance of a riding room to store riding gear when she was terrified of horses? Pippa was the only one who rode, and that wasn't often.'

'Family money,' Fiona replied. 'What was Rowena's father? CEO of some huge financial institution?'

Harvey nodded, making room for the food being displayed in front of him. 'The trouble is, Rowena's trying to squeeze the maximum money out of this divorce; clearly an attempt to bleed me dry. She's not satisfied with the millions in family trusts and assets. I can see myself with not even two twenty-cent coins to rub together once her lawyers have finished.'

'That's not fair, if you want my opinion.' Fiona offered Harvey a sympathetic look. 'You've worked hard over the years to get to where you are now. It's a blessing you're living in Sydney, distancing yourself from Rowena. Sorry to say, but she and I never really clicked.'

'I don't know what I originally saw in her,' Harvey confessed. 'She's revealed a dark side I never realised existed. Marriage brings out the worst in some. Let's change the subject; Rowena has consumed enough of our thoughts for one night.'

Harvey raised his glass. 'Here's to the future, Fi. Who knows what that might bring, but I have a strong feeling my troubles will soon be over. Cheers.'

Fiona clinked her glass with Harvey's. 'To a brighter future; here's hoping Rowena won't get everything you've worked hard for.'

'Fat chance of that.' Harvey's blue eyes sparkled in the evening light. 'Poor Rowena. I get the distinct impression she's in for a bit of a shock. Now, enough chatter; let's eat.'

***

Devon, England

'Thanks for picking me up; I could have phoned for a taxi.' Mallory threw her overnight bag on the back seat of Will's car, clambering into the passenger seat.

'My pleasure.'

Will pressed "start" and manoeuvred the Jag out of St David's carpark into the busy pre-Christmas peak hour traffic.

'I thought it best we have a briefing before tomorrow's meeting with Pettigrew,' Will informed Mallory. 'He's jumping up and down, wanting results on all task force investigations. Word's going around that a female clot of a Home Secretary personally rang Pettigrew. We believe she's under some sort of pressure from the Minister.'

'I bet he is.' Mallory chortled. 'You can count the number of hairs left on that scaly scalp of his, ageing lines to boot.'

'And he's not even sixty,' Will added. 'Not much prospect for the poor sod, is there?'

'Doesn't look that way. Hey, we could chat over dinner if you like. I'm starving, and Bruce is working until nine.'

'Thinking the same. Lenny's Bar and Grill is just around the corner. How does a steak sound? Cook your own night, half-price happy hour cocktails.'

'Sounds great.'

Mallory sat back, watching the city pass by as Will drove the short distance to the restaurant. Once inside, they ordered T-bones, throwing them on the open grill. Will then updated Mallory on everything she needed to know before tomorrow's meeting.

After finishing their main course, Will relaxed, intrigued, watching Mallory make short work of a large portion of sticky date pudding. Mallory seemed to shove a tonne of food away, still managing to easily maintain a curvy, yet trim figure. *Genes are everything*, he surmised.

'How was London?' Will ventured at last.

'It was busy as usual, but you know me, Will. I love London, having spent many years there. I don't mind the hectic lifestyle. I mostly stayed around Kensington but did venture to the East End on a couple of occasions to catch up with friends.'

'Get much shopping done?'

'Yes, blew my credit card. Funny though, Oxford Street and the retail districts didn't have their normal buzz. A lot of shops are vacant; crowds are down, a bit depressing. Even the Christmas lights were not what I remember.'

'I always find it strange being back in Devon, surrounded by unspoiled countryside and the slower pace of life. But, you know, Will, London isn't the city I grew up in; frankly, I could be in another country. I don't feel entirely safe on the streets or catching the tube. Must admit, I get a little more anxious venturing up there now.'

'Get to see your parents?'

'Yeah. Dad's in fine fettle; he has his little classic car restoration project to keep him busy and loving retirement. He and Mum are off again on another cruise next month. When they get back, it's down to Malaga for a few weeks in the sun; wish it was me.'

'I could handle that.'

Mallory attempted to stifle a yawn. 'Sorry, I've been on the go since six.'

'You can always stay the night at my place,' Will suggested. 'Message Bruce, tell him you won't be back, had to stay another night in London, missed your train, something like that.'

Mallory looked hesitant. 'Best if I don't. Bruce is starting to get suspicious. I get interrogated about everything nowadays, especially my need to work such erratic hours.'

'Next week perhaps. You could say you have to go to a conference.'

'We'll see.'

***

The Spit, Sydney Harbour, Australia
One Week Before Christmas

'Come on, this way, second to last boat at the far end.' Linton pointed, leading Fiona out along the yacht club marina. 'Growing up in Devon, I reckon you know your way around a boat. Done a bit of racing in your time, eh? The Fastnet, Cowes Week?'

'I can't lie, Linton. Truthfully speaking, sailing boats are my worst nightmare. When I was ten, my brother borrowed a friend's Salcombe Yawl for the day. We got caught in a gale at the mouth of the estuary. James capsized it, and we ended up being rescued by a passing fishing boat.'

'You guessed it; neither of us had life vests on. I was in the water for twenty minutes in freezing Channel water, hanging on to the rudder. James didn't have a clue. I almost drowned. To this day, we never talk about it.'

'You're kidding me, right?'

'Haven't stepped on board anything with a sail since.'

'Then today is the day we finally get Fiona Sinclair out of this nightmare she's been stuck in and discover what she's been missing for the past thirty years.'

Fiona stopped at a vintage 33' cruiser/racer with unmistakable classic pedigree, moored in a club berth. 'Wow, is this yours?'

'Yeah, not bad, huh. Very rare; only a handful were built worldwide. You know what they say about racing a boat, "It's like standing in the rain tearing up dollar notes," but she's worth it.'

As Linton helped Fiona aboard, she looked around, puzzled. 'Are we early? The guys aren't here.'

'Guys? Oh, you mean my crew,' Linton answered, poker-faced. 'Today, it's just you and me.'

The blood drained from Fiona's face.

'Right, if you can go down below, switch on the electrics. Red dial beside the steps. Whilst there, bring up two inflatable vests from the locker above the settee.'

Doing as instructed, Fiona took a few moments to look around, impressed at a beautifully fitted-out, warm, seductive interior, handcrafted from Tasmanian hardwoods and celery top pine. Catching her eye, a plaque proudly announcing the boat's racing successes, mounted on the bulkhead.

Fiona poked her head out into the cockpit. 'So, we're just going out on the motor, with no crew, to admire the view.'

'What? No. A great day for sailing, a light nor'easter 10 to 12 knots is expected. Not a lot of boats on the harbour, we can relax. A piece of cake, to be honest. We can handle the gusts, no problem. I often take her out by myself, just for the solitude, escape from the rat race.'

'But I don't know the first thing about sailing.'

Linton broke into a smile, amused at Fiona's body language, simultaneously turning the ignition key, causing the motor to spring into life, sending the characteristic lumpy diesel exhaust note vibrating through the hull.

'You could circumnavigate in *Synergy*, safe as houses. Now, I want you to do most of the work. Just do exactly what I say, and things will start making sense. The wind will blow us out; go upfront and cast off the mooring line and springer. Then come back into the cockpit and take over the tiller for a second while I go below. Just head her straight out.'

Linton's voice carried a relaxed air of authority and encouragement within it, an assuredness calming Fiona's anxiety and infusing confidence. Following his concise instructions, Fiona hoisted the mainsail straight out of the boom bag, securing the halyard around a winch, allowing Linton to turn off the motor, leaving only the mesmerising sound of the waves rushing past and the wind whistling through the rigging.

Linton then unfurled the genoa, and in a heartbeat, they were beating out of Middle Harbour, past secluded beaches and exclusive multimillion-dollar residences at a steady 9 knots, revelling in a strengthening nor'east sea breeze. Very soon, Linton had his student tuning the sails to the slightest changes in wind speed and direction, easing or pulling in the sheets as *Synergy* effortlessly sliced through the harbour chop.

With every minute, Fiona's apprehension diminished as she worked with Linton, feeling the boat respond to her input, mystified why she had been so fearful for so many years. Reaching Sydney Heads, they tacked to starboard, steering towards Manly, the breeze increasing, the boat heeling in the gusts, showing her speed, Linton and Fiona laughing and joking as they raced a ferry, responding to the waves of passengers on board.

Reaching Manly Wharf, they turned round, and with the wind now behind, the sails were eased.

'Sure you haven't done this before,' Linton questioned, handing the tiller to Fiona and heading below. 'Coke or mineral water. Your turn; want to take her under the Bridge?"

'Really, I don't think that…'

'Pick a compass heading or line up a landmark. Keep the sails full by bearing away or coming up into the wind; watch the telltales. You'll get the idea.'

***

Exeter, Devon, England

'I found this draft summary on the Copeland murders, tucked away in the back of Wallis' locker,' Mallory announced to Jock, sitting hunched over a laptop, the only other police officer in the operations room. 'How John Wallis made it to DI level is anyone's guess. I don't even think he'd make the grade as a desk sergeant. It sure beggars' belief.'

'Incompetence is always promoted.' Jock focused on his computer screen, fingers moving swiftly over the keyboard. 'Any chance of a coffee, Mal? I wouldn't normally ask, but I've been stuck here since five this morning to get these wretched statements typed for Pettigrew, and I keep finding my concentration lapsing. Be a pal and check if someone fiddled with the heating thermostat. Bloody freezing in here.'

'Of course, tell you what; I'll nip across the road to Carl's Kiosk, nab us two large caps and a couple of Danish pastries.'

Mallory bolted out the door, always effervescent, no matter what the time of day, returning fifteen minutes later, placing a Styrofoam cup and Danish in front of Jock. She then slid in behind her own desk, studying Wallis' report whilst sipping her hot drink.

After ten minutes of silence, except for the occasional expletive emanating from Jock and the ever-present background hum of the aircon fans, Mallory let out a loud exclamation, 'Wow, how did we miss this!'

'Um, what?' Jock muttered, still typing away.

Mallory started reading aloud, 'According to this report, it states here: *Shirley Copeland argued with her nephews two days before their demise. She admits to owning a gun, which she kept in a secure area at home, and claims the gun was stolen sometime before the murders. She also reported a wad of cash, totalling around 100K, taken from her office safe.*'

'Sorry, not quite sure what's amiss there,' Jock confessed, munching slowly on his apple Danish. 'Will and I obtained all this information from Shirley on a recent visit. We know about the gun and money being taken. That dickhead Wallis failed to mention any of this to us before he pissed off back to London, but we're well informed now.'

Mallory continued reciting the statement provided by Shirley Copeland, '*My home was broken into prior to my nephews being murdered, but initially, I didn't report it to the police; I didn't feel it was important. It was only after the murders that I thought it may be of interest, especially when I realised my guns were missing.*'

'Still not getting it,' Jock admitted, shoving the last piece of Danish into his mouth.

'It could be a typo, but why does Shirley mention guns in the latter part of the statement when before, she says she owns *a* gun, in the singular sense?'

'Like you said, a typo,' Jock offered an explanation. 'Easily happens.'

'Or it could be this investigation was a complete cock-up by Wallis from the start, and he didn't scrutinise anything properly.'

'Now, that I can believe,' Jock responded. 'The problem is, Mal; Albert and Reg died several weeks back. *If* and I use the word loosely, *if* Shirley had any involvement in the death of her nephews, she will quickly backtrack, stating she only ever owned *one* gun.'

Mallory sighed before continuing with her analysis of Shirley's statement. 'It also has conflicting information on where Shirley was when her nephews were killed. Firstly, it states she was at KC's; the second part of the report says she was in Newton Abbot getting her hair coloured.'

'Shit, we ought to have been asking these questions from the beginning, but instead, we headed merrily off down a different track, thinking Wallis had it all covered.'

'Whatever you do, don't let Pettigrew be privy to any of this,' Jock warned. 'Wallis is long gone. If Pettigrew wants to point the finger at a botched investigation thus far, he'll be turning the blowtorch on us.'

Mallory bolted down the rest of her cappuccino. 'I feel like a complete idiot. I've got my head in the sand, not focusing properly.'

'Distracted perhaps?' Jock glanced up at Mallory for the first time, a knowing look on his face.

'Meaning?'

'Nothing, forget it.'

'No, go on; if you've got something to say, Jock, spit it out.'

'People are speculating, Mal, about you and Will. Don't let this get out of hand. You're a level-headed detective, but if you start making mistakes, it *could* cost you everything.'

Mallory turned to face Jock, her anger rising. 'Mind your own business; you have no right…'

'Morning, comrades,' Will walked into the office, plonking his oversized briefcase onto an empty desk before opening it and retrieving antacids and a file. 'Briefing in half an hour. Anyone want breakfast?'

Jock shook his head.

Mallory stood up, heading for the door. 'No thanks, I need some fresh air. It's getting stuffy in here.'

Lying in bed, suffering from another violent attack, and with both children at school, Ruth thought about what she would do to her husband; the best way to get rid of him.

She didn't own a gun; besides, she wouldn't know how to use one. Poison seemed a safe option, but what if it didn't kill him? That would make matters worse. She needed something swift and effective—a knife.

Chapter Fourteen

West New Britain Province, Papua New Guinea
Christmas Eve

10:10 Hours: The two men lounged in the shade of a small, demountable corrugated tin building masquerading as the mine site airstrip terminal, engaging in idle conversation. The taller of the two, a thick-set individual with a fair complexion, bearing the unmistakable stance of an ex-military type, casually cradled an Armalite AR15 automatic rifle in his grasp.

The other man; slimmer, olive-skinned, dressed in khaki mine site corporate work fatigues, stared out across a coconut palm fringed lagoon, anxiously scanning the horizon and talking into a hand-held two-way radio. Both men turned around expectantly as a Toyota Hilux full cabin 4WD bearing the logo of the New Britain Gold JV emerged out of the dense rainforest along a red dirt track at the far end of the airstrip.

Stopping in front of the building, two local Melanesian mine workers jumped out, armed with shotguns. The fairer of the two men walked over to the 4WD, waving a friendly greeting and throwing an arm around both. Conversing in broken "pidgin," he directed one of the natives to a forklift just visible inside a large equipment shed adjacent to the "terminal."

'Ten minutes, all good,' the slimmer man announced, pocketing the radio, checking the time, and joining his comrade. 'Better do the bar count reconciliation now and sign off the paperwork. I want it all stowed on board and on our way by 11 am at the latest. The forecast is for a few early afternoon storms, moving in from the Vitu Islands.'

10:20 Hours: Both men, alerted by the sudden high-pitched shrill of gas turbine engines and throb of rotor blades, looked up as a large helicopter in dark red livery flashed overhead at treetop level, down-blasting the immediate area with warm air and the pungent smell of jet fuel, scattering flocks of seagulls and noddy terns, sending all four men ducking for cover.

'Coates, you bastard... He did that deliberately,' the thick-set individual sniggered, raising a middle finger in the air.

10:30 Hours: Terry Coates eased the Bell 212 heavy lift helicopter charter down close to the Hilux and switched off systems. Jumping out of the cockpit, with the large rotor blades still turning, he sprinted over, head down, to join the small group watching on with interest.

'Solomon not here?' A concerned Harvey enquired.

'Hi chaps. Yeah, sends his apologies from Moresby; something came up urgently in the parliament, a vote or something. Says he'll ring you when we stop to refuel in Lae.'

Harvey and Ryder threw an anxious look at each other. 'Can't be helped, I suppose. Where do the boys load the boxes?'

11:15 Hours: 'Been lucky with the weather,' Terry announced, admiring the scenery from the left-hand pilot's seat. 'Next week might have been problematic; the weather models are predicting an early onset of the monsoon.'

Harvey turned around, raising an eyebrow at Ryder in the rear seat. If he was going to make a move, it had to be soon. Ryder, taking the hint, unbuckled his seat belt, carefully unhitching the Beretta from its holster.

'Sorry about this, Terry. Just do as you're told, and you won't get hurt. Ryder's got a 9mm two inches from the back of your head, and he's a little trigger happy. Now, take her down to 50 feet and head out to sea. I'm switching the autopilot to 310 degrees; maintain the heading for the next twenty minutes.

Drop IAS back to 80 knots; and just to let you know, I'm fully qualified on 212s,' Harvey nonchalantly announced, switching off the VHF and all radio communications on the overhead panel. Reaching under the seat, he then manually disabled the transponder sender. As the chopper descended, ahead the early vestiges of a tropical storm appeared on the horizon.

11:35 Hours: 'What's going on, Harvey? There's nothing out here except a few small uninhabited islands. We'll run out of fuel if you maintain this heading. That's a rain squall ahead.' Terry tried to remain calm; inside, he was panicking.

11:40 Hours: 'In two minutes, give or take, you'll sight a horseshoe-shaped coral atoll out to starboard. Take her up slowly to 200 feet, drop back to 30 knots, and scout around for a place to set down. On the beach if necessary.'

11:45 Hours: 'That's a clearing about 30 metres in from the beach,' Harvey announced. 'Bring her around to 180 degrees and take her in. Careful, mate, don't try—'

At that moment, noticing Ryder was distracted, looking out the window, Coates yanked the cyclic to the left and pushed down hard on the collective, pitching the helicopter over into a violent half-inverted turn. Ryder, thrown sideways, slammed hard against the cockpit door, temporarily losing consciousness.

The Beretta automatic flew forward into the cockpit, discharging; the bullet ricocheting off the instrument panel, striking Coates in the neck, causing him to slump forward, releasing his grip on the collective and cyclic controls; blood splatters spraying the windscreen. The Bell immediately entered a slow spin, pitching forward, rapidly losing altitude.

11:47 Hours: Fighting the high negative g force, Harvey pushed Coates off the cyclic control and grabbed the collective, pulling it hard up, slowing the rapid descent. Counteracting the spin with the torque pedals, he gradually brought the Bell under control, but it was too late.

The chopper lurched over the palm trees and crash-landed well above safe landing speed in the clearing, bouncing twice before settling on its side, the rotors disintegrating against the hard coral sand, sending deadly metal fragments spewing into the undergrowth.

Severely shaken and winded, Harvey reacted on pure instinct a few seconds later, blindly shutting down the jet turbines and switching on emergency extinguisher systems, with a last gasp effort, releasing his seat belt before blacking out. An eerie silence returned to the atoll.

***

Exeter, Devon, England
December 23rd

'Don't forget, everybody, before you go: the CID Christmas party's tonight at "The Blue Boar" in Exmouth, combined with the leaving party for Magnus, of course; thirty-five years in the force and bald as a badger.' Charles grinned, addressing the room at lunchtime. 'Kicks off around seven; if you're bringing a gift, leave it on the bar when you enter the venue. Should be a fun night.'

Will turned to Mallory. 'Are you going?'

'Er, yeah, but I'm bringing Bruce. He's getting annoyed I never seem to be home; it seemed the right thing to do.'

'You can't keep stringing him along.' Will lowered his voice.

'Now is not the time to be having this conversation,' Mallory hissed back, turning her back on Will. 'Didn't you hear Rudy Jenks earlier? They're expecting to see partners.'

Will, not one to be put off easily, moved his chair around to a position now facing Mallory head-on. 'We need to sort things out, Mal. I don't want this to be some casual affair; a convenience to indulge, whenever it suits you.'

'What did you expect, Will? I'm engaged; I've made a commitment to Bruce. I don't see how our relationship can be more permanent.'

'You have choices.' Will lowered his voice a further notch, aware his colleagues were close by, with every possibility of overhearing the conversation.

'Yes, and?'

'Ah Parker, Wakefield. All set for tonight's shindig. Looking forward to it. Chance to relax after a few hectic weeks. Now, if you've got a moment, I'd like an update on your current cases. Shall we?' Pettigrew was all smiles, leading the way to his expansive office at the far end of the corridor.

'You need to make a decision,' Will whispered to Mallory as Clive disappeared behind the water cooler. 'It's me or him; you decide.'

***

Exmouth, England
The Blue Boar Restaurant

Mallory eased through the noisy work mob, making her way to the bar. She'd already attracted the attention of one of three waitresses frantically pouring drinks. She ordered two large dry white wines, meandering back through the throng to a relatively quiet area in a back room, adjacent to the bistro, away from the crowded benches and makeshift dancefloor, where Bruce sat waiting.

'Your workmates are a rowdy lot,' Bruce complained, taking his drink and instantly downing half. 'Worse than a football crowd.'

'We like to let our hair down, that's for sure,' Mallory agreed. 'Possibly due to the intense, stressful nature of the job.'

Mallory spied Will Parker, immaculate in a blue suit and matching cream silk tie, doing the rounds, chatting to various people. Eventually, he worked his way up to Mallory and Bruce's table. Approaching the couple, he smiled broadly.

'You remember Bruce.' Mallory turned to Will. 'Roger Kincaid's funeral back in June.'

Will nodded, reaching out his hand. 'Of course, nice to see you again, mate. I hear on the grapevine you've finally picked up your own radio time slot, scheduled early next year. Congratulations.'

Bruce nodded, deftly extracting another drink from a young lad circulating the room with a tray.

'Quite an achievement,' Will continued. 'I often tune in to Breakfast and Drive Time Radio on my way to work. Great presenters, entertaining chats, and pleasant music to boot.'

'Yep, lucky to have a great team at the station, and we've got lots of exciting deals in the pipeline. I must have you as a guest on my new show one day, Parker; perhaps we could discuss why my fiancée works such long hours, being rostered on heaps of late shifts. You're her boss, Parker; surely there are other coppers who can pick up those crazy after-hour stints.'

Will twitched uncomfortably, aware of Mallory prodding Bruce sharply in his left side, urging him to switch the conversation.

'We try and allocate the workload fairly, but at the same time, when heavily involved in homicide investigations, we often don't have anywhere near enough of the resources required. Everybody's aware morale in the force is at an all-time low,' Will explained.

'Unfortunately, when you're a senior detective, such as Mallory, with specific expertise, over twenty years on and off in CID, they're needed more than others.'

Bruce let out a throaty chuckle. 'I suppose I ought to be grateful she's at work and not screwing around, huh, Mal?'

Mallory took a sip of her drink, avoiding eye contact. Will could tell how uncomfortable Mallory was feeling, but there was no way Bruce could know about the affair; he was just being an arrogant arsehole.

Bruce continued his spiel, 'I always said to Mal, if you ever cheat on me, it won't be the bloke that gets crushed, it'll be you. Sounds reasonable, wouldn't you agree, Parker?'

Will managed a forced smile. 'Great to see you again, Bruce. I'd better be a bit more sociable. Glad you could make it tonight. Enjoy the rest of your evening.'

'Yeah, you too, Will. You should seriously think about coming on my show. I know crime is on the rise; our listeners would be interested in all the latest technology and strategies used for catching the bad guys.'

'Sure, maybe someday,' Will replied, before strolling to the other side of the room. He turned around a moment later to see Mallory reprimanding Bruce. Will felt angry, more than guilty. Mallory deserved better than to be stuck with such an irrelevant, conceited prick.

***

Sydney, Australia
Christmas Day
News Update

News is coming in of a helicopter down in a remote part of Papua New Guinea. Anne Cummings, our correspondent in Cairns, has just filed the following report:

The Bell 212 was on its way from West New Britain Province to Lae to refuel, thence on to Port Moresby when the alert was raised. A search and rescue team has been deployed to the last known location before it disappeared off radar at approximately 11am AEST on Christmas Eve.

The chance of finding any survivors is believed to be minimal. A spokesman for the New Britain Gold Joint Venture Mine in Port Moresby confirms three men were listed on board when it went down: two Australian nationals and an ex-US marine.

Our sources are saying the helicopter was on the first leg of a flight transporting a large quantity of gold from the mine site on New Britain, in the Bismarck Sea. We will bring you further developments as news comes to hand.

***

Papua New Guinea
Vitu Islands. The Bismarck Sea

'Welcome aboard the MV Oceania Crystal Blue,' the tour guide beamed, leaning against the stern rail of the boat. 'On the dive today, you will experience a magnificent expanse of soft and hard coral reefs, brilliantly coloured fish, sharks, and dolphins; a truly magical experience; a garden of underwater delights.'

'If we are lucky, turtles and perhaps a majestic manta ray or two. Lying within the Ring of Fire, this undersea habitat contains the most diverse marine life in the world. Have your cameras at the ready; this tropical marine paradise supports twice as many marine species as the waters of the Red Sea and up to five times as many as the Caribbean. Pleasant diving.'

Elaine listened intently to the enthusiastic tour guide, heart rate rising in anticipation, being reminded why she'd chosen this part of the world for the trip of a lifetime, venturing all the way from North Carolina. She was finally fulfilling a long-held ambition to dive in the crystal-clear waters of Papua New Guinea, a country known around the world as the "Land of the Unexpected.".

Once all safety checks had been carried out and signed off by the dive master, Elaine, with her diving partner, Lynne, advanced to the platform at the stern, checking air supply and mask breathing one last time before stepping off together into the water.

***

Exmouth, Devon, England
Nick Shelby's Apartment

Nick felt around on the bedside table, searching for his watch. Picking up his cherished Longines aviation chronograph, he struggled to make out the luminous hands in the dark, waiting for his vision to adjust. 'Jesus, three in the morning.'

He weighed up whether to ignore the interruption, in no mood to listen to his sister droning on, especially as he'd only climbed into bed two hours ago. Reluctantly, he sat up, switched on the overhead reading light, and picked up.

'She's fixated on the old man who's living next door,' Helen explained to Nick. 'She thinks the old guy's our father. What if history repeats itself? What if…?'

Nick took a deep breath. 'Mum's got dementia, Helen; for God's sake, I doubt she remembers what happened all those years ago.'

'Yes, but they say—'

Nick, frustration growing, tried to calm his sister down. What was he expected to do from twelve thousand miles away? Helen was the one living in New Zealand; *she* was the one who needed to deal with the situation.

'What if Mum starts bringing up stuff from the past?' Helen questioned. 'How are we going to explain what happened? Nick, we *could* go to prison.'

Nick let out a long-drawn-out sigh. This was the last thing he needed right now. He was just hanging on, desperate to get his life back on track and kick a few bad habits. His sister regurgitating old events like this would only fuel his addiction.

'If Mum does start talking, nothing will make much sense,' Nick offered reassurance. 'Everyone will think it's part of her condition, the furthering stages of her dementia. Relax. Look, if things get worse, I'll fly over for a few days. In the meantime, try to stay calm. We have enough money for you to organise a carer to visit Mum each day and help out around the house. She'll soon forget about the chap next door. Don't stress.'

'I hope you're right; I really do.' The phone went dead.

Nick buried his head in his hands, the incessant sound of wind-driven sleet pelting against the corrugated roofing exacerbating the pounding in his temples. Realising sleep was an impossibility, Nick headed downstairs into the cold confines of his kitchen and peered out the window from the top-floor apartment into a pitch-black night, unable to spot the

215

flashing lights of the channel markers out in the estuary mouth.

The seas continued to build, fed by an abnormal Christmas tide and a force 8 gale sweeping down the Channel. Waves crashed over the seawall, sending spray the length of a deserted esplanade. Grabbing a wine glass off the shelf, Nick recovered a half-full bottle of pinot noir from the fridge and sank down on a stool, reflecting on Helen's agonising words; he knew they were treading on dangerous ground. His mother had killed once; what if she did it again?

***

The Bismarck Sea

After climbing back on board the Oceania Crystal Blue and stripping off her diving gear, Elaine glanced at her Seiko Diver; a picnic lunch was scheduled for one o'clock on the beach. With Lynne in tow, Elaine jumped off the inflatable into the warm tropical water, walking along the beach to join other members of the crew and dive party setting up towels, picnic hampers, and drinks coolers in the shade of a lone palm tree.

Elaine flung herself down on the coarse white coral sand, soaking up the midday sun. Glancing further into the sparse vegetation just beyond the she-oaks, something large and shiny caught her eye. 'Do you see that?'

A few members of the dive party looked to where she pointed. 'Can't be much; these atolls are deserted.'

'A chopper, a big one,' a party member remarked, venturing further into the undergrowth to investigate. 'Appears to be a crash site.'

Within ten minutes, the entire boat crew and guests stood at the edge of the clearing up by the wreckage, morbidly fascinated, intrigued by the scene of destruction confronting them.

'Be careful. I suggest everybody step back and don't touch anything,' the tour guide instructed. 'Looks like this might be the missing chopper the Navy has been searching for. I'll phone it in.'

Elaine, craving solitude and not the least bit interested in a helicopter crash, wandered off along a narrow sandy path, dodging boobies nesting in the branches, noisily protesting the intrusion, hoping to get a better view of the water from a different part of the island. She'd come here to dive and take lots of photographs and videos, wanting lasting memories of her two-week holiday.

She revelled in the dappled sunlight filtering through the canopy, warm on her back as she strolled along, tempered by a cooling breeze blowing in off the sea, suddenly grateful for the wide-brimmed hat and the ever-present SPF 50 shielding her fair complexion. Being a GP's receptionist, Elaine was well acquainted with the devastating effects of ultraviolet rays.

After walking about fifteen minutes, Elaine stumbled across a body, snagging her foot on an arm protruding onto the path; a male lying prostrate, concealed in the vegetation to one side of the path, half hidden by fallen branches, head turned to one side. Ants and other insects swarmed over the victim's bare skin; sand crabs fought each other for tasty pieces of flesh.

Elaine froze, momentarily unable to move. Eventually, her feet decided to cooperate, allowing her to run back along the path.

'Over here,' Elaine shouted, hoping to be heard, tripping on an exposed tree root, grazing both knees.

Reaching the tour group, she breathlessly informed them of the gruesome find, a small group electing to make their way back to where the body lay.

'He's dead,' the tour guide proclaimed, kicking the body gently, dislodging angry crabs, staying well clear of the ant swarm. 'Come on, let's head back to the boat; a team is on their way; there's nothing we can do for this poor chap.'

***

Bovey Tracey, Devon, England
Moorland Forensic Consultants Facility

Javier sorted through the various evidence bags spread out before him on the examination table in the Moorland lab, the phone conversation two days ago with Dr Margo Betteridge fresh in his mind:

Javier, dear boy; seeing MFC is contracted by Police Scientific to assist on forensic work in the Lisa Marshall matter, I have instructed Jan Stafford at the mortuary lab to have a technician drop over some pertinent physical evidence for you to take a look at.

Sorry for the imposition; Nick's Forensic Centre Lab is snowed under with biochemists on leave, the flu, or tied up in court evidence appearances, it looks like. I would probably have weighed in and done some DNA and biological tests, but my department at the hospital is undergoing relocation.

What's the urgency on this stuff, Margo? James and I are flat to the boards on commercial and private client legal business. Are you certain it can't wait? What about the government outsourced boys in Bristol?

Corrupt. I don't trust them. What's that? No, absolutely top priority I'm hearing. Liaise with Will Parker. I'm coming down with a bug. Going home.

In that case, I suppose it can fit somewhere into—

No mucking up; the police are desperate for any foreign DNA confirmations from the reservoir to follow up on, Margo warned, sneezing several times, as if on cue. Sort it out with James. This is your perfect chance to gather vital evidence, Javier.

***

From casual discussions Javier held with Margo and Derek Ingalls over the past two weeks, all three now agreed unequivocally: Lisa was poisoned; someone had then tried to drag her into the reservoir before deciding that wasn't an easy feat, eventually dumping the body alongside the embankment.

***

Moorland Forensic Consultants Facility

Javier examined the hair under both a light microscope and an electron microscope. Initially, he was able to rule out the hair strand as human, clearly of animal origin. Noting the morphological characteristics, what he found himself looking at was a dog hair, confirmed particularly by the medullary and cuticle patterns, rather than micrometric measurements.

Consulting the literature and a recent extensive paper on dog breed hair analysis, he concluded the hair strand was an unequivocal match with that of the German Shepherd breed.

'You've made an early start,' Katie observed, a sudden wave of nausea creeping over her. Last night's suspect a vindaloo takeaway, inflicting mayhem on her digestive system.

'You okay?' Javier commented. 'You look a bit pale.'

'Stomach virus going around. Nothing serious.'

***

Sydney, Australia
NSW Forensic Laboratories
08:30 Hours. Staff Canteen

Jacinta, leaning over the vending machine and sorting through change, looked over her shoulder, noticing an anxious DCI, mobile to ear, hurrying towards her.

'Hi Linton, my God, did you just climb out of bed? Can we get you sustenance?' Jacinta offered. 'The croissants are freshly—'

'No time for that,' Ansley interrupted, putting his arm in the small of the forensic technician's back, guiding her towards the door, signalling for Fiona to follow. 'Sorry ladies, time to earn our pay cheques. Too bad, but I'm not here on a social visit. We have a helicopter crash in Papua New Guinea; two Aussies and a Yank on board, one confirmed dead.

'Jaz, you and Fiona will have to attend the scene. We fly up there this evening. I've spoken directly to an expat contact in the PNG Police, and confidentially, he's saying the crash is shaping up as political dynamite, the government desperate to keep a lid on things. They have requested immediate assistance from Canberra, and we've drawn the short straw.'

Fiona tried to hide her shock, thoughts immediately turning to the twins and who would look after them if she had to leave Sydney.

As if reading her mind, Jacinta offered a solution: 'My sister isn't working right now; she's great with kids. I'll arrange for her to collect the boys from school and look after them whilst we're away. We can sort out logistics when we return.'

Fiona felt a wave of relief creep over her. That was one problem solved.

'Linton will arrange the flight, visas, and all the intricate details,' Jacinta continued as they ambled out into the bright sunlight of the carpark. 'In the meantime, we need to get hold of your passport and throw a few belongings into an overnight bag. You never quite know how long one of these trips will take.'

'Sounds like you've undertaken a few before,' Fiona remarked.

'Yep, one or two.' Jaz sounded wistful. 'Don't look so glum; they can be fun—all expenses paid, and you get to see a new country. Plus, relaxing evenings without children around. I'm sure it won't be as bad as you envisage.'

Ruth toyed with the Japanese sashimi knife, turning it over and over, looking at its razor-sharp blade. This seemed the obvious choice, but now, she needed to determine when and where she would plunge the knife. Hearing the door shut, she shoved the knife under the bed; she couldn't risk being caught.

Chapter Fifteen

Newton Abbot, Devon, England

Tom, flustered and caught in a heavy downpour, barged through the large doors of the *Star* head office, clutching a Styrofoam cup, a soggy folded newspaper, and an oversized portfolio case. Discarding his soaked trench coat on the reception lounge, he entered the main news office, scowling at his employees lounging behind desks, watching cartoons on the wall-mounted television.

'Warms my heart to know everybody's busy pumping out the news. Perhaps one of you would be so kind as to put the kettle on; I'm in need of a very hot, very strong, black tea.'

His youngest recruit stood up hastily, moving towards the kitchenette. 'Er, yes, Mr Markham, sir, but don't you already have a drink?' Oliver pointed to Tom's cup.

'Oh, you mean this?' Tom held the cup aloft before tossing it into the nearest wastepaper basket. 'Like me, it's freakin' cold, and you know *why* it's freakin' cold, young Olly?'

Oliver, just turned twenty, new to working in a busy office environment and not used to being around mixed personalities, especially one as unique as Tom's, froze to attention, slowly removing hands from pockets.

By now, someone had tactfully switched the TV to streaming news services, the journalists retreating to their laptops, making a half-hearted attempt to look like they were engaged in meaningful news gathering.

'I'll tell you, shall I?' Tom was now towering over Oliver, making him look even more diminutive than his 5'3".

Before Tom could continue, Lana strolled in, heading for her large glassed-in office at the rear, seemingly oblivious to the scene unfolding, phone in hand, engrossed in texting.

Tom gave her a scathing look before continuing, 'Olly, I left my house nice and early, seven-thirty to be precise. I drove twenty minutes along the A38, hardly any traffic, a breeze. At the Newton Abbot exit, I stopped at the service station, grabbed my usual beverage and the *Daily Mail*; God knows why, because frankly, most of the news in that rag is crap; however, let's not be nasty.'

Tom paused briefly, accepting a speedily brewed steaming hot English Breakfast. He then continued, 'I arrived at the office carpark shortly after eight, and then it hits me: some arsehole has parked in my reserved spot. Yes, would you believe it?'

'You know, the big sign that reads "Editor in Chief— Private Parking," and lo and behold, if there's not a bright orange Lamborghini Aventador occupying the space where my Volvo Estate should be.'

You could hear a pin drop in the office, everyone waiting with bated breath. Oliver wanted to sit down but didn't dare; instead, he stood there in the middle of the office, not daring to move, resembling a stone water feature.

Markham resumed the story, 'So, dear colleagues. I then notice not only has *my* spot been taken, but all the other spots, ostensibly due to the weather and everyone arriving early to work, which, I hasten to add, is not a bad thing. But *where is Tom going to park?* I hear you thinking.'

'Practical question, which I will happily answer: I drive back down the road, finding a spot five streets away. Yep, five fuckin' streets away. I then proceed to walk back to the office with my drink cup, newspaper, and case.

'Now, I expect you're all wondering why I didn't toss the cup in a bin along the way and pop the paper in my briefcase to stop it getting wet.'

Lana was now paying full attention to Tom's rant and offered a suggestion, 'Because I expect you wanted to make a point.'

'Ah, do I detect one intelligent person among us?' Tom grinned. 'You bet. You are correct, Lana, my love.'

Tom turned to look directly at Oliver. 'Me, being a hotshot journalist and a bit of a detective, Olly, I notice a set of shiny keys on your desk. Can I confirm you drove that orange go-kart into my parking spot this morning, which one assumes is for a photoshoot to go with an article we're writing?'

Oliver had now turned a deep crimson colour, looking around for support. 'Er, yes and no, Sir.'

'Which is it, yes or no?' Tom offered a sickly-sweet smile.

'Yes, I did drive the Lamborghini into your parking spot, but it's not for a photo session, Sir, it's…'

'Lambo's mine,' Lana piped up. 'I'm unable to drive two cars at once, clever though I may be, so I requested young Oliver, who normally catches the bus, to pick up my new prized possession and drop it off at work for me.'

'Where's your Lotus? The canary yellow one?' Tom asked.

'Parked out front in the delivery bay. The dealer is coming around in half an hour to pick it up. Couldn't resist the trade-in offer.'

Tom, still with a sickly smile on his face, now directed his invective towards Lana, 'Fascinating. Oliver, you are momentarily off the hook. Lana, my office, NOW.'

***

Richmond RAAF Base, Australia
17:00 Hours. December 28th

Linton led the team into a private room at the base for a brief meeting. Clearing his throat, he began to address his colleagues, 'Our aim is to attend the crash site and obtain crucial forensic evidence, which will then hopefully lead to a full investigation into what caused the aircraft to crash. We will be in PNG for approximately five days, staying at a dive resort at Kimbie on New Britain, accessible to the mine site and also to the crash site off the coast.'

'Now, for those unfamiliar with PNG, here's some important information you need to take on board: Where we're headed is a dangerous place, hence the need to take our own security team. PNG is known for its violence, criminals often using the ubiquitous bush knives (machetes) and guns.'

'You always need to be alert to your surroundings and never break away from the group. Avoid going out after dark and keep all doors and windows locked. The crash site is on an uninhabited coral atoll, and Kimbie, on New Britain, is relatively safe, so I don't envisage any problems in that regard.'

'Civil unrest and tribal conflict are common and can occur without warning. Criminal groups operate in remote areas, but mostly in the Highlands and on Bougainville. Always be on your guard.'

'As if that isn't enough to contend with, the weather pattern in PNG can be extreme. Heavy rains, flooding, landslides, earthquakes, and tsunamis. We may find some roads impassable, needing to take a different route, especially as this is an emergency trip, and we've not had much chance to check things out.'

'Medical facilities are poor. This is a third world country, folks; make sure you only drink boiled or bottled water and avoid bathing in freshwater sources. PNG is rife with insect-borne diseases such as malaria, Zika virus, dengue, chikungunya, and, oh yes, I forgot, Japanese encephalitis.'

'Always use insect repellent. The good news is we have an RAAF doctor, Captain Jackie Minter, accompanying us, but let's not give Jackie additional work. On the plus side, before you all signed work contracts, we made sure your vaccines were up to date, anticipating travel to remote places may occur. Any questions? One other thing. Captain Minter will be dispensing antimalarials immediately after this briefing. These are mandatory.'

One of the specialist photographers put his hand up. 'The landings in PNG, I've heard they can be bloody dangerous; is there a risk?'

'Yes, Mervyn, there is a particular risk in flying aircraft in Papua New Guinea, which necessitates strict adherence to procedures and extensive training. If I could pass this question on to Squadron Leader Hew Thomas from the RAAF.'

Hew Thomas stepped over to a digital whiteboard displaying a map of the South West Pacific, featuring Australia and PNG. Dressed in a standard issue RAAF khaki flight suit, well over six feet, he spoke confidently and with amiable authority, 'Rest assured, we have published parameters for each airstrip, which considers topics like the wind, temperature, surface condition, slope, and surrounding terrain.'

'There is a fair bit of margin built into these parameters. Also, all pilots flying in and out of PNG are required to have stringent training, ensuring we are competent. Here, on my left, is Flight Lieutenant Curtis Emery, one of the best pilots I've met.'

Curtis gave a brief nod before Hew continued, 'One thing unique about flying in PNG is what we call the committal point. This is a point along the approach path that is our last opportunity to safely conduct the landing. For example, if we continue past that point, we must land; there is no option to abort!'

Fiona began to feel sick, reaching for a water bottle. She wanted to stand up and walk out, opting to abandon this trip. What on earth was she doing here, sitting in a claustrophobic briefing room at an air base somewhere in Western Sydney, ready to board a military transport aircraft, resigned to placing her life in the hands of others? Her preference was to be at home with the twins, leading a dull and boring life. She gulped down the water, trying to focus on Hew's speech.

'Before we continue past the committal point, we need to be confident the winds are suitable, the runway will remain clear, and that any turbulence will not destabilise our approach. Occasionally, we may experience unforeseen changes to the wind or turbulence that occur past the committal point, but remember, safety margins are built into those operating parameters.'

'The take-off equivalent of the "committal point" is the "safe abort point." This being the latest point along the take-off run at which we can safely abort the take-off and stop in the amount of runway remaining.'

Thomas paused briefly, amused at the blank looks on his passengers' faces.

'I apologise if all this makes you a little apprehensive, but every flying decision Curtis and I make during this trip will be well thought out and considered; we will not be taking any chances. We will be actively engaged during the flight with communication and our surroundings.'

'If we go to land or take-off and have to abort, we are still in full control, and safety will be foremost in our minds.'

'Yes, and to add to that,' Curtis interrupted. 'We may encounter harsh weather, poor visibility, and even have to abort a take-off or landing; yet, we urge you to always remain calm and let us, the pilots, do our job. That's partly why we provide this lecture, to make you all aware of procedures and provide reassurance.'

Linton stood up to take over. 'Our aircraft is an RAAF C-130H Hercules turboprop military transport. Not as comfortable as a commercial flight, sorry.'

A collective groan rang through the briefing room.

'I know, I know, a bit noisy.' More groans mixed with expletives. 'However, I suggest everyone try and get some sleep on board and wear ear protection. Our flight path takes us directly to New Britain, flying time six to seven hours, right, Hew?'

'Once we arrive at the crash site, probably tomorrow, early afternoon, we need to work fast, due to the unpredictable weather conditions and knowing how dangerous PNG can be in so many ways. The navy has sent an Armidale Class patrol vessel to the area as backup and provide a quarantine area around the atoll to ward off unwelcome guests.'

'You have all been given set tasks and need to carry those out swiftly, yet with due diligence. Each morning and evening, we will be transported to the atoll and back to our accommodation by RAN helicopter. Right, boys and girls, gather your belongings; let's go.'

***

Newton Abbot, Devon, England

Lana sat in Tom's office, inspecting her well-manicured fingernails. 'Get a grip, Tom, you're overreacting yet again. Poor Olly was nearly wetting himself out there. You need to calm down.'

'When I want your advice, I'll ask for it. I don't understand what's going on with you, Lana, but your work ethic and general journalism have not improved since our last chat. Why is that?'

'Overworked and underpaid,' Lana retorted, still studying her nails.

Tom snorted. 'Clearly not underpaid if you can afford an almost new Lamborghini.'

'In case you'd forgotten, my friend, we ran exclusive stories on Lisa and Christina. We got paid big bucks, so it was well worth our little trip down under. I told you it would pay off.'

'That's as maybe, but your standards are slipping, Lana. You're not setting a good example for the others.'

'At least I *have* standards, Tom. This rag would be nothing without me.'

'Oh please. How many times have I heard that old chestnut? If the *Star* is not meeting your requirements, leave. Secure yourself a job with a much larger paper. You keep telling me you're accomplished enough.'

Lana stood up. 'You know what, Tom; I might just do that.'

Lana stormed out of the office, slamming the door in her wake.

***

Papua New Guinea
Helicopter Crash Site. Next Day

'It's very unlikely any more bodies from the crash will turn up,' Linton proclaimed, alighting with his team from the RAN chopper on the coral sands of the atoll, before guiding his team to the crash site, fifty metres in, past she-oaks lining the shore.

A small contingent of RAN personnel with Steyr rifles guarded the scene, now cordoned off with tape. 'We already know there was one body, along the path to our right.'

Fiona, a little apprehensive, approached the scene of destruction, treading carefully, wary of the alien environment: a large, downed helicopter, a potentially dangerous proposition. They were greeted by the first response team who'd flown in the day before, headed up by legendary Australian forensic consultant, Evan McMillen.

'Welcome.' Evan reached forward to shake hands, instantly recognisable by his short, rotund stature, trademark goatee beard, and jovial façade, crisscrossed with deep ageing lines. Fiona estimated about sixty, but later learnt only early fifties, thick head of hair completely white.

'To fill you in, we had a forty-eight-year-old male pilot on board, Terry Coates. Residing in Port Moresby but originally from Brisbane, a commercial pilot who usually does the daily milk run from Moresby to Wau, Bulolo, and Lae. There were two others on board: Harvey Driscoll, an English mine manager with Aussie citizenship based in Sydney, and Ryder Albero, an American national, also domiciled in PNG.'

'Searching through the debris and low atoll vegetation in the near vicinity to the crash site, we haven't encountered any bodies, but as you are aware, there was a deceased male a reasonable distance away, believed to be Mr Coates.'

McMillen paused briefly, reaching for bottled water, passing a critical eye over the new arrivals.

'Now, a number of scenarios. Did the other two men miraculously manage to climb or jump out of the burning wreckage and are still on the atoll somewhere? This overgrown hunk of dead coral is slight, lying only about a metre to two metres above sea level at high tide, the undergrowth sparse; you can walk around the island in under an hour. Won't take long to check it out. Any questions?'

'Sorry, did you say Harvey Driscoll?' Fiona questioned, her voice faltering.

Evan nodded. 'Correct. Why, do you know him?'

'Yes, he's a close friend. Um, sorry, this is devastating news.' Fiona took a moment to regain her composure. 'Sorry, I'm fine. Please continue.'

Linton stepped forward. 'This bloke, Terry, do we know much about his experience as a pilot? I heard you need extensive knowledge to fly these routes. Was this an accident waiting to happen?'

'Personally, I would think it highly unlikely,' McMillen answered, squinting against a blinding mid-afternoon glare radiating off the coral sand. 'Coates was one of the best; clocked 10,000 hours flying for Qantas on the long-haul trips from Brisbane to Japan and China. Prior to that, eight years of service as an RAAF attack helicopter pilot.'

'Well, the weather on the day of the crash was basically clear,' Linton commented, having already conducted some research. 'I'm surmising it must have been mechanical failure that brought the chopper down.'

'We'll see,' Bruce remarked, never one to speculate. 'The specialist aviation team will be flying in shortly to work on the aircraft. Now, if there are no further questions, let's get on with the job. It'll be dark before we realise it, and I don't fancy being stuck out here after the sun sets.'

***

Papua New Guinea
Kimbie, Dive Resort. 02:00 Hours

Fiona found the haven of sleep hard to come by. Concern for her boys weighed heavily on her mind; she longed to be back in Sydney; thankfully, she had Jaz for company. They were sharing a twin room, basic in furnishings with two single beds, but it did the trick.

A small kettle was provided on a bench, allowing them to make hot drinks, along with a modest assortment of packet biscuits for hunger attacks during the night.

Fiona tried to shift into a more comfortable position; despite the air conditioner on high, she felt her body overheating, hoping this wasn't the onset of a summer cold.

'You awake?' Jaz whispered from her bed, a few feet away. 'Can't you sleep? If you're worried about the twins, don't be; they'll be fine. My sister will take excellent care of them.'

'I'm not used to this remote work, that's all.' Fiona stretched out a hand to switch on the bedside lamp. 'I'm hoping we won't be here for too long, praying we'll get an early mark.'

'Perhaps. Now, tell me, Fiona, how well did you know this Harvey guy? You looked pretty cut up when you heard he was involved in the crash.'

'Well enough,' Fiona responded, propped up on one arm, idly studying the native spears and ceremonial fetishes displayed on the opposite wall. 'We were friends back in the UK for a number of years.'

'What do you think happened to him? I can't get my head around the fact that the pilot was found some distance from where the helicopter went down, even weirder that there's no trace of your friend and that American.'

'I expect we'll find out more tomorrow when we take another look at the wreckage and get updates from the aviation team,' Fiona whispered back, afraid they would wake those sleeping in the next room.

'What sort of chap was Harvey?' Jaz had a lot of questions; Fiona was not sure how much information she wanted to part with. It was a shock to hear Harvey was missing, presumed dead. She found it hard to talk about.

After a few moments, she responded, 'Complicated.'

Suddenly, Jaz sat up in bed. 'Hey, that autopsy we conducted before we left Sydney, the one on Brenda Carr. Didn't she work with Harvey Driscoll? I vaguely remember reading something about Brenda working for Pacific Rim Mining.'

'Yes, she did.'

Jaz let out a huge exclamation, 'OMG! If I were Linton, I'd be looking into these events very carefully. Surely, it can't be coincidental that Brenda gets murdered and now Harvey has been involved in a major aviation accident and probable gold heist. It would appear someone was out to get them both; what do you think?'

'It's certainly starting to look that way.' Fiona sighed, turning off the lamp. 'Let's try and get some sleep. I can't see tomorrow being easy for any of us.'

***

Papua New Guinea
Third Day. 06:00 Hours

Fiona and Jaz joined the investigation team early in the dining room; ahead lay an exhilarating helicopter flight out to the crash site, both having no illusions as to the gruelling day that would follow.

'Everyone, your attention please,' Evan instructed, standing up to address the subdued team members, quietly attacking a full buffet breakfast. 'I've had a chance to catch up with the aviation techs from the RAAF, and this is what they've told me: this was no unfortunate accident.'

Everyone started speaking at once. Eventually, Evan had to silence them by banging a spoon against a cereal bowl and raising his voice. 'Righto. This is what we believe happened: The pilot, Terry Coates, was forced to bring the chopper down in a hurry, and once it crash-landed, the scene was made to look like a tragic accident; the aircraft set alight and left to burn.'

'As for the gold bars, no trace of them or the ammunition boxes, even after a thorough search of the immediate vicinity. Evaporated into thin air.'

'No way,' Jaz piped up. 'But why? Do we know more about the death of the pilot, who may have killed him?'

'Most likely he was executed,' Evan replied. 'Immediately after arrival yesterday, I transferred his body onto the navy patrol boat for refrigeration. First thing, you people need to do a preliminary autopsy on board the patrol boat and check our theory.'

Linton took over the conversation, 'My firearms guy identified a bullet lodged in the cockpit roof as 9mm. The type

236

of gun used points to a US military standard issue 9mm Beretta automatic, which Ryder Albero was known to be carrying, which clearly puts Albero in the frame, and possibly Harvey Driscoll; although Driscoll could well be another victim, we don't know.'

Fiona started to feel sick.

'We'll be heading out to the crash site in thirty minutes, so finish breakfast and collect anything from your rooms you want to take with you,' Evan instructed. 'We've a long day ahead.'

***

HMAS Benalla. Armidale Class Patrol Boat: 09:45 Hours

'Tell you what we'll do, Doctor,' Commander Jeff Dawson announced, engrossed with his second-in-command poring over the large GPS Navionics chart plotter screen display, prominently mounted in the bridge operations room. 'I'll bring my boat inside the reef and out of the sou'easter swell. Be aware and keep in mind we'll have less than one metre of water under the keel, and that, I'm not even confident of. The navigation data for these remote islands is extremely unreliable at best.'

'Understand perfectly, Commander.'

'I can only give you till 12:30 hours maximum, before the tide turns, and I'm pulling the anchor and taking my boat back outside, regardless of where you two ladies are at,' Dawson continued.

'Sorry to put you to so much trouble,' Fiona acknowledged. 'Thank you, Jeff.'

'Forget it. Least we can do. Glad the navy can help. Anything you want, my medical officer will get it. Good luck, Dr Sinclair.'

10:33 Hours: 'You heard what Commander Dawson said, Jaz: two hours,' Fiona reiterated. 'Unwrap the plastic and cut off Terry's polo shirt. I'll start cleaning the face and body and take an overall view of what we've got. Definitely no time for any serious dissection, maybe none at all. I'm betting a preliminary examination will give us the answers. Ready?'

12:15 Hours: Fiona and Jaz stepped off the ladder and into the inflatable just as the Benalla's diesels rumbled to life. Speeding away, they waved cheerio to Dawson, clearly visible standing just outside the bridge, the inflatable dropping them off on the beach where the navy crew was setting up an impromptu BBQ.

12:25 Hours: 'You join the others, Jaz. Might take a walk, be by myself for a while. To be honest, I'm not that hungry. Need to clear my head and come back down. The water looks inviting. Tell Linton I'll brief them after lunch.'

With that, Fiona walked off along the beach in the shade of the trees, her mind struggling to come to terms with the events of the last days, unable to comprehend the bizarre coincidences and the possible implications of Harvey's involvement.

13:15 Hours: Reaching the other side of the atoll, ignoring advice not to swim in the dangerous waters, Fiona stripped off and sat on the sand, staring blankly out across the lagoon, the warm tropical waves washing gently over her feet, time slowing.

14:00 Hours: Brought back to reality by a noisy seabird overhead, Fiona glanced at her watch, realising the team might be getting anxious. Quickly gathering her things and stuffing them in the kit bag, she hurried off along the path. Deciding to head straight into the vegetation and cut diagonally across the atoll, she calculated this would bring her right back to the site and the team camp, saving twenty minutes.

14:10 Hours: Plunging through the she-oaks and undergrowth, Fiona suddenly entered a small clearing about twenty metres wide and halted, at the end of which was a large object half-buried in the sand. Moving closer, Fiona soon realised what lay before her was the remains of a World War 2 aircraft.

Although the aluminium airframe was now in a severe state of corrosion, its brown and green wave pattern camouflage was plainly discernible under a mass of branches and vines. Clearing away the sand with her boots, Fiona stepped onto the wing, noting the faded blue and white rondel markings peppered with what she recognised were machine gun bullet holes, and peered into a closed cockpit, unable to see inside through degraded Plexiglas.

Using all her strength, she forced back the canopy, encountering a tragic scene undisturbed for eighty years. The mostly skeletal remains of an Allied fighter pilot, shreds of pale khaki uniform and leather helmet adhering, still secured by his belt, skull hard forward against a remarkably intact optical gunsight.

An identification bracelet hung from a wrist, along with the faded photo of a loved one in a metal frame attached to the gunsight. Ignoring the ghostly scene, the professional pathologist in Fiona took over, recording the scene on her smartphone; to her trained eye, the cause of death was immediately apparent: the front of the skull bore severe trauma indentations from shrapnel of an exploding armour-piercing shell entering through the front of the canopy.

***

Papua New Guinea

20:30 Hours Evan rose from the dining table at the dive resort, ready to address the noisy, ebullient team seated around him. As the chatter slowly died, he scanned the faces, a broad smile slowly spreading across a sunburnt visage.

'Ladies and gentlemen, can I ask you to please raise your glasses, whatever you're drinking, in a toast to our pathologist, Dr Fiona Sinclair?'

An almighty cheer rang through the room, followed by yells, clapping, and stomping of feet on the floorboards, lasting for well over a minute.

'I received a communication from the RAAF half an hour ago, confirming our discovery of an important war grave, for which we have the lovely doctor to thank.'

More cheers erupted.

A team member broke in, excitedly holding up a YouTube video on an iPhone, 'Hey Doc, you've gone viral on social media. Already on the late news breaking back home.

240

Everybody's streaming you talking, standing near the Boomerang.'

Jaz hugged an incredulous Fiona, who, uncertain whether to laugh or cry, rose briefly. 'I was only doing my—'

Drowned out by more cheers and yells, Fiona sat back down and raised her glass.

Evan continued over the hubbub, 'Got the details here somewhere. Yep, an RAAF CAC Boomerang ground attack fighter, supporting the 5th Division AIF's campaign against the Japanese on New Britain-15 May 1944. Didn't return that day from a mission. Listed as lost, the pilot, a flight lieutenant, MIA, presumed killed.'

'This is one the War Memorial and RAAF have been hoping might one day turn up, and also, of course, for the family to finally get closure. The pilot was an ace with 7 "kills," one of our few; this is big news. From what the aviation crash guys tell me, they reckon the Boomerang most likely tackled a Japanese Navy Zero fighter, coming off second-best.'

Ruth was losing all the courage she'd built up over the past few weeks. He seemed to be gaining strength, more manipulative. He even had her starting to believe she deserved the abuse.

Chapter Sixteen

'You brainless imbecile. Please, please tell me you didn't take Scotch and Soda to the reservoir when you followed Lisa Marshall. Of all the fucking dumb things to do.'

Shirley paced up and down, gesticulating wildly, breathing fire, her face distorted with anger. Desmond retreated behind crates of beer in the storeroom for protection, suddenly realising the impact of what he'd done.

***

Salcombe, Devon, England

Lana Gibbs checked the Satnav on her smartphone, confirming the address, and swung the *Star's* pool Corsa into a spacious driveway, parking directly outside the modest fifties holiday home. Situated halfway down a steep, winding back street of Salcombe, hidden behind a mature boxwood hedge, the white-painted cottage offered broken views back out across the estuary to Kingsbridge in the distance.

Unlike the summer months, the first touches of winter ushered in the return of sanity to the streets and fields of South Devon, especially to the now-quiet coastal communities like Salcombe; tourists magically transported back to the cities and crowded suburbs, mundane jobs, coupled with long cold nights.

Striding up a flight of steep steps to the front door of the property, a normally uber-confident Lana admitted to feeling a little more than anxious. It had taken several weeks to get hold of Basil Hammond, who normally resided outside London, preferring to make the trip down to Devon just twice a year at Christmas and in August.

He had reluctantly agreed to meet up, confirming the visit by email, acquainted with Lana from his time as a senior detective in special investigations, attached to New Scotland Yard. She wasn't even 100% sure Basil remembered her; maybe he wouldn't turn up, the drive down from *Newton Abbot* possibly shaping up as a complete waste of time.

What was it, ten years ago, when they last conversed, when Lana was a fledgling journalist with one of the national papers in London, before securing her job with the *Newton Abbot Star*, which in her mind had hardly ever been the career choice she'd sought?

Somehow, she'd gotten stuck in a rut, and here she was, several years later, still churning out the same boring copy for a small-time regional paper.

'Not for much longer,' Lana muttered to herself, dismissing doubts to press the doorbell.

The door flew open almost immediately, Basil quickly urging her inside and closing the door with a firm push.

'Blasted winter weather,' he grumbled, leading Lana through to a cosy snug where a fire burnt brightly in a stone fireplace. 'Lana, isn't it? Make yourself at home. Won't be a tick, get rid of the coat. I've a plunger of coffee on the go. I presume you're partial to the local croissants.'

Throwing her coat over the lounge, Lana took a quick look around. Attracted to a stunning cabinet in burr walnut veneer on an ebony stand, she moved over to take a closer look, carefully opening its doors, failing to notice Basil re-enter the room, placing a tray on the coffee table. When he spoke, she jumped.

'Oh, sorry, I couldn't help touching. Such a beautiful piece of furniture, surely valuable.'

'High five figures, I believe. Rare item that, circa 1906, Arts & Crafts. Probably by the Barnsleys or Grimson, I saw a similar one on Antiques Roadshow. Passed down from my grandmother, or maybe my great-grandmother; I can't remember. Anyway, I don't tend to keep many items of worth here in Devon, but this one suits the period feel of the house and decorative fireplace.'

Basil poured two mugs of coffee, placing one on a side table next to where Lana was sitting. 'Milk and sugar?'

Lana obliged, waiting for an opportune moment to make her move.

Basil, cradling his own mug of coffee, leaned back in his chair, eyeing her with amusement. 'Yes indeed, your face is familiar. The Charing Cross Tube fire? Long time since we met; ten years I'm deducing?'

Lana responded, 'More recently, we briefly chatted at a police charity event I was covering in Plymouth for the *Star*, Easter 2020.'

'Sorry, my memory's a bit rusty. Just before I retired from the Yard, maybe. Um. Now, tell me, what's this meeting about? You were very vague when we spoke on the phone. All I managed to unravel was something about cold cases, am I right?'

Lana blurted out the reason for the meeting, studying Basil's expression to gauge if he would be willing to part with anything useful. At the end of her long-winded speech, he got up, threw another log on the fire, poured himself another coffee, and reached for a chocolate croissant. Lana waited patiently whilst he tended the fire vigorously with a poker.

Finally, Basil looked up, offering her a broad grin. 'I must say, Gibbs, you're very direct, which is one of your finer qualities. That's half the reason I gave you the exclusive news release of those arrests, years ago back in London. You don't hold back. Whether I can assist you today is a totally different matter, but let's give it a go.'

Lana sat with bated breath, watching Basil pour a third cup of coffee.

'Occupational hazard,' he advised. 'Working crazy long hours and being involved with some of England's most infamous events turned me to coffee, and perhaps the odd tipple of wine.' A twinkle flashed in his eye. 'I can see you're a one-cup wonder, Gibbs.'

Lana waited for Basil to continue, hoping he would provide her with the information she desperately sought.

'There are two fairly recent cases the department has consigned to the *too hard basket*; homicides that had us completely baffled,' Basil informed her. 'The first one was the hit-and-run death of little Ryan, discovered by the side of a country lane, discarded like some stray animal.'

'No one saw or heard anything. That was a little over four years ago, about two years before I retired. We had very little evidence to go on. His family was strange: mother, a drug addict; Ryan's father, a known alcoholic. Neither seemed too upset by the lad's death. It was Ryan's older brother who made the most noise, saying he'd eventually find out who killed Ryan and seek revenge; all hype if you ask me.

'Anyway, we worked hard on that case, but we didn't find anything that told us where to start looking for a suspect. No one ever came forward with game-changing information.'

Basil stopped to catch his breath. At sixty-nine, he still cut an impressive figure, sitting there reminiscing about his previous cases.

'I think this case will be the one of most interest to you,' Basis finally continued. 'If you dig up any new information in this matter, Gibbs, it will certainly nudge your career to another level.'

Lana sat up in her chair, notebook at the ready. 'This happened shortly before I left the force. It revolves around the death of one of England's top research scientists, found dead where she worked. The coroner's ruling: accidental death by asphyxiation. However, I was not convinced.'

Lana took another sip of her drink, waiting for Basil to continue. When he did, she noticed his hands shaking, a possible sign of Parkinson's.

'Take this down,' Basil instructed. 'Doctor Kimberley Marshall, thirty-five at the time, double degree, Honours. Imperial College London. PhD, Georgia Tech, I'm sure you can get the details off the internet.'

Lana obliged, writing the name down as a heading.

'To me, Kimberley's untimely death reeked of foul play and cover-up,' Basil informed Lana. 'A very attractive young woman, with a bright future ahead, who was a lead scientist on a top-secret project for the MOD. A Wednesday evening, early November from what I'm remembering.

'Kim was working late in an experimental defence facility outside Yeovil, phoned her husband, advising she would be home, and was found dead the next morning in what was left of the facility destroyed in a massive fire and explosion. This woman was an exceptional engineer and chemist.'

'I appreciate accidents happen, but to die under such horrific circumstances looks more like a deliberate attack to me. No eyewitnesses, missing evidence, restricted access to classified files, sends all the wrong signals. Read my mind.'

'Why didn't others feel the same way as you?' Lana quizzed.

Basil shrugged. 'Less drama, I suppose, plus I didn't have much to back up my theory. This matter often keeps me awake at night. Almost three years on, there's no interest at the top level anymore. Everyone progresses with their lives; for Kim's family, life stands still.'

'Do you still have access to Kim's file? Is there a chance I can take a peek?'

'I thought you'd ask. Gibbs, if you have a role in kickstarting this case, you'll be a bloody hero.'

Basil paused, taking a deep breath. 'I'll make a few calls enabling you to take a look at the records, but remember, Gibbs, this whole matter is very sensitive. I also want you to update me on anything of interest you find. If the Yard deems it warranted to reopen the case, I'll certainly weigh in with any influence I can still muster.'

***

Sydney, Australia
Early January

On Fiona's first day back in Sydney, the nightmares began. Every night without fail, causing her to wake in panic, underwear soaked in sweat, her temples pounding from incessant headaches. There was no official or unofficial update on Harvey's whereabouts or the American and the missing $40 million mine gold bar shipment.

It was now patently clear that the pilot, Terry Coates, died from a bullet wound to the neck, thanks to Fiona's preliminary examination. Either by accident or in a deliberate move, the investigation team now leans heavily towards the latter, thus pointing the finger right at the American or Harvey, or both.

No trace of the bullion was found on the island or any evidence of the missing men. Harvey was either at the bottom of the Bismarck Sea or somewhere he didn't want to be found, a possible party to the biggest aerial gold hijack scheme in history.

***

Sydney, Australia

Glancing at the bedside clock flicking over to 5am and the realisation she had at least two further hours of rest before it was time to rise and confront a new day, Fiona turned over, pulling the sheets up. She'd only just started to drift off when a loud clatter finally forced her out of bed.

Treading softly across the carpeted floor, in a half trance, Fiona tried to work out the origin of the noise. The boys were fast asleep in their beds in the room down the hallway; it sounded like it was coming from outside the main door, across the hallway, perhaps from Hayley's apartment, whom Fiona knew to be away for a few days.

With her heart beating loudly in her chest, Fiona undid the security locks on the front door, peering out into the dimly lit corridor. A male figure stood outside Hayley and Jordan's apartment, Fiona's appearance making him jump.

'Christ almighty, you scared me!' He exclaimed, the key he was holding falling to the ground.

'Sorry, I didn't mean to startle you,' Fiona apologised. 'I heard a noise; I know Hayley and Jordan are away and thought someone was trying to break in.'

'Apologies, just on my way up the coast, I needed to pick up my diving gear. I forgot to inform anyone I might call around. Can't seem to get the keys to fit. I'm Dylan; I was best man at Hayley and Jordan's wedding.'

Fiona let out a sigh of relief. 'Ah, of course. I've heard all about you, how you and Hayley once dated, and she broke up with you in the Brindabella National Park.'

Dylan looked surprised. 'No, not me. I've never set foot in the—what did you say?—the Brinda something; I've never heard of it. Hayley and I were never an item; you must be mistaking me for someone else.'

Now, it was Fiona's turn to look bemused. 'Right, I must have heard wrong. Sorry to put you through the third degree.

Well, now I've learnt you're not a burglar; I'll head back to bed.'

***

Bovey Tracey, Devon, England
Moorland Forensics Consultants Facility

'Sorry guys, gotta go.' Nick announced, scooping up car keys and wallet, before extracting the black leather suitcase stowed under a desk in the Moorland office. 'My flight leaves Heathrow at nine tonight.'

'And you'll be away how long?' James asked, pressing the button to open the courtyard gates.

'Only a couple of weeks,' Nick answered. 'I need to sort out Mum's affairs and get her settled into a nursing home.'

'It'll be a weight off your mind, knowing she's properly cared for,' Javier piped up, busy at the photocopier. 'My mother's in care, back in Cebu. It gives our family peace of mind.'

'Yep, I'm sure it will be a blessing.' Nick glanced anxiously at the railway clock in reception. 'There's only so much one can do from the other side of the world. The coach leaves Exeter in an hour; better be off. See you both in a few weeks.'

'We'll be fine here,' James reassured Nick. 'Javier and I finally have our client backlog under control. And don't concern yourself with the dramas at your lab. I'll keep an eye on things. If you need to stay longer, just give me the heads-up.'

'Thanks, I appreciate your support.' Nick made his way to the front door, pulling the black leather suitcase in his wake.

'Safe travels,' Javier called out. 'Text when you land in Auckland; let us know you've arrived safely.'

Nick, zipping up his ski jacket, stepped out into the chill of a howling northerly sweeping down from the icy wastes of the Arctic and across the high Dartmoor plateau.

Throwing the luggage in the rear of his 280SL coupe, he sat for a few minutes, waiting for the vintage Mercedes to warm up, looking out through the windscreen, watching windswept snowflakes swirling around the courtyard. He was not looking forward to the flight of almost twenty-six hours, and even less the arrival into Auckland. Too many memories.

***

Devon, England

Mallory looked up at the surveillance camera monitoring their approach and pressed the buzzer to the right of the doorway, resulting in a loud chime clearly audible in the entrance foyer on the other side.

'Will, there was no real need for both of us to visit Mrs Roundtree for a routine interview. A DCI and an acting DI, a bit of overkill, wouldn't you agree?'

'Don't stress, Mal; besides, I needed some fresh air; I've been stuck in the office all week. I intended to sneak out anyway to pick up a burger.'

Will stepped back from the doorway to take in the three-storey property. 'Bloody imposing. Hell, how big is this place?'

'Isn't it? Don't be fooled by the 16th-century exterior. It's Edwardian. Built for Rowena Roundtree's great-grandfather, complete with the mock Tudor exterior.'

'You *are* a wealth of knowledge.' Will sounded suitably impressed. 'No wonder you're up for promotion. Very thorough, Mal, efficient—that's what the upper echelon is looking for in a DI.'

Mallory blushed, pushing gently on the door to see if it was unlocked, but it wasn't.

'Perhaps no one's home; they're no longer able to afford the heating bill,' Will jovially remarked, moving his feet to counteract creeping numbness in his toes.

'Got a bit of fascinating history, this one,' Mallory continued. 'Last night in bed, I flicked through the autobiography of Percival Roundtree, who built the place. Apparently, the old boy was one of the backers of Howard Carter, the famous Egyptologist who discovered Tutankhamun's tomb. Didn't everyone associated with the expedition die premature, gruesome deaths?'

'Thanks for that, Mal. Made my day.'

Mallory pressed the chimes once more. A few moments passed before the door opened and Rowena stood in front of them, power dressed to kill, in a pale blue, figure-hugging, satin trouser suit unbuttoned almost to the waist, revealing more than ample cleavage, long blonde hair restrained in place with a tortoiseshell comb.

'Yes, how can I help you?' There was no warmth in her voice.

Will briefly explained the reason for their visit, asking if they could come in.

'Of course, I remember now. Vivian, my secretary, took your call. Sorry, I've had a lot going on lately. Something to do with Harvey, you said?'

Reluctantly, Rowena stepped aside, showing them into a vast circular entrance hallway; the floor in local polished stone, leading to a sweeping pink marble staircase immediately opposite. Ancient Egyptian artefacts, in glass viewing cases, were strategically positioned around the room, including free-standing sarcophagi complete with original mummified royal personages.

She then led them into a grand sitting room on the ground floor, asking them to remove their shoes. 'Apologies for the entrance hallway; it has that effect on people. Unfortunately, one of the stipulations in grandfather's will is that those antiquities must remain on display in perpetuity.'

'Quite all right, Mrs Roundtree, very impressive. Like the British Museum,' Will replied.

'Yes, well, I promise you, Detective Parker, the rest of the house is not like that.'

'More worried about her shag pile than any missing husband,' Mallory whispered, taking up residence next to Will on a soft, cream sofa, whilst Rowena puffed up a couple of cushions.

'Missing a few days, you say,' Rowena questioned, sitting down opposite the detectives. 'I'm sure Harvey will turn up eventually; sadly, he always does.'

'We found the crash site and no sign of your husband,' Will continued.

'Ex-husband, well, soon-to-be,' Rowena corrected, gazing down at long, well-manicured, iridescent blue fingernails. 'Harvey and I have not been together for a very long time. You should probably be having this conversation with his sister, who lives in France; she's listed as his next of kin. I washed my hands of Harvey a while back. He had these awful habits, I mean.'

'When did you last hear from Harvey?' Will quizzed.

'Oh, probably six weeks ago. Informed me he was in the process of signing the divorce papers, but there would be a slight delay as his solicitor was away on leave. Frustrating.'

'You weren't aware of Harvey's planned trip to Japan?' Mallory asked.

'No, not my business.' Rowena's voice took on a bored tone, indicating she really wasn't interested in what the police officers had to say.

'Do your children have much contact with their father?' This question was posed by Mallory.

'Certainly not. Harvey is focused on his career; he always has been. That's why we separated in the first place. Well, that and the fact he couldn't keep his eyes or hands off other women, disgusting. I'm not bothered if I never see that dreadful man again.

'I certainly don't need him financially, with all my assets. Look around you, detectives. The value of the antiques in this room alone is worth well into six figures. Take the Chippendale secretaire and matching dresser over there; current value, well, it would be rude of me to quote that figure.'

In response, Will and Mallory looked around at the furniture and other decorative items, mostly high-end

Georgian design pieces and contemporary landscape paintings, tending to agree with her summation.

'Yes, well, if you do hear from your soon-to-be ex-husband, do get in touch.' Will rose to his feet, Mallory following suit, concluding that a disinterested and reticent Rowena Roundtree had nothing more to offer.

'And if we should hear any news of Harvey's whereabouts, we'll be sure to inform you,' Mallory advised.

'Don't bother,' Rowena snapped, impatiently waiting for her guests to put their shoes back on.

Outside in the cool air, Will heaved a sigh of relief. 'Now, that's a bitter female. I can't see any bloke wanting to shack up with her.'

Mallory tucked her arm into the crook of Will's elbow. 'Yep, the focus is solely on herself and money. Now, me, on the other hand.'

Will, ensuring they were out of the direct line of sight of any windows, pulled Mallory into a warm embrace. 'Oh, I know all about you, Mallory Wakefield, and I like what I see.'

Each night, Ruth would retrieve the knife from under the bed, holding it tight. Tomorrow, she kept telling herself, it had to be tomorrow. Always tomorrow. But in reality, tomorrow never came.

Chapter Seventeen

Sydney, Australia
Central Command CID. February 3rd

Linton, looking out from his office window back towards Central Railway and beyond to the iconic buildings of Sydney University in the distance, was in two minds whether to duck out for a pub lunch or suffer the consequences of the staff canteen fare when the tablet on his desk flashed up a Zoom notification.

'Doctor Fiona Sinclair, I presume. Big day for you. Just caught the ceremony from the War Memorial on the news direct from Canberra. I expect everybody back in Devon was watching the presentation on GB News.'

Linton focused in on Fiona, her face beaming from end to end, proudly holding up a large gold medal hanging around her neck.

'My God, Linton, I've never been through anything like this before. Still shaking.'

'You looked fabulous. Sorry I couldn't travel down with you.'

'Don't worry. The RAAF flew me down with others from the crash investigation in their VIP plane. Lots of celebrations happening soon, including a big dinner event tonight to coincide with the opening of the War Memorial's new WW2 wing. I believe they have plans to make the Boomerang centrepiece in a recreation of the crash site.'

'Well done, Fi, proud of you. You truly deserve it.'

'You really think so. Tell you what, I'm due back on Thursday; I'd love to catch up. You can take me out for dinner somewhere special; surprise me. Have to rush; can you believe I have media interviews scheduled the rest of the afternoon? Text me. Cheers.'

Watching Fiona's image fade, Linton shut down the iPad, his thoughts returning to lunch and the growing urgency of the backpacker investigations, the failure of the CID to achieve any meaningful breakthroughs weighing on his mind. Pressure from both the media and the Assistant Commissioner continued to mount.

As Linton made his way to the lift, his mobile vibrated in his coat pocket. 'DCI Ansley.'

'Lint, it's me, Graeme, Graeme Brosch. How the devil are you, mate?'

'Good grief, "Broschy," this is a blast from the past. What are you up to nowadays, buddy? Has to be at least two years since we last spoke, too bloody long.'

'Nearly three,' Graeme answered. 'I've been assigned some cold cases to go through. The area commander over here thinks it's the ideal opportunity to pass on my experience to some of the younger detectives. Not that I particularly mind. I don't care how long it takes to put the crims away, so long as we get the bastards in the end.'

'How's the injury?' Linton enquired. 'Last time I saw you, you could hardly walk.'

'Still giving me trouble. I've ditched the walking stick finally, thank God, wearing leg braces a majority of the time, and hanging out for the pension. Thankfully, only a few months left to go.'

'Sorry to hear about the leg; it can't be easy. Bloody bad luck you got involved in that firefight with those two indigenous thugs at the farmhouse siege. A blessing they're inside for life. Console yourself with the realisation you're close to retirement; unfortunately, I can't see myself anywhere near getting out of the force. I'll be stuck here at least another five years, possibly more. Anyway, what can I help with? I presume your phone call is work-related, eh?'

An extended pause prevailed before Graeme came back on the line. 'Sorry about that; had to pop a couple of analgesics. Back to business: I'm currently working on the disappearance of one Wayne Brenner, originally from Perth, twenty-two when he went missing, roughly eleven years ago, in the Brindabella National Park in the ACT. Not sure if you recall the case; were you around then? Regardless, I've spotted a few similarities with the current backpacker murders; I thought you might be interested.'

Linton sat up straighter, placing the mobile in a holder and switching to speaker. 'What you got, mate?'

'The synthetic cord used to tie Wayne all those years ago is identical to the cord now being employed by the current backpacker killer. An unusual construction, quite distinct in colour and fibre composition, polypropylene.'

'As a bonus, photos from the crime scenes confirm the binding method used on all three victims employs an identical sequence of clove hitch and bowline knots. Now, don't tell me that isn't coincidental.'

Linton cleared his throat. 'Only trouble is, my victims were all women, raped and then murdered. I don't see how Brenner's murder is linked.'

'Ah, well that's what *I* thought at first,' Graeme explained. 'Hear me out here; let's suppose Brenner was the first victim, killed for a totally different reason, then later, this guy goes on to murder women.'

'A serial psycho, I don't know.' Linton sounded doubtful. 'If you dig a little deeper, you'll probably discover the cord isn't that unusual in—'

'That cord was only sold through one ship's chandler outlet in Sydney for a few months, twelve years ago, before the Korean manufacturer went out of business. The MO is *exactly* the same,' Graeme persisted. 'Do me a favour, take a look into Brenner's case, and call me back.'

'I suppose it won't do any harm,' Linton agreed. 'Lovely to hear from you, my man. Drop round sometime if you're ever on a plane to Sydney. By the way, how's Perth treating you?'

'Great, I'm enjoying the weather and slower pace of life.'

'Excellent. I promise I'll take a look at the Brenner data. Speak soon.'

Linton ended the call and headed out across the street, opting for a kebab. Once back at his desk, he pushed all other work aside and started trawling through the Brenner file he had requisitioned up from archives.

He then went online, searching for any relevant news articles, publications, or YouTube docos that covered the murder, shy on eleven years. What he discovered was interesting; perhaps there was something in the theory Broschy came up with after all.

***

Plymouth, Devon, England
A Secure Psychiatric Facility

Christina sat reading, propped up in bed in a corner of the room, an element of surprise crossing her façade when Javier walked in. She had a feeling he would turn up asking questions, but not this soon.

'You must be Blake's friend?' She stated, resting the book on her lap. 'What exactly do you want to know?'

Javier nodded in reply, taking up residence on the bed next to Christina. 'I want to know where Lisa hid the memory stick.'

'She didn't tell me. Your guess is as good as mine.'

'Where do you think she hid it?' Javier pressed. 'It's important we find it; put an end to the mayhem those "Big Pharma" mongrels are planning in Australia.'

'What, and get us all killed, the same way Lisa was murdered?' Christina opened her book once more.

Javier, not one to be put off, took the book from Christina, placing it on the bed next to him. 'I will personally guarantee your safety, but no one is going to be safe with the USB missing. Origan will leave no stone unturned to get the damn thing. If I can find it, make the contents public, it'll put an end to what's been going on. Surely you can see that.'

Christina blew out her cheeks. 'I honestly don't know where the stick is. If I did, I would tell you. Now, if you don't mind, I'm trying to read.'

Javier stood up, turning Christina around to look at him. 'Where do you think she might have hidden it? You knew

Lisa very well. Where would she secret a petite object she didn't want anyone to find?'

'In her shoes, perhaps. Straight out of a bad spy movie plot, you'll say. Bizarre, but it's true, the go-to place when she wanted to conceal something.' Christina stopped briefly to retrieve a carton of soft drink from the bedside drawer, Javier watching intently.

'Lisa's grandfather owned a bootmaker shop; he taught her how to remove the sole of a shoe where the inside section was hollow. Of course, you can only use a certain type of shoe or boot and only store small items. Lisa had Jodhpur boots, and these were ideal for storing drugs and tiny amounts of cash.'

Javier leapt to his feet, giving Christina a peck on the cheek. 'Thank you. I'll be back, not sure when, but I'll be back to get you out of here.'

Christina giggled. 'I quite like this place. No rush. Oh, and say 'hi' to Blake for me. He's a top bloke.'

***

Auckland, New Zealand

Nick removed the cardboard boxes from the basement, placing them near the front door. Brewing up a plunger coffee from what little stores remained in the kitchen, he sat on the floor, methodically beginning to sift through the contents of the boxes, disposing of any items no longer required. He came across a confidential file pertaining to his mother.

Ruth Shelby has been diagnosed with schizophrenia. It's recommended she receive the correct medical and psychiatric treatment to assist with her condition. A referral request has been put in for Mrs Ruth Shelby to be seen by the head of the psychiatric unit at the Neville Foley Institution in Auckland, where, in my opinion, Ruth should be admitted.

If her condition goes untreated, it may very well escalate; Ruth then poses a risk to herself and others.

Several hours later, punctuated by an extended break for a homemade sandwich and a one-hour kip on the lounge, brought on by jet lag, Nick came to the last shoebox, full to the brim with letters, along with old newspaper cuttings and miscellaneous documents.

With a heavy heart, he picked up one of the articles, yellowed and frayed around the edges, dated August 1989:

Forty-three-year-old father of two, Howard Shelby, was found dead last night, throat cut, in a bathtub, in his Mount Eden, Auckland home. Police are treating the death as suicide.

Family members disclosed Howard Shelby suffered a life-long battle with addictions to prescription pain medication, coupled with chronic bouts of depression.

***

Sydney, Australia

Unable to resist any longer, Linton shut the laptop, pushed aside the leftover takeaway chilli chicken order from his favourite Chinatown eatery, and buried his head on folded arms, intending to doze briefly for ten minutes.

One hour later, he woke with a start and a parched throat to the whine of police sirens rising up from the streets below. Yawning loudly, he rose from the desk in his office on the 7th floor, opened the last can of sparkling-infused raspberry soda, and downed it in one motion before moving over to the window to peer down through the wooden blinds at the lights of traffic streaming out of the city in all directions, now thinning rapidly as midnight approached.

His thoughts switched for an instant to Fiona, tempted to shoot off a quick SMS, wishing he could join her and the team; no doubt they were having a great time at after-dinner drinks as celebrations continued well into the early hours; no need to interrupt.

He returned to his chair, placing both feet up on the desk, picking up the large notebook listing all the relevant points he'd jotted down from his recent search, and a brief cryptic handwritten summary.

According to reports, at the time of his disappearance, Wayne, a twenty-two-year-old postgraduate student from the University of WA, was studying engineering at Sydney Uni on an exchange research scholarship. Wayne, along with his twenty-year-old girlfriend, Leigh Crompton, embarked on a hiking trip during his mid-year break, intending to walk in the national parks around the ACT and the Alpine regions of southern NSW.

Four days into their ten-day trip, Wayne disappeared. Leigh was found on day five, picked up by a national park ranger, who found the young woman wandering about dazed on a fire trail with a large cut to her forehead, suffering severe exposure, and requiring a number of stitches. Leigh was transferred to Queanbeyan for treatment and observation.

Two days later, after intensive police and army searches, Wayne's body was located off a track near their planned hiking route, tied and bound, shot in the back of the head with a small handgun, probably a .32 calibre pistol.

Leigh claims to have no recollection of what happened to Wayne. She gave a brief statement to police but refused to attend any press conferences, speak to counsellors, or liaise with any members of Wayne's family. This fuelled media speculation as to whether Leigh was involved in her boyfriend's murder.

Two months after the discovery of Wayne Brenner's body, Leigh disappeared. At this current point in time, after eleven long years, no one has been able to locate her current whereabouts, and there remain to this day grave fears for her safety.

***

Exeter, Devon, England
One Week Later

'Mallory, so glad I caught you. I have some new information pertaining to Lisa and Christina; may I come in?'

Mallory opened the door, allowing Lana Gibbs entry to her modest bungalow in a neglected, run-down, seventies residential development close to an industrial estate on the outskirts of the city.

'Couldn't this have waited until tomorrow?' Mallory grumbled, walking back down the hallway, with Lana close on her heels. 'I was in the middle of dinner.'

Mallory resumed a seat at the kitchen table, ready to continue her attack on a large plate of fettuccine carbonara. 'If you want some, there's a bowl on the side.'

'Nah, I'm fine. I ate on my way over. Wouldn't say no to a drop of that red, however.'

'Go for it; you can top mine up whilst you're at it. Well, go on, what's the latest?'

Lana pulled out a wooden country chair and sat down, facing Mallory. 'According to Spen, my journo friend in Sydney, Lisa and Christina worked for a large Sydney-based drug concern, Origan Pharma. Employed there for three or four months.'

'Origan, an offshoot of a large Swiss pharmaceutical company, Advance SA, among other things, undertakes drug trials for cancer patients. Anyway, just before they both got fired, yes, fired, not voluntarily resigned, Lisa happened to stumble upon highly confidential progress data indicating those participating in these in-house trials were becoming very sick. According to his source, she threatened to go public and expose what was going on.'

'So, you think what happened to the girls might be in some way related to this pharmaceutical company?' Mallory quizzed, her fork not quite reaching her mouth.

'I'm almost certain of it.'

'Has anyone questioned the company, tried to find out their side of the story?'

'Spen looked into it but ran into a brick wall. He couldn't even get past the receptionist.'

'Are the police in Australia acquainted with any of this?'

'Seems they have little enthusiasm or lack the resources to follow up.'

'What do you expect *me* to do?' Mallory remarked, continuing to eat. 'I can't really get involved if the Australian police aren't showing much interest.'

Lana reached for the half-empty bottle of Shiraz, draining the contents into both their glasses.

'I thought you could contact Fiona Sinclair; she's working closely with DCI Linton Ansley in Sydney. Fiona might be able to give Linton a push in the right direction. He certainly won't give the time of day to an English journalist who's looking for a cover story.'

Mallory finished her last mouthful of pasta, pushing the bowl to one side. 'No, get someone else to do your legwork, Lana. I'm not interested.'

'Actually, it's your job to show an interest,' Lana persisted. 'These young women were from Devon; it's technically your case. One has been murdered, and the other is under surveillance in a mental institution. If you don't show an interest, it's your arse on the line. If I were to let slip you knew about this and failed to follow up, well, kiss goodbye any promotions you may be thinking about.'

Mallory lifted the glass to her lips. 'Email me what you've got so far, and I'll see what I can do. Now please, finish your wine and leave me in peace.'

***

Sydney, Australia
One Week Later

Linton opened the door to be confronted by the beaming, larger-than-life, thick-set features of his long-time detective friend, standing in the entrance vestibule.

'You must be intrigued with Brenner's disappearance to have me fly over from Perth,' Graeme mused, giving his friend a firm hug. 'What's on your mind?'

Linton led the way into the lounge room of his stylish Northern Beaches apartment, Graeme making himself comfortable on a red recliner, resting his leg on a cushioned footrest, taking in the view through gum trees out over the idyllic blue expanse of Pittwater.

'This.' Linton handed over a manila folder. 'After Brenner's body was discovered, a further two persons went missing: Zelda Watkins from New Zealand and Siobhan Murray from Ireland. Both women were nurses on working holiday visas, residing in Canberra, last seen in the Brindabella National Park, their bodies turning up several days later.'

'Zelda in a vacant caravan in a camping ground on the Far Southern NSW Coast and Siobhan in a motel room in Broken Hill. You failed to mention this fact when we first spoke.'

'I wanted you to read the file, which you did,' Broschy responded, with a "gotcha" smile, repositioning his leg on a footrest. 'Makes for interesting reading, doesn't it?'

'Sure does. How did the investigation pan out? I can't seem to find anything more; even the autopsy results are pretty vague; they allude to the same method of murder, but that's about it. Inconclusive at best.'

'After a thorough investigation, all three cases were closed,' Graeme announced. 'Insufficient evidence, no suspects, zero eyewitnesses. Like Brenner's murder, we came to a dead end with Zelda and Siobhan. Back then, we had fewer resources than we have now.'

'It was also a time when the Litchfield kids went missing; more time and energy was put into that; other cases weren't given such attention. The whole thing became the victim of a power struggle within the force hierarchy, not to mention the whole circus turning into a political "hot potato," being tossed around among feuding state governments.'

Linton took this on board. The Litchfield case was huge; three young children taken from their grandparents' house in Adelaide. The discovery of their bodies coming two years later in a shallow woodland grave. It had taken a further year to convict and charge the children's grandfather of these brutal murders, a very sad outcome, which tore a loving family apart.

'Do you think all three cases might be linked?' Linton asked, turning his attention back to Broschy. 'Abundantly clear to me the same person or persons murdered Wayne, Zelda, and Siobhan. What do you think?'

'Without a doubt, but I was the only one with these thoughts.' Graeme remembered the tough time he had encountered trying to convince others of his hypothesis. 'None of my colleagues felt the same way. They thought I was delusional, relying on so-called "meaningless coincidences."'

'I have more questions: how did Brenner's girlfriend disappear without a trace?'

'Now, that remains a mystery. Leigh's family claims she keeps in touch with immediate family members but doesn't wish to disclose her whereabouts.'

'Do you think there's a possibility Leigh knew what happened to Wayne?' Linton probed.

'That idea had crossed my mind,' Graeme answered, accepting a cold beer from his host. 'The statement Leigh provided to the police, after Wayne disappeared, seemed constructed and lacked any emotion.'

'You have no idea where Leigh might have ended up?'

'Nope. If she doesn't want to be found, one assumes she changed her name and headed overseas—who knows? It definitely looks like she knew something.'

Ruth finally realised she couldn't bring herself to do it. How could she kill someone? A contravention of the Christian beliefs and morals drummed into her from an early age. It made perfect sense to stab the bastard, but somehow, it didn't seem right. God would never forgive her.

Chapter Eighteen

Exeter, Devon, England

'Hi, Javier, come on in.' Margo greeted him at the entrance to her part-time office in the Exeter Forensic Centre. 'I'm running very late this morning; have to return to my lab at the hospital shortly. Tell James I'm truly grateful he agreed to you assisting us today. Doesn't help I've been on sick leave for two weeks.'

'No problem at all, Margo; always glad to help where I can. What would you like me to tackle first?'

'If you don't mind, I was hoping you'd take a look at Lisa Marshall's clothing and see if you agree further tests are warranted. I ran through the preliminary conclusions from Derek Ingalls but was keen for a second opinion.'

Margo pointed to a small workbench and a bulging file in an envelope labelled "Javier.".

'That's for you, Javier; you can work in the spare lab. Sorry, got to rush; I have a heap of urgent matters to take care of. Chat with you next week. Bye.'

Margo disappeared out the fire door exit, towards the carpark. Javier inwardly breathed a sigh of relief. He hadn't envisaged events being this easy; handed the task he so desperately wanted on a silver platter.

He walked into the cool confines of the lab, donning protective gear, before making his way to the evidence bags, housing Lisa's clothing. It was the boots he was particularly interested in, but he would need to work swiftly in case anyone walked in.

***

Devon, England

'You eaten?' Will quizzed Mallory, seated next to him in the staff canteen. 'These salmon rolls are surprisingly fresh. Care for a bite?'

'Ah, no thanks. My stomach's playing up today. I need to cut back on the alcohol.'

Will snorted. 'Right, like that's about to happen.'

Mallory shot him a death stare. 'If you think I'm such a weak character, why bother—?'

'What? Hang on a second.' Will sounded offended, discreetly signalling for her to lower her voice. 'I'm jesting. Whatever I say nowadays seems to be taken out of context. You always bite my head off.'

Mallory took a sip of water. 'Sorry, overtired, I guess. Did you manage to get hold of DCI Linton in Australia?'

'I sure did.'

'And?'

'He's happy to go and speak with the bosses at Origan Pharma, but he'll need to tread carefully. We'll have to wait and see if he manages to unearth anything.'

'That's a start. Will, sorry for being such a grouch. I'll make it up to you. Promise.'

'Now, you're talking.'

Instinctively, Will, about to reach out under the bench for Mallory's hand, quickly decided against it. The staff canteen at lunchtime was not the place to demonstrate affection towards a member of the opposite sex, especially a work colleague, one betrothed to another man.

Mallory pushed back her chair, about to rise from the table when she had a light bulb moment. 'Of course, how on earth did we miss this one? Holy shit!'

Everyone around turned to stare.

'Miss what?' Will demanded.

'Didn't Shirley Copeland tell us her brother Davey manages a large pharmaceutical company in Sydney? I'm betting it's the same one Lisa and Christina worked for; that would make sense, especially as Lisa worked at KCs for a while.'

Will stared, open-mouthed. 'You're right. Oh my God. Our lovely Shirley could be behind the attack on the girls and most probably mixed up in Lisa's murder as well. Bloody hell.'

Will reached for his mobile; he didn't care what time it was in Australia. He had to make a call, even if it meant waking Linton Ansley up in the middle of the night.

***

Sydney, Australia
Origan Pharma, Macquarie Park

Linton casually leaned against the reception desk. 'I'm here to see the CEO, Davey Copeland. Is he around?'

'I very much doubt it,' the young blonde retorted. 'It's Tuesday.'

'Yes, it is, very observant of you,' Linton confirmed, checking his watch.

'Tuesday is golf day. Mr Copeland plays golf on Tuesdays,' the woman explained.

Linton turned to his officers, who were occupying nearly all the recliners in the spacious reception area of Origan Pharma Inc. 'Hear that, people. Tuesday is golf day. Perhaps we should implement that back at the station.'

Restrained laughter broke out, Linton leaning closer to the young blonde. 'Shame Davey's not about. We promise not to make too much mess.'

'What do you mean? Who are you? I've already told you Mr Copeland's not around. That's your cue to leave.'

Linton pretended to search all his pockets before finally producing a folded piece of paper from the inside of his jacket. He waved the paper in the air, simultaneously producing ID. 'That's a relief. For a moment, I was worried I'd misplaced the magistrate's search warrant.'

The young receptionist's eyes nearly popped out of her head. 'I'm sure that won't be necessary, Detective Ansley. Let me see if I can get Davey on the phone.'

Miraculously, within five minutes, Davey Copeland emerged from the lift, dressed in a tailored dark grey three-piece suit, a dark green tie with a matching breast pocket handkerchief, and shiny patent leather handmade Italian shoes; the family resemblance to Shirley was plain to see.

'What's all this about?' Davey demanded of Linton. 'You there, I'm guessing you're Linton Ansley? You can't come barging in here with all this entourage; this is a private business.'

'Oh, I'm sorry.' Linton's sarcastic tone coming to the forefront. 'I'll head back to base, informing my boss you refuse to allow a search on these premises on account of it being golf day.'

Davey shot the blonde receptionist a murderous glare, forcing her to refocus on the computer screen and busy herself with typing.

'We'll be off then,' Linton continued. 'Carry on, Mr Copeland.'

Linton made his way across the open foyer before halting and turning back, addressing one of his policewomen, 'Constable Hunter, would you kindly like to drop the cuffs on Mr Copeland, or shall I? He's refusing to let us take a peek inside these four walls, which he claims technically isn't permitted and might just mean he has something to hide. Oh dear, we seem to be stuck with a dilemma.'

Davey Copeland scowled, snatching the court order from the DCI.

'A murder investigation, unbelievable. Righto, you win; search all you like, but you won't find anything that shouldn't be here. Blatant abuse of taxpayers' funds. Regardless, I will be having our legal team lodge a formal complaint with the Police Minister and the Premier's Office without delay. Heed my warning, Detective; this won't go down well with our parent affiliate, Advance Pharma's head office in Basel.'

'Be my guest.' Linton smirked. 'Once again, we do apologise for this inconvenience, Mr Copeland. In the meantime, please assign a relevant manager to accompany our search of each section. Don't worry; we won't be interfering with any manufacturing operations or the like.'

'Just want our technicians to have a little look around, check everything is kosher. Why don't you take yourself off for a nice cuppa and add a dash of brandy? You look like you could do with a pick-me-up.'

Linton divided up the small team of police officers and forensic chemists to conduct the search of the Origan facility, a stark modernist concrete monolith of three levels, with reception and manufacturing on the ground floor, three laboratories on the mezzanine level with administration, and management offices on the top level. Linton headed to Davey's office first, with Constable Hunter following closely behind.

'Nice office,' Linton remarked, taking in the nearby cityscape through a full-length floor-to-ceiling window. 'Wouldn't mind this outlook myself, instead of a claustrophobic view of downtown Chinatown. Right, Hunter; let's get started. Mr Copeland, what do we have in that filing cabinet?'

'What in the devil's name are you looking for, Ansley? This blatant, spur-of-the-moment intrusion is highly illegal, and you know it; no solicitors present and no advance notification. Where's the evidence for this so-called "search warrant"?'

I assure you, we are a fully accredited drug manufacturer, complying with all the relevant government and statutory industry regulations. For Christ's sake, if you wanted access to our files and manufacturing procedures, why didn't the police just ask? I would have been happy to provide details for any formal request in a legitimate murder investigation.'

Sydney, Australia

Combing the premises of Origan, they found nothing of consequence relating to the attack on Lisa and Christina or subsequent events. The personnel files on both girls provided by HR were accurate, fully listing their employment, salary, and personal details during their time at Origan.

As far as the technical search was concerned, a random, cursory check of computer manufacturing protocols and inspection of the facility revealed nothing untoward.

'All above board, then,' Davey Copeland remarked smugly, triumphantly facing Linton in the boardroom. 'I guess that means you'll be off, leaving me and my Origan staff in peace.'

Linton, determined to salvage something from the failed intervention, marched back to reception, leaning in towards the blonde female, busily affixing labels on courier packages.

'What?' She snapped, trying to cover up her name badge.

'If you know anything at all, Janine McLachlan, you'll contact me.' Linton passed across his business card. 'Here's the thing: we *will* uncover damning evidence against Origan, and when we do, you'll be out of a job. If, on the other hand, you cooperate and provide us with the information we need, I'll personally see to it that you find secure employment elsewhere. That is, so long as you're not caught up in whatever's going on here.'

Janine looked uncomfortable, avoiding eye contact with the DCI. 'Of course I'm not involved in anything underhand; I'm the bloody receptionist, answering calls, organising refreshments, typing, filing, and warding off advances from male co-workers.'

'You have my details.' Linton pointed at the card now in Janine's grasp. 'You can call me anytime.'

***

Sydney, Australia

Linton, slouched over his desk in his office on the seventh floor, cast a weary glance over the pile of documents spread out in front of him and tossed up where to start.

Mentally drained from an intense briefing with Scientific, struggling to come to terms with topics like "standard deviations for the Anglo Saxon genome population" and "interference considerations in X-ray fluorescence spectra interpretations for common heavy metals," Linton contemplated whether it was worth the trip down to the 2nd floor canteen for another double espresso black. Deciding in the affirmative, he rose from his chair, about to exit the office, when his internal desk phone sprang to life. He answered on the fifth ring.

'Okay, right, down in reception you say. Thanks, Russell. Show her into interview room one and have Constable Hunter in attendance.'

Linton grabbed his jacket draped over the coffee table before heading down the rear flight of stairs, two at a time. When he entered the interview room, Janine McLachlan, playing nervously with her smartphone, looked up, offering a pensive smile.

'Can I get you anything?' Linton asked, taking up residence opposite Janine. 'We're just waiting on one of my colleagues, Constable Hunter. You met her briefly the other day when we came to your office.'

'I'm fine, thanks.'

Almost immediately, there was a brief knock at the door, and Constable Juliet Hunter walked in. 'You wanted me, Sir.'

'Take a seat,' Linton instructed. 'You remember Janine McLachlan, don't you?'

Juliet nodded, sitting down next to Linton.

'Before we start, I want to reassure you, Janine, you are not under caution for anything. You have come to us on a voluntary basis. However, if you feel you'd like to have a solicitor present, that can be arranged.'

'It's all good,' Janine responded. 'I thought long and hard over the weekend regarding your comments the other day, and to be honest, there are some facts you need to be told about in relation to Origan Pharmaceuticals.'

'Great, and that job offer still stands. If you help us out, Janine, we'll make sure you're taken care of. Also, if any of the information you provide us with today runs the risk of putting you in any danger, we will ensure your safety. I promise.'

Janine took a deep breath. 'I've been with Origan nearly four years; I went there after barely surviving two years of a university pharmacy degree. I had enough by then; not for me. My dad plays golf with Davey; that's how I got the job in the first place.'

'The company manufactures a wide variety of drugs, some under licence from its part owner, Advance Pharma, in Basel, but also undertakes its own research and development of new therapeutics independent of Switzerland, which are then marketed worldwide to the medical profession.'

'There's one new particular drug designed to help cancer sufferers. The technical specs are not important. I won't even bother trying to pronounce the chemical name, but around the office, it's referred to as Miracle Zee. The directors at Advance and Origan have been talking it up for the last twelve months. Now that production is underway, the hype around the office at senior management level is crazy.'

'Go on,' Linton urged.

'Various people voluntarily trialled this drug over a six-month period, mostly in NSW, with a few in Victoria. At first, everything seemed to be going smoothly. Then, people started getting sick, with bouts of diarrhoea, liver toxicity, and breathing issues.'

'A decision was made to pay these people large sums of money to keep quiet and help their symptoms go away by giving them an antiemetic, etc. They figured—'

'And these people were willing to take the money, even with their health clearly deteriorating?' Linton interrupted.

Janine nodded. 'All of the people in the trial were already stage three, probably dying within a few months, a year tops. They were realistic: the drug would only provide a bit more time. Miracle Zee was really designed to help those in the early stages of cancer.'

'Blake was not all that confident it should initially be given to stage one sufferers. He always erred on the side of caution. Anyway, the money the company handed out to those trialling the drug meant they could provide for their loved ones when they passed away. Quite depressing really.'

'I see. How exactly did you come across this information?'

'Mostly, I hear things. People forget a receptionist has ears; they think I'm a dumb blonde. Very few staff realise I completed two years of a pharmacy degree. I overheard the directors talking on several occasions. Mostly after hours, whilst I was packing up to go home. You can't just leave the reception area; you need to tidy up and switch the phone to night mode. It all takes time.'

'Unfortunately, hearsay won't help us much,' Linton remarked. 'As you're aware, we searched the offices and labs, looking for evidence of malpractice or illegal procedures as a possible link to our current murder investigations, but our scientific people certainly didn't come across anything like this.'

'Yes, because it's all stored at Davey's private residence in Double Bay,' Janine explained.

Linton reached out, reassuringly patting Janine on the hand. 'And you know this for sure?'

'Yes. About five months ago, Davey was on sick leave with the flu and was working from home. He asked me to drive over and drop off some sealed archive boxes for him. On the way, I ran my car into the kerb; nothing serious, but enough damage for me to have to call my boyfriend, Blake, and ask him to pick me up.'

'When Blake arrived, we transferred the boxes into the boot of his car, and during that process, came across the confidential progress reports pertaining to the drug's side effects and a list of all the trial subjects. It was a breakthrough for Blake, as he'd been suspecting foul play for a very long time.'

'And who exactly is Blake?'

'Blake Carleton worked as chief chemist for Advance Pharmaceuticals, overseeing the drug manufacturing. Before you say anything, yes, he's a fair bit older than me, but we get on well together.'

Linton raised his hands. 'Hey, I'm not one to judge. Please continue.'

'Blake and I took a few photos of the documents we'd discovered, also seizing a USB that contained a record of everything we had discovered in the boxes. We then dropped them off at Davey's home and left, hoping he would be none the wiser. A risk, but we had to do something.

'However, what happened next was disastrous. Blake left the USB on his desk that night, and the following day, it was gone. We tried to find out who had taken it, and eventually, Lisa Marshall owned up to being in possession of the USB. You'll be aware Lisa and Christina worked for Origan during their time in Sydney.'

'The reason behind our search of Origan,' Linton explained. 'We learnt Lisa and Christina worked at Origan for a few months; Lisa as a technical assistant in the lab and Christina in accounts. Correct?'

'Yes. Anyway, Blake begged Lisa to give the USB back, but she insisted on confronting Davey with everything she knew. She was after money.'

'That's why Lisa and Christina were attacked out in the bush,' Linton surmised. 'Davey and his cohorts pursued them in an attempt to recover the USB.'

'Yes, silly girls. It certainly looks that way.'

'Tell me more about Blake Carleton. Where is he now?'

Janine gave a weary smile. 'Blake flew to England. He has a Filipino friend, Javier, who's based in Devon, the same place Lisa comes from. Between them, they were hoping to get the USB back from Lisa. Javier is a medical expert with contacts. They planned to expose the Origan cover-up and shut them down before they did any more harm.'

'Have you spoken with Blake?'

'Too risky. When I heard about Lisa's murder, I knew things weren't looking good. Davey Copeland and his "mates" are dangerous. He must have realised Blake had betrayed him; there's now a price on his head. I overheard Davey chatting on the phone about a week ago.'

'I wanted to warn Blake, but I have no idea how to get in touch with him. The same goes for this Javier guy. Blake disposed of his mobile phone before boarding a flight to London. Emails are also out of the question.'

Linton leaned back in his chair, taking in the information Janine had provided them with.

'You were brave to talk to us today, Janine; thank you. It won't be safe for you to return home; we'll arrange temporary accommodation elsewhere until everything gets sorted. In the meantime, take a couple of weeks off work, compassionate leave or something.'

'How long will it take to get everything sorted?' Janine was wringing her hands together, her expression one of angst.

'To be honest, I have no idea. I need to get in contact with my counterparts in England. See what they know. Right, well, if there's nothing else, let's get your accommodation worked out, and once again, thank you.'

***

Double Bay, Sydney, Australia

'This is bloody well not on,' Davey exploded, trying to block DCI Ansley from accessing his property. 'Fuck off, or I'll report you to your superiors for harassment.'

'Go ahead, because, like it or not, I have a search warrant, and we're coming in, Davey Boy.'

One of Linton's senior officers shoved Davey aside, clearing the way for Linton to walk into the wide entrance hall.

'Lovely place you've got here,' Linton remarked, scanning the elaborate interior. 'I always wondered what homes in this part of Sydney were like. Very flashy and tastefully decorated, if you don't mind me saying so.'

'Oh fuck off!' Davey started to walk into the lower-level kitchen area, trying to escape the onslaught of police officers invading his home.

'Er, sorry, sir, you need to wait outside whilst we do a full sweep of these premises,' Detective Upwood announced, coming up behind DCI Linton and walking up to Davey. 'We apologise for any inconvenience, Sir. By the way, that goes for all members of your household.'

Davey let forth with a lurid tirade of expletive-loaded language, waving a mobile phone menacingly at Linton, causing a nearby policewoman, dressed in blue police fatigues, to blush.

'Who in fuck's name authorised this? Who's your commanding officer? What's the police hotline number?' Davey screamed.

'It's a warm night; I suggest you either go for an invigorating walk or perhaps sit and relax by your infinity pool, enjoying a cold tinnie.' Detective Upwood continued, completely unfazed by Copeland's aggressive response.

'On your head then, Detective, just to add, I'm on first-name terms with the Police Minister; that's his place two doors down the—'

Upwood then followed Linton up a wide set of stairs where the search team assembled, ready to begin an attack of the upper floors, ignoring the rant echoing up from the kitchen.

'You couldn't get this place for less than ten million,' Linton announced to no one in particular. 'Impressive view.'

Everyone stopped what they were doing to gaze out across Sydney Harbour, crisscrossed by the lights of ferries. The expansive, sweeping walls of floor-to-ceiling glass revealed a stunning panoramic view back towards the city skyline, Harbour Bridge, and Opera House.

'New Year's Eve would be spectacular from up here,' Linton continued. 'Not sure how Davey will cope tucked away in a pokey prison cell, pity. Perhaps we could buy him a poster of the harbour to stick up on his wall. Might feel more homely.'

A few officers sniggered.

'Right, let's see what we can find,' Linton instructed, entering the first of six bedrooms and opening the top drawer of a bedside cabinet. 'We need incriminating evidence to lock this bastard away for a very long time.'

Ruth started putting pills into his evening meal, each night watching him slowly drift off into a peaceful slumber. This resulted in her being able to lead a relatively normal life; it brought a modicum of joy back into her world, rendering him too drugged to abuse her.

Sadly, it all ended when he decided he'd head to the pub for his dinner, no longer wanting the 'muck' she dished up or the boring company. Had he become suspicious of Ruth's actions? She wasn't sure.

Chapter Nineteen

Exeter, Devon, England
KC's Nightclub. 01:00 hours

'Hi Shirley, have I caught you at a bad time?' Will barged into
the nightclub, not waiting for an invitation. The last patrons
began drifting out into the side street, searching for a cruising
taxi. 'I have more questions pertaining to your nephews and
Lisa Marshall.'

'I'm getting a bit fed up with you lot, no results, yet more
damn questions,' Shirley shot back, busily supervising staff
placing chairs on tables. 'Can't whatever's bothering you wait
till tomorrow? Do you ever sleep? I have to fix up the band
and finish closing; I have no time for idle chit-chat. Go home,
William; the cleaners are due in shortly; you'll be getting in
the way.'

'Shall we go somewhere more private to chat?' Will
pointed to a table near the bar, occupied by one of the security
team, quietly enjoying a pot of tea.

'There's nothing you can't say in front of Ardi; he's
practically family.'

'Just as well, considering both your nephews are dead.'
Will perched himself on a high bar stool. 'I'll have a light

beer, please, Shirley. I'm not officially on duty; this is more of a social call.'

Shirley's face mirroring displeasure, nodded to a curvaceous redhead behind the bar in a black leather, cut-away latex mini dress, to fix the detective a drink. Ardi, the mountain-like Samoan, shifted his chair to the other side of the table, rolling up his shirt sleeves to reveal arms the size of tree stumps, determined to keep a close eye on unfolding events.

'Interestingly enough, I've been liaising with a senior police officer in Sydney,' Will continued. 'Apparently, he and Davey are recent acquaintances. Well, perhaps he doesn't know him as such, but they've had a few dealings of late. Have you spoken with Davey recently, Shirl?'

'No, I haven't.'

'Ah, just as well. He probably can't make long-distance calls from prison. Too bad.'

Shirley fiddled with a chequebook and keys, shifting uncomfortably. The waitress plonked a full pint of beer in front of Will, a large amount splashing out onto the padded vinyl bar top.

'Cheers.' Will raised his glass. 'What do I owe you for the beer?'

Shirley forced a smile. 'Nothing, it's on the house.'

The DCI put away his wallet. 'Very kind, very generous. Thank you, Shirl.'

'Oh, for fuck's sake, Will, stop this childish playacting and tell me why you're here. Get to the bloody point. I've got work to do, and staff are hanging around waiting to wrap up for the night.'

Will took another drink from his beer, a tiny white moustache forming on his upper lip.

'Like cooking, Shirl?' Will asked, giving her a sweet smile. 'Capable of making the odd quiche?'

'What are you on about?' Shirley probed. 'When do I get time to cook?'

'Perhaps when you want to kill someone.' Will once more drinking from his glass, before firmly placing it back on the tabletop.

'It was a money thing, wasn't it?' Will surmised, leaning back in his seat, eyes making direct contact with Shirley's. 'That's why you had your nephews disposed of. They couldn't wait for their inheritance; they decided to help themselves, and Aunty Shirl got angry. Am I right, pet?'

'What a lot of rot!' Shirley opened a fresh packet of cigarettes. 'What cretin back at CID thought that one up?'

Waiting patiently for Shirley to light up her cigarette, Will nonchalantly pushed across the ashtray. Shirley's hands visibly shook as she raised the cigarette to her lips, drawing deeply several times and exhaling in Will's direction.

'Oh, I don't expect you to admit it, far from it.' Will informed her. 'But, eventually, Shirl, I'll get to the truth with a little assistance from our forensic people. Tell me, I'm puzzled how you disposed of the bodies; a petite woman like you couldn't manage all that physical stuff by herself.'

Will glanced across at the burly Samoan, all three hundred pounds of him, who returned the stare and a barely perceptible smile. 'Ah, of course, your colleague Ardi came to the rescue. Well done, you, Ardi. A very loyal and dedicated employee. Not many of those about nowadays. You should see some of my lot; they stroll into the police station at all hours, clothes dishevelled—'

The giant Samoan leapt up, slamming a fist hard down on the table, causing Will's beer to jump.

'Temper, temper,' Will taunted, quickly demolishing the rest of his beer. 'I'd come clean if I were you, Ardi; admit your guilt. Accessory to murder will get you a prison sentence, but if you admit your involvement, the time will be greatly reduced. Think about it. Here's my card.'

Will tossed a business card next to his empty glass. 'Thanks for the drink, KC's. I'm sure our paths will cross again before too long.'

Will eased up from the table, reaching forward to pat Shirley gently on the arm. 'Take care, Shirl. I must say, you're looking a bit stressed.'

Will then headed out of the nightclub, back to his car. He knew Shirley had committed the crimes; the only thing left was to prove it.'

***

Devon, England

Katie urged Polo Mint forward and into a gentle canter along the embankment pathway, now becoming narrower, curving perilously closer to the unprotected river's edge as it approached Tavistock. The breeze picked up, gusts swirling through trees lining the bank, her favourite pony sniffing the air and imminent danger. Katie's sixth sense detecting the anxiety in her mount.

'You daft thing,' Katie lightly scolded. 'The wind can't hurt you.'

Polo Mint threw back his head and, within a split second, broke into a frantic gallop, cutting headlong through the hedge towards the safety of the road. Katie, suddenly involved in a desperate attempt to maintain control, Polo, on a mission.

Before Katie realised, her feet slipped out of the stirrups, Polo Mint rearing suddenly. Losing balance, Katie catapulted out of the saddle, instantly making a sickening impact with the road's hard surface, where she lay, dazed, severely winded, gasping for breath, before attempting to get to her feet.

'Hey, you okay?' An unseen female voice asked. 'You took quite a tumble. My husband is taking care of your horse. Best you get checked out at the hospital. I live a few minutes away. Don't move; I'll fetch my car.'

***

Exeter, Devon, England

'Where's Charles Haig?' Will barked, in no mood to go searching for one of his junior officers.

'Sniffing around Helsa, who's heading up cold cases,' Jock answered. 'He's been down there nearly two hours.'

Will turned on his heels. 'Jock, when you see that baboon, tell him he's working with the task force, not hanging out distracting Senior Constable Helsa Pedersen.'

'Got you, Boss.'

***

Sydney, Australia

'Busy day?' Linton asked, poking a head round the door of the lab annex, catching Fiona in a lab coat encamped in a corner of the room on a quick break, ravenously devouring a toasted sandwich. 'You look done in.'

Fiona offered him a rueful smile. 'Tell me about it. Been here since seven this morning and probably won't get home until after seven tonight.'

'Er, I don't suppose you fancy meeting up for a drink when you eventually finish? I really need to chat about a couple of things.'

'Sure, why not. That sounds good.' Fiona glanced at her watch. 'Sorry Linton, I must be off; I have a meeting in five minutes. Let's catch up at, say, around seven-thirty. Does that suit? The kids can look after themselves for one night.'

'Sweet. I have to drop down to the yacht club to check the boat's batteries; how about the Mosman Arms, just around the corner from your flat? Till later.'

Linton disappeared, leaving Fiona mildly puzzled as to what could be so important he felt the compulsion to talk after hours. Her head was fuzzy with so much work, compounded by bureaucratic government indifference and the wildly unrealistic workload expectations; she was beginning to wonder how long she could sustain this frantic lifestyle. Things were never this hectic back at MFC.

***

Devon, England

'James, it's Will. Did you get my SMS? Apologies about the rush, old boy. Trust I've given you sufficient warning. Lance Waring has scraped together a scratch team from Scientific at the last minute and will be over to pick you and Javier up within the hour.'

The Court order is only valid for twenty-four hours. No surprise Shirley's solicitors are jumping up and down. It might be revoked at any time. Can you liaise with Waring's boys to go through the nightclub, plus Shirley's residential property on Exmoor? Find me the forensic evidence needed to lay charges. It's a matter of urgency. Uniformed officers, as we speak, are sealing off both properties. We're holding Shirley here at CID under a temporary restraint order.'

'Yeah, no problem, William, all organised. Thanks for the heads-up,' James informed him. 'Flick me over your latest updates on the Copeland investigation, including any additional info you think may be of interest. Guess we can look forward to a long night, huh?'

'Good man, thanks.'

***

Sydney, Australia

Fiona arrived at the fashionable pub close to her Mosman apartment almost at the same time as Linton.

'Perfect timing,' Linton mused, leading the way through an outdoor beer garden filled with locals enjoying the warmth of a balmy, late summer evening. He then negotiated a path inside to a vacant table close by an open BBQ grill, filling the space with the aroma of sizzling steaks. 'My shout.'

Fiona took a seat, whilst Linton headed to the bar.

'I think we're in for a weekend deluge,' Linton remarked, returning a few minutes later with half-price, happy hour cocktails, easing into a seat. 'A "Southerly Buster" is forecast for tonight, bringing gale-force winds up the coast, turning into an East Coast Low on Sunday. That rules out any chances of sailing this weekend. Must make a mental note to check the mooring lines and fenders on my way home tonight.'

'I'd like to come with you, if that's alright,' Fiona stated. 'A nice night to be down on the water.'

The conversation continued on the topic of sailing, Linton reminiscing on his early sailing years as a youngster racing dinghies on Sydney Harbour, later crewing for his father in keelboats, and eventually skippering his own boat, complete with the adventures, drama, disappointments, and euphoria, before a reluctant Linton returned to the real reason for catching up.

'Davey Copeland is in custody and likely to be locked away for a very long time. By the way, have you received the drugs for analysis?'

Fiona nodded. 'We're in the process of running a series of tests, but we'll need to take blood samples from all those involved in the drug trials and do cell pathology screening for cell damage and mutations. My boss, Trinni, and toxicology are organising that, in coordination with cancer specialists from ANU and Sydney University.'

'Look, Fi, you're not going to like this, but I have grave concerns regarding your neighbours.'

'Hayley and Jordan, are they in danger? What's happened?'

'Not concerns about their welfare, more worries about what they might have been up to,' the DCI replied. 'Police hotline recently received an anonymous tip-off; a science teacher at a Sydney college allegedly caught on video, spotted on a number of occasions, following a student home from class.'

'We traced this back to a college in the city; the name Jordan Paterson came up with a red flag. He was reported by a female student for sexual harassment, but Jordan's superior, Dylan O'Rourke, dismissed the claims, stating this woman had a crush on Jordan and wanted to discredit him when he refused her advances.'

'Dylan was best man at Jordan and Hayley's wedding,' Fiona broke in. 'I ran into Dylan by chance when he visited Jordan and Hayley's apartment a couple of weeks back. What in God's name?'

'It gets worse,' Linton continued. 'We discovered Jordan was camping in Brindabella National Park when an ex-Sydney Uni student, Wayne Brenner, disappeared eleven years back. It may be coincidental, but I'm saying—'

Once more, Fiona interrupted, 'Oh Christ, Jordan and Hayley told me at a dinner party just before Christmas that they originally met in Brindabella National Park when Hayley gave her boyfriend the flick. Could that boyfriend be Wayne Brenner, and if so, were they responsible for Wayne's disappearance?'

'Murder,' Linton updated Fiona. 'Wayne's body turned up days later, and yes, possibly.'

Fiona was aghast. 'No, no, certainly this can't be right. Hayley told me she and her ex are still in contact. None of this is making sense.'

'And you had no reason to doubt her story?' Linton asked.

'I didn't think much about it at the time, just the usual dinner party chit-chat stuff, but now, I'm not sure. If what you're telling me is factual, Hayley's story can't be true, can it?'

'Try not to engage with either Hayley or Jordan, should you come across them,' Linton instructed. 'I've dedicated two officers to delving more into their backgrounds, but if my theory stacks up, they're both very dangerous. We're trying to locate them to initiate a surveillance program.'

'I think they're still away, but if they come back, I'll be sure to provide an update,' Fiona advised, trying to take in this disturbing news, picking up her cocktail and taking a big gulp.

Linton's phone pinged a notification. He looked at the screen. 'Right, I can now confirm Hayley Paterson is in fact Leigh Crompton; she changed her name to Hayley Paterson when she married Jordan. We've been endeavouring for a long time to track her down.'

'Latest info from Foreign Affairs and Passport Tracking indicated she may have been living in Vietnam on and off. When I spoke with Graeme, an old detective colleague, he informed me that a Leigh Crompton was the girlfriend of Wayne Brenner and was with him when he vanished from Brindabella National Park.'

'The puzzle pieces are starting to fit. It now appears Hayley, and possibly Jordan, could have been involved in Wayne's murder. We'll do all we can to track them down, but remember, in the interim, if you see either of them, you are to contact me immediately on my personal mobile. Do I make myself clear?'

Fiona nodded.

Ruth's nose was broken; she knew it instantly, the bottle crashing down with such force, the impact of the break sending shockwaves through her skull, causing momentary blackout. Grabbing a towel from the bathroom, Ruth applied pressure before going in search of an ice pack.

He showed no remorse. Once more, he blamed her for the abuse.

Chapter Twenty

Devon, England

'I'm sorry, the fall caused you to lose the baby.'

Katie stared at the doctor, disbelief taking hold; it had never once crossed her mind that she could be pregnant. Suddenly, she was submerged in an overwhelming sense of loss.

***

Devon, England

'Fluorescein spray detected moderate traces of blood in one of the storerooms at KC's, smears and splatters,' James informed Will, speaking with a mouthful of toast. 'Someone made a half-hearted attempt at a clean-up and tried to hide it with cartons of beer.'

'So, we'll run some initial blood typing back at the lab, trying to match it to the victims. If encouraging, I'll program urgent DNA analyses on the samples; there might be enough residue to avoid any lengthy PCR replication. Say, three days for unambiguous results.'

Having arrived back at his duplex around 3am, James, with barely three hours of sleep, was semi-comatose, fighting to string words into meaningful sentences.

Placing his mobile on top of the coffee machine and switching to speaker, he continued to blurt out a semi-legible update: 'I suspect Reg and Albert were killed in the storeroom before the bodies were moved to the disused area behind the bar at KC's. Furthermore, who would have thought, a clear plastic bag of mushrooms discovered at the bottom of the nightclub's deep freeze, very suspicious.'

'Won't take long to check those out, microscopic examination and a couple of thin-layer chromatograms. No sign of any hemlock, but that's hardly surprising. Doubtless, any excess hemlock would have been chucked away.'

'Excellent work, thanks, James.'

'No trace of a firearm or ammo at the club,' James continued. 'Lance is picking me up for the drive up to Exmoor in twenty minutes to check out Shirley's property. That should be interesting.'

'Keep in mind Waring's team must finish up and be out of the place by midday,' Will confirmed.

***

Sydney, Australia

Fiona came in from the outside balcony, closing the sliding doors behind her, pulling across the drapes, shutting out the moonless night, with it the lights of the last Manly Ferry disappearing in the distance behind Dobroyd Head and into a late-night rain squall. Her watch indicated nearly eleven; the twins had crashed an hour ago, excitedly looking forward to the weekend.

Declining the option of a hot chocolate nightcap, as the haven of sleep beckoned, Fiona padded across the hallway, checking on the twins one last time, then towards her bedroom. She'd barely taken a couple of steps when her sharp hearing detected a muffled sound, followed by whispered voices, then a blood-curdling scream, suddenly cut short, leaving an eerie silence. Fiona froze.

***

Devon, England
Late February

Katie needed to work. She was appreciative of support from family and friends, but right now, her top priority was to focus on keeping both mind and body busy, reinforced by a positive attitude. Matt had been a tower of strength, reminding her of their bright future together and their upcoming wedding.

'You're fit and healthy, we can have fun trying for another baby. The main thing is, you're okay. Blimey Katie, that was a nasty fall, did you think you were competing in an equestrian event, or something? Any idea what made Polo react in such a way?'

Katie smiled. 'We can't blame Mint. Polo's always been headstrong, he got spooked. Bless him.'

'Bless him, my arse. The little shit needs to go back to school, learn a few manners.'

Katie wrapped her arms around Matt's neck. '*You* could always ride him, show him what a macho man you are.'

'Yeah, right. You'll never get me on that donkey.'

Katie unwrapped her arms, picking up her shoulder bag. 'I need to get going or I'll be late.'

'Come on, you're not working today? Thought you were having some time off.'

'One week's more than enough. I'm getting bored. Besides, I've an easy day planned; I'm visiting Christina in the psychiatric unit.'

'Is that wise? I mean, that female's a bit unpredictable; I don't want you putting yourself in more danger.'

'Stop acting like a mother hen. See you tonight.'

Katie planted a kiss on Matt's cheek before heading out of her thatched cottage to the Punto in the garage.

After a relaxed forty-five minute drive along traffic-free B roads and lanes, Katie arrived at the private facility where Christina was now almost a permanent fixture. Kate was signed in by security and escorted to Christina's room on the ground floor, east wing.

'What do you want?' Christina deliberately turned away from Katie, her gaze focusing on the walled garden.

'To talk.' Katie sat down on the side of Christina's bed.

'Why? I'm a threat to life and limb. I'd be careful, Sinclair; you shouldn't have anything to do with me.'

'That's what you want everyone to believe,' Katie responded. 'I've grasped the real reason you attacked Dr Finch. You were afraid; you wanted to be locked up, to stay safe.'

Katie watched a tear slowly roll down Christina's flushed cheek. 'What will happen to me? I don't want to stay here forever, and I don't want to go to prison.'

'I'll conduct a full report on your psychological state of mind. What happened wasn't your fault, Chrissy. With the right treatment, you will eventually be able to go home, I promise. I'm on your side.'

'It's a fucking mess.' Christina sobbed. 'Lisa and I had no idea what we were getting into when we worked for Origan Pharma.'

'I know. Javier filled me in on everything.'

'Is Blake okay?'

'He's lying low for the time being, but once everyone involved is rounded up and in custody, he'll come out of hiding.'

Christina reached for a tissue, her face visibly relaxing. Katie caught hold of her hand, sensing her inner release.

'Let's get cracking on this report. I have a series of questions, and you must answer them honestly. Once completed, I'll try for a release date. It's about time I called in a few favours from people in high places.'

***

Sydney, Australia

Fiona remained silent, rooted to the spot, senses highly attuned, straining to detect the slightest sound, primeval instincts on overdrive. In two minds what to do, she quietly discarded her pyjamas on the floor, pulling on a light grey tracksuit and slipping into a pair of worn boat shoes.

She dialled DCI Ansley; his phone went straight to voicemail; he was possibly already in bed. Fiona left a brief message, urging him to call, before venturing stealthily out into the mostly darkened apartment corridor, save for the LED ceiling light, shining down the far end of the corridor, above the lift.

The door to Hayley and Jordan's apartment swung open, the light spilling out, illuminating the corridor. Hayley appeared in the doorway, half in shadow.

'I think I heard a noise.' Hayley spotted Fiona, coming to stand next to her. 'Did you hear anything?'

'Er, yeah, I thought the sound was…'

'What are you two up to?' Jordan exited the lift, walking towards them, grinning broadly. The back of his polo shirt soaked in sweat. 'I could murder a drink. Care to join us, Fi?'

'Honestly, I shouldn't; it's been a tiring day; the boys are—'

'Ah, come on.' Jordan reassuringly wrapped an arm around Fiona's waist, a strong smell of vodka on his breath. 'One wee drink won't hurt. It's Friday night. Surely, you're not working tomorrow.'

'Thankfully, no.'

'Come on then. Hayley's got a superb bottle of red, a gift from a client. I popped the cork earlier to allow it to breathe. At its peak, needs drinking.'

Under the circumstances, Fiona was in no mood to engage in a drinking session with Hayley and Jordan, but if she refused, they might become suspicious something was up. Reluctantly, she agreed, following them into their apartment.

Once seated in the living room, Fiona watched Jordan disappear into the kitchen, returning almost directly with three glasses of red. 'Here's to adventures. Hayley and I are off again tomorrow.'

'I thought you'd just been away,' Fiona questioned, sampling the powerful Shiraz.

Jordan broke into laughter. 'True, that was just a "mini break," the accommodation too good to turn down. This trip will be a bit longer. Not a bad drop, eh? Where's your glass? Let me top you up.'

Fiona felt her eyelids starting to close. 'No, I really should be…'

***

Devon, England

'You seen Detective Wakefield?' Will Parker enquired of the desk sergeant.

'Mal? Yep, here about half an hour ago; got an urgent call and requisitioned a pool car. Mumbled something about a nuisance at home and hurried off. Do you want me to try and call her?'

'Yes, please, I'll wait here.'

After three attempts, Stephan shook his head. 'Sorry boss, it goes straight to voicemail. I can keep trying if you like.'

'Don't bother. I'll catch her later. There's an envelope sitting unopened on her desk. I believe it may be about the promotion she went for; I just thought she might like to know.'

Stephan smiled. 'I hope it's good news. If anyone deserves a promotion, it's that lady. She's worked damn hard over the years, yet always seems to miss out for some reason.

Her promotion would be a welcome morale boost for everybody here at HQ.'

'Couldn't agree more. Night, Stephan. Call me if anything urgent crops up.'

'Sure thing. Night, Will.'

Will pulled his jacket in tight, stepping out of the lift into the dank, frozen emptiness of the rear carpark, scanning for the Jag. He tried Mallory once more before giving up.

***

Devon, England

Mallory listened to the voicemail again, hoping and praying her golden retriever, Tonic, was okay. She wasn't well acquainted with her new neighbours, due to irregular working hours, but appreciated one of them getting in touch to advise that Tonic had escaped out of the back garden and was wandering aimlessly along the narrow country lanes. Her immediate, greatest fear: Tonic being hit by a passing car.

Mallory's first thought was to contact Bruce, but tonight, he was staying back in an emergency production meeting, unable to leave the studio any time soon. Mild panic setting in, Mallory elbowed the pool Honda through peak hour traffic, every minute counting, the only immediate option being to search for Tonic herself. Thankfully, there were no roadworks, and traffic was lighter than usual, avoiding any delays in getting home.

Arriving in her driveway within half an hour of leaving work as the last vestiges of light faded away in the western sky, Mallory jumped out, grabbing the pencil torch from her backpack. Quickly checking the garden and turning on the outside lights, she headed out the side gate and up the dark lane, calling for Tonic.

Ten minutes of calling brought zero response; Tonic wasn't anywhere in sight. Deciding to have a quick chat with the neighbours, Mallory retraced her steps, hurrying back down the lane and onto the sparsely lit roadway, probing the darkness with the torch beam.

Rounding the corner, Mallory didn't see the car; lights turned off, accelerating off the grass verge, rocketing straight towards her. With a sickening thud of impact, Mallory was catapulted into the air like a rag doll, bounced hard against the roof, and flung back onto the road, ending up on her back, where she lay motionless on the hard gravel surface, the noise of the vehicle fishtailing away on the wet surface, tyres fighting for traction, fading from her consciousness.

***

Devon, England

Will pushed the digital key into the ignition, about to press the "Start" button, when he felt the vibration of his mobile phone. Hoping the caller was Mallory, Will quickly extricated the device from his trouser pocket, switching to speaker. He was slightly deflated hearing James Sinclair's familiar voice on the other end of the phone.

'Apologies for calling so late; thought you'd like to know the blood typing and DNA sequencing found in KC's storeroom matches both that of Reg and Albert Copeland. In addition, the mushrooms found in KC's freezer exhibit the morphological characteristics of the Death Cap fungi.

'I'm running chromatograms on solvent extractions of the fungi tomorrow to confirm the toxins, but it's a given. I can email you a full report soon. That's the good news: the bad news: this doesn't prove Shirley's a murderer. Will— William, are you there?'

A long delay transpired before the DCI replied in muted tones, 'What's that, Jim? Yeah, no problems. Shoot something over tomorrow. Stellar stuff. Bye.'

***

Sydney, Australia

Fiona stirred on the bed, waking up groggy and disoriented, bathed in sweat. She went to sit up, but her head refused to cooperate. Her body was on fire, despite a cool draught washing down from an overhead fan.

'Hey, take it easy,' a male voice instructed. 'You're badly dehydrated.'

Fiona looked around, not recognising her surroundings. 'Where am I?'

'Safe,' the male answered, passing Fiona a bottle of water. 'Drink.'

Fiona grasped the bottle, gulping down the water to quench her thirst and ease her dry throat. She gazed at the bloke kneeling in front of her. 'Jordan, where are we? What's going on?'

'I think you had a little too much red last night,' Jordan mused. 'Actually, that's not entirely true. I spiked your drink.'

'What!'

'Come on, don't sound surprised. I think we both know you've been speaking with DCI Linton Ansley. What is it with detectives and the need to uncover the truth?'

Fiona was about to respond when Hayley called out to Jordan from an adjoining room. 'Shit, the little bitch bit me.'

Fiona looked up as Hayley entered the room, eyes adjusting to the low light, starting to focus more clearly on her surroundings: a windowless annex room housing another single collapsable bed, wash basin, and toilet.

'Ah, our guest has chosen to wake up,' Hayley mocked, turning to Fiona. 'Good of you to join us on our little adventure. How did you sleep?'

'What are you on about? Where are we?'

Hayley eased herself onto the floor, sitting cross-legged, opposite Fiona. 'Camping in the Brindabella National Park, where else would we be? We've been using this old lodge for quite a few years now, complete with all the mod cons, well, the essential touches one really needs, like electricity and running water.'

'Yes, but why are we here?' Fiona's eyelids started to feel heavy again. 'Where are my boys?'

'Do you want to explain, or shall I?' Hayley turned to Jordan.

'Oh, *you,* my love.' Jordan chortled. 'You're so much better at fundamentals than I am. Oh, but wait. I think our guest is drifting off. Come on, let's go for a nice long walk before the light fades; apparently, our guest requires more time to sleep it off.'

Ruth finally made up her mind to leave. There must be people to help her escape the onslaught of abuse, and she was desperate to protect her two young children and get them away from this living hell.

One evening, whilst he dozed, Ruth crept to the phone in the hall. The woman on the other end of the line was friendly and helpful. Everything was organised; she would make contact again next week.

Chapter Twenty-One

Devon, England

'How is she?' Will posed the question, observing Mallory's fiancé, clearly distraught, frenetically pacing the hospital corridor outside the Intensive Care Unit, his face puffy and tear streaked.

'It's early days, but she has a lot of broken bones and internal bleeding, and they are not sure if she sustained a head injury.'

Will, for the first time, genuinely felt a kinship with Bruce. 'We're going to do everything we can to catch the mongrel.'

'You're saying it was a deliberate attack?'

'In our line of work, someone is always looking for payback. A little too coincidental in my opinion; Mallory happening to be right in their path, especially that time of the evening, it doesn't add up.'

'I don't understand what she was doing.' Bruce sighed. 'Why go wandering along the narrow lanes at night? What possessed her to do such a stupid thing?'

'Could she have been taking the dog for a walk? Mal told me you guys recently bought a new puppy, a golden retriever.'

Bruce stared at the DCI. 'No, my sister's currently looking after Tonic. I told Mallory the other day that Tonic would be staying at my sister's place for the week; at least I *think* I did. Life's been a bit crazy for us both of late, what with my hectic work schedule and Mallory putting in for promotion.'

'Tonic's a cute bundle but tends to keep us awake at night. I felt we needed a break. Besides, we don't walk Tonic after dark. One of us usually gets up early to let him out and do the dog run stuff.'

'I see; I guess we'll know more when Mal regains consciousness,' Will announced. 'Here comes the doctor now.'

A man of unremarkable appearance, shortish stature, outfitted in mandatory surgical scrubs, strolled up to the men, fatigue mirrored on his face, intense blue eyes lighting up in recognition. With one swift movement, he removed his surgical cap, revealing dishevelled, cropped hair, heavily flecked grey.

'Don Crossfield, the consulting surgeon. Which one of you is Ms Wakefield's partner?'

Bruce stepped forward. 'I'm Bruce, her fiancé, and this is DCI Will Parker, Mal's work colleague.'

'Right, well, I'll give it to you straight. Unfortunately, Mallory sustained some severe injuries. The spleen was ruptured, so we removed that and stopped the internal haemorrhaging. She has a broken arm and a broken leg. At this stage, we can't be sure if she has any spinal cord damage, neck injuries, or permanent brain damage.'

'Haven't seen evidence of a brain bleed, but she'll need close monitoring over the next forty-eight hours. As soon as we are confident Mallory's out of the woods, we'll initiate a series of tests. I'm quietly optimistic, but she took quite a tumble.

'Luckily, she's healthy and a fighter. From the extensive torso bruising, clearly she impacted hard with the road surface. At some stage, we're looking at synthetic skin grafts to repair damage to the right outer thigh where a large portion of skin was torn away by the impact; the sort of thing we see a lot in motorbike accidents. Then, of course, there'll be the psychological treatment. In my estimate, the car was really moving to cause these types of injuries.'

Will looked grim. 'Thanks, Doctor, I've got my work cut out, but we'll catch the rogue eventually.'

The surgeon walked off, promising to keep Bruce updated and advising he would be able to see Mallory in about an hour.

'You will keep me posted on how she's doing?' Will turned to Bruce.

Bruce's eyes narrowed, his expression harsh. 'I'm not sure that's a good idea, do you?'

Will looked stunned. 'Er, I just thought in the circum…'

'Mallory is *my* responsibility, Parker. Perhaps you should take a good look at your professionalism when at work. I'd hate for you to get into strife for overstepping boundaries. I will happily contact your superintendent in relation to Mallory's medical progress but not *you*. Mallory is happy in her relationship; best you not interfere, huh?'

Will turned red, remaining silent, Bruce's words a stinging slap in the face.

'Oh, and a word of warning, Detective; come anywhere near my fiancée again and you'll live to regret it. Now fuck off; your mere presence is pissing me off.'

Devon, England

'All I want is to be told how she's doing,' Will grumbled to Katie. 'That weasel Bruce has made it perfectly clear I'm to stay away. It's almost like he's trying to make me feel guilty for what's happened to Mal.'

'And with good reason he's dirty. You *were* sleeping with his fiancée,' Katie responded, offering little sympathy.

Will looked sheepish. 'Yeah, point taken, but I care about Mal; it's not just a casual fling. I want her to realise that.'

'Perhaps now is not the best time, Will.'

Noticing Will's despondent look, Katie returned a caring smile. 'Look, I'll drop by the hospital when I can and see what I can do, but she may not want to discuss her relationship with you; Mal's been through a lot lately.'

Will reached for Katie's hand. 'Thanks.'

***

Australia
Brindabella National Park

Fiona awoke, now migraine-free and in total recall, to a primeval sound emanating somewhere from within the room. Fiona prayed it wasn't rats, her abhorrence of rodents of any kind legendary, especially when she was in no position to ward them off.

An attempt to sit up was thwarted by the thick cord binding her arms behind her back. Her eyes struggled to adapt to the darkened surroundings, feebly lit by the faint early morning glow filtering into the room from a narrow-slit window directly overhead.

Again, the sound, this time she discerned to be a muffled sob from near the other bed.

'Who's there?' Fiona called out. 'Are you okay?'

'I'm over here, tied to the bed. Can you help me? Please, for the love of God, I have to get out of here.' Graphic fear, verging on panic, in the woman's voice.

'You and me both,' Fiona muttered to herself, then raising her voice, 'What's your name?'

'Aoife, my name's Aoife. I'm twenty-two, on a working holiday from Galway in Ireland. Who are you?'

'Fiona Sinclair, I'm a forensic pathologist, working in Sydney. How long have you been here, locked up in this hellhole?'

'Only a few hours. I was given a drink of orange juice, which must have contained a strong sedative; when I woke up, I found myself in *this* ghastly place. There's another room beyond this one; that's where they've been keeping me.'

Fiona absorbed this information. 'Aoife, you need to tell me everything. For starters, how do you know Jordan and his wife, Hayley? Where did you meet them?'

Aoife let out a loud sob. 'I want to go home. I want to get out of here.'

Fiona tried to remain calm, offering words of encouragement. 'Yes, I know. We will get out of here, but first, talk to me about this couple. The more I know, the easier it will be to work out a strategy and plan our escape.'

Aoife sniffed, clearing her throat. 'I was scouting around for a part-time job and saw an advertisement for a receptionist at an English language college in Sydney's CBD.'

'Don't tell me; *English for All*, was that the name of the place?' Fiona asked.

'Yes, how do you know?'

'Jordan happens to be my neighbour. Anyway, keep going.'

'There's not a lot to tell really. I started working there three days a week, and yesterday, Jordan asked if I would drop off some enrolment forms at his place in Mosman; he organised a taxi for me.

'I arrived at his apartment about six in the evening. Jordan took the papers and suggested I come inside for a drink of juice as it was such a warm night. I thought nothing of it, so I followed him inside the apartment. That's when I met his wife, Hayley.'

'She brought me a large glass of freshly squeezed orange juice, after which, I think I must have crashed on the settee. I remember waking up feeling nauseous, my head spinning, unable to stand; it was about midnight, definitely recall checking my watch and then being half carried, half dragged out of the apartment into the lift, doing my best to get away.'

'Must have been comatose for a long time. Next thing, I'm waking up here, with my hands and feet bound and thick tape across my mouth. Who are these people, and what do they want from us?'

Fiona silently puffed out her cheeks. She didn't dare tell Aoife the truth; *Hayley and Jordan were serial killers, targeting overseas travellers.* That would only freak her out.

'They're clearly not well,' was the response she offered.

Sidmouth, Devon, England

'Glad you could make it.' Bruce leaned against the Citroën estate, watching the foam-capped waves crashing onto the desolate beach.

'What do you want?' Charles Haig shouted back, over the roar of the pounding surf, shielding from the wind-driven salt spray behind the seawall, a lightweight sailing jacket ineffective in preventing Arctic cold from seeping into his bones. He wore his uniform underneath, having driven to the remote location straight from work.

'To talk, Chas, old boy.'

Bruce, by contrast, was appropriately attired in an all-weather drover's coat and hood. 'We need to get our stories straight, Chas. I want you to go back to that turd of a boss, Parker, and tell him the night Mallory was hit, I was at the radio station in Plymouth; that will ensure my alibi checks out.'

'And if I don't want to comply with this form of bullying?' Charles questioned.

Bruce took a step towards Charles, their faces only inches apart. 'Simple. I disclose your cocaine habit and name your dealer. Won't that go down a treat? You'll be out of the force quick smart, lying in the gutter, where quite frankly, you belong.'

'You wouldn't dare.' Charles tried to remain poised, his fists ready to let fly at any moment.

'Try me.' Bruce inched back a few steps, a broad smile spreading across his harsh features.

'What if he doesn't believe me?' Charles remarked. 'What's the Plan B?'

'Of course, he'll believe you.' Bruce retreated to the warmth of the Citroën.

'Why wouldn't he? Besides, he's got so much on his plate right now, he'll believe anything anyone tells him. Now, fucking well get out of my sight and leave me in peace. Text me when you've spoken with Parker.'

***

Australia
Brindabella National Park

'I hope you're both rested; we're off for a hike later, team building,' Hayley pronounced sarcastically, coming to sit next to Fiona. 'I also hope you've kept that little bitch in line. Snivelling little cow bit me earlier.'

'You'll live.' Fiona's tone was icy. 'Look, if it's all the same to you, I need a pee.'

Hayley reached for a rifle leaning against one of the cabin walls before untying Fiona's hands and feet, forcing her to stand. 'If you try anything funny, I'll blast a hole in your skull, got that?'

'Yep, I think so. I only want a pee,' Fiona reiterated.

Hayley dragged Fiona out into the bright sunlight, causing her to close and reopen her eyes several times until her focus adjusted to the light. She then headed to an area a short distance from the hut, squatting to relieve herself.

Taking time fastening the zip of her jeans, Fiona studied the firearm Hayley bore, loosely swinging from her shoulder.

A formidable AK-74 Soviet design Kalashnikov, the ubiquitous international symbol of revolution and resistance. One Fiona was familiar with.

'Hurry up,' Hayley instructed, pushing Fiona back inside the cabin. 'As soon as Jordan returns in the waggon, we'll make a move.'

'Where are we going?' Fiona asked.

'Somewhere you'll never be found,' came the chilling reply, a shiver running down Fiona's spine.

***

Mosman, Sydney, Australia
11 a.m.

Linton sprang up the steps to the entrance of the apartment block, looking forward to joining Fiona for a few hours of precious relaxation. The plan is to catch up for a harbour walk before driving over to Manly for lunch and maybe a dip in the surf after dropping the boys off at a friend's birthday celebration. Humming softly, Linton knocked firmly on the door of Fiona's apartment, surprised there was no answer.

Then, he tried the buzzer. Perhaps she'd forgotten, gone off somewhere with the boys. Linton was about to walk away when the apartment door opened slowly and one of the twins poked his head out.

'Mum's not here; we're not sure where she is. Can I help you?'

'Ben, isn't it?'

'No, I'm Alex.'

'My apologies. You're saying you're uncertain where your mum is? Did she leave any messages? Any missed phone calls?'

'No, we already checked our phones; it's weird she's not here. It looks as if Mum's bed hasn't even been slept in.'

Alarm bells started to ring. Linton reassured Alex his mother wouldn't be far away; perhaps she'd woken up early, ducking to the shops. He then headed across the hallway, pressing the button on Hayley and Jordan's door. There was no reply.

Linton tried turning the door handle, surprised when it turned easily, and he was able to push open the door. Cautiously, he stepped into the living room, suddenly regretting leaving his 9mm automatic in the car.

***

Mosman, Sydney, Australia

'We've got scenes of a struggle,' Linton informed the officer. 'I want a forensic team here immediately. Shut down access to the building; no one's to leave.'

***

Australia
Brindabella National Park

It felt like they'd been walking for hours, the sun high in a cloudless sky, its rays penetrating through Fiona's fair Celtic complexion. Fiona calculated they were on an old, overgrown fire trail, no longer used by national park personnel or the general public; cleverly chosen by their captors to avoid other walkers and possible detection.

'How much longer?' Aoife asked, dragging her feet.

Out in the daylight, Fiona finally managed a good look at Aoife, taken aback by her natural beauty: hair long and blonde, stretching down her lower back, large, pale blue eyes, perfect porcelain skin, and a lean, athletic body.

'We need water,' Fiona instructed. 'Surely you can't expect us to keep walking in this heat; we haven't eaten since yesterday.'

'Stop whingeing,' Jordan piped up. 'You're going to die anyway; water won't make much difference.'

Aoife stumbled on a large rock, colour draining from her face. The ragtag group pushed along the roughshod track, gradually climbing higher. By reference to the surrounding landmarks, Fiona judged the group was now well into the remote and more rugged regions of the park, near the summit of one of the mountains girdling the ancient caldera, within which sat the sprawling Capitol.

'It's okay,' Fiona whispered in her ear. 'Try to keep going; stay focused. I won't let either of us die, I promise.'

Aoife managed to get back on her feet, continuing along the narrow debris-strewn track. Eventually, they halted at a clearing.

'Right, this is where we leave you,' Hayley announced. 'Hands behind your backs, please.'

Fiona deliberately positioned her arms in a crisscross fashion, forcing Hayley to tie the rope further up her bare arms, rather than the usual method of tying the rope around her wrists. A trick she had learnt at a self-defence course she'd attended with Harvey years ago at a gun club safety tutorial.

'You won't need both guns,' Fiona remarked, pointing to the assault rifle weighing down Hayley's right shoulder. 'It looks cumbersome. A few kilos, huh?'

Hayley swung the rifle away, leaning it against a nearby gum tree, ensuring to engage the safety. 'You've got a point, gal. Besides, it's not like you'll be able to reach for it with your hands tied behind your back. I doubt you even have the faintest knowledge of how this beauty works. Too bad if a wild boar comes for you out of the grass; oops, a gun so close, yet so far away. Shame.'

'I want to go home,' Aoife wailed, collapsing to her knees. 'Let us go; we won't say anything, we promise. Don't leave us here.'

'Oh, *you're* not staying.' Hayley cackled. 'Get the fuck up, stupid Irish mole. We've not finished with you yet; you're coming with us. Now, start walking, bitch. Jordan's dying to get to know you better, aren't you, Jordan? Just like he got to know Astrid, Renata, and Beatriz.'

***

Devon, England

'You'll be severely reprimanded if Will Parker finds you hanging around down here again,' Helsa scolded. 'Heaven knows what you find interesting here anyway, just a load of boring cold cases, which I very much doubt we'll ever solve. Task force is heaps better. Lots more intrigue with up-to-date information.'

Charles leaned forward against Helsa's desk. 'I've been asking you out for the past five months, Helsa. If you agree to one tiny drink, I might leave you to work in peace.'

'Go on then, Friday at seven, you can pick me up from my flat. I'll text you the address.'

Charles beamed. 'Perfect. Now, tell me, what are you currently working on?'

'An elderly woman attacked in her Dartmouth home five years ago, a teenager who died of a suspected overdose four years ago in Chudleigh, which to me looks like murder.'

'Anything else? What are these files?' Charles pointed to half a dozen boxes stacked neatly on a shelf adjacent to the desk. 'May I look?'

Helsa nodded consent. 'Sure, but don't be long. I don't want Parker on the warpath looking for you.'

Charles skimmed through the names on the boxes before moving to another shelf. Eventually, he came across what he'd been looking for. He waited until Helsa had ducked to the bathroom before reaching for the box and pulling out the file.

Tucking it into the inside of his jacket, he sent Helsa a quick message to her mobile, vanishing up the stairs back to the locker rooms, where he carefully removed the file, placing it into a Sainsbury's zip-up shopping bag.

Nick stumbled upon the knife by chance, wrapped in a small towel, concealed under his mother's bed, when searching for a piece of Lego. Nick turned the knife over and over in his hand, morbidly mesmerised, now fully realising his mother's intentions.

How desperate was the driving force within, his own mother harbouring the need to kill?

Chapter Twenty-Two

Australia
Brindabella National Park

Fiona watched Jordan and Hayley disappear along a narrow trail, Aoife being dragged in between them, the gun always visible. Swiftly, Fiona started working on the rope binding her hands together, desperate to be free and aid Aoife. She worked furiously, finally releasing her hands, rubbing them together to restore circulation.

Knowing time was of the essence, Fiona reached for the rifle still resting at the base of the tree. She flung it over her shoulder, making her way along the dirt track in an attempt to catch up with the others. It was paramount she tread lightly, not alerting them to her presence.

After tracking them for half an hour, Fiona wondered how much longer she could keep walking; her throat was dry and itchy from the heat, blisters forming on her feet, and her eyes were starting to sting. Sheer willpower kept her forcing one foot in front of the other.

Fiona seriously thought about giving up the chase when she spotted Hayley ahead, halted to rest at the edge of a clearing, Jordan doing the same and Aoife lying half prostrate, stricken with advanced dehydration.

Fiona estimated their distance, 100 to 120 metres, just within her marksmanship ability to put a 6-inch cluster of shots on target; something she had achieved many times at the gun club range at home practicing with Matt's prized Czech-made AK74.

Dropping silently to the ground, Fiona flicked off the safety, pulled back the charging handle, injecting the first 5.56mm cartridge into the chamber, and swung the Kalashnikov in the direction of the group, sights locked on Hayley's right leg.

Without hesitation, Fiona fired off a shot for range, quickly followed by a second, right on target, watching Hayley collapse to the ground, screaming in pain. Jordan, realising what had just taken place, grabbed his rifle, instinctively pulling Aoife in close by his side, wrapping one arm around her neck in a choke hold.

'You try anything and she's dead,' Jordan shouted, catching sight of Fiona entering the clearing.

'Let her go, Jordan, it's over. Give yourself up.'

'Shit, do something,' Hayley panted, rolling around on the ground in agony. 'I need help; my fucking leg is ready to explode.'

Fiona advanced slowly to within a few metres of the couple. Jordan looked awkward, trying to keep Aoife in a firm hold whilst struggling to aim his rifle at Fiona. Fiona raised her own rifle at Jordan, who let out a shallow laugh.

'You shoot, and you'll kill my friend here,' he mocked. 'Go on, do it, bitch.'

'Shut up,' Hayley hissed. 'We didn't even think the silly cow knew how to use a gun, and look what's happened to me.'

Now, it was Fiona's turn to laugh. 'Yes, sorry about that. I forgot to mention, well, it doesn't really matter. By the way, Jordan, your safety's still on.'

Distracted, Jordan momentarily relaxed his grip around Aoife. In the blink of an eye, Fiona took aim at Jordan's exposed left leg, pulling the trigger. With his hold on Aoife ceasing to exist, Jordan dropped to the ground, moaning in disbelief. 'The fuckin' bitch shot me; fuck you.'

'Charming.' Fiona edged forward, letting her rifle slip onto the grass, reaching for Aoife, and pulling her in close. 'Listen to me, you're okay, you're okay. Grab the water bottles and their phones; let's find an exit out of here.'

***

Exmoor, England
Shirley Copeland's Residence

Finding Shirley's door ajar, the DCI encountered Shirley in the kitchen, concocting a cocktail in the blender.

'William, do come in. This is a pleasant surprise. Just in time for a drink. Pull out a bar stool.'

'Not for me, thank you. We must talk, Shirley, you and me. Time to come clean, own up to what you've done.'

Shirley swivelled around, looking the detective in the eye. 'Will, I don't know what medication you're taking, but it's not helping your…'

'Enough of these games, Shirley,' Will broke in, mid-sentence. 'We have plenty of forensic evidence leading to your doorstep; now I need a confession. A confession for the murder of Lisa Marshall and your nephews, Reg and Albert.'

Shirley let out a long-drawn-out sigh. 'Will, I am not about to admit to crimes I didn't commit. You've got it all wrong; you really have. I haven't killed anyone.'

'Oh, for the love of God, why are you constantly in denial? Aren't you tired of these games? I am.'

'Will, how could I have killed Lisa Marshall when you know damn well I was out of the County when she was found? As for my darling nephews, no one's come up with hard evidence I had *any* involvement in their demise. They were poisoned, for Christ's sake; anybody could have whipped up a quiche or bought one and mixed the hemlock through it. Same with the quiche poor Lisa ate.'

Shirley opened a fresh packet of cigarettes, purposely offering one to Will, despite being perfectly aware that he had recently kicked the habit.

'You'll keep fighting till the end, won't you, Shirl?' Will acknowledged. 'Perhaps if I were in your shoes, I'd do the same.'

Shirley lit up with a gold Cartier lighter, drawing in deeply, watching the smoke rise leisurely to the ceiling. She took a deep breath, offering Will a sympathetic smile.

'William, sweetheart, why are you flogging a dead horse? Even if I did have some minuscule involvement with these unfortunate events, the boys in blue are going to have a hard job proving it. Move on; believe me, your health will deteriorate if you don't. You've given more than enough to the force. Enjoy your last few years at CID; let some other dick do the hard yards.'

Will felt his anger rising, wanting to throttle Shirley Copeland with his bare hands. He knew she was guilty as sin, but proving it would be difficult or impossible. Shirley had been clever in covering her tracks, allowing others to do the dirty work for her.

'Sure, have it your way.' Will stood up to leave. 'I won't stop trying for a conviction, you do realise that, Shirl?'

Shirley smiled, raising the cocktail to her lips. 'Are you sure you won't have one for the road?'

Will Parker shook his head.

'You're a decent copper, Will; I've told you that before, and you're welcome to keep trying all you like, but I will always outsmart you. See yourself out, pet. I think our little chat is over, don't you?'

***

Exeter, Devon, England
Police Head Quarters. Staff Canteen

'We don't have enough evidence to charge her.' Will sighed, pushing the sugar dispenser across the table to a bemused Rudy Jenks seated opposite. 'James Sinclair has confirmed the find of Death Cap mushrooms in KC's freezer, but there are no prints on the bag, which means we can't testify Shirley put the mushrooms in the freezer or used them in any way.'

'Unfortunately, Shirley has a multitude of people accessing the club on a weekly basis: cleaners, bookkeepers, security personnel, bar staff, and strippers—all would have access to the deep freeze at some time or another.'

Will paused in the update, adding two sugars to a lukewarm cup of tea and stirring slowly.

'Even though we have reason to believe the gun used to kill Albert and Reg belonged to Shirley, it was registered in her late husband's name. Roger Tudor thinks he may be able to run down the type of firearm on the internet and has offered to dig around, maybe come up with a ballistics match, but it...'

'We probably don't need to go there,' Rudy interrupted. 'Tudor's bloody expensive. The task force budget is already blown to pieces; Izzy Bax is already looking around for someone to blame.'

'Sorry about that.' Will muttered softly. 'The trouble is, not one of Shirley's employees is saying anything. It's doubtful any of them used the gun; Shirley would have hired an outsider.'

'Plus, some old blood spots we also found in the storeroom don't link Shirley directly to the scene, as she owns the damn place; she has a solid alibi for the night her nephews were killed. The same goes for the murder of Lisa Marshall; Shirley was away in London for two days.'

***

Exeter, Devon, England
CID
One Week Later

Jock cornered Will as soon as the DCI entered the room. 'Boss, earlier this morning, we found the body of Desmond Mottle at his mother's terrace in the centre of Exeter. First indications are he died from a heroin overdose.'

Will threw his mobile phone across the room, a perverse litany of swear words flowing forth from his mouth. 'We basically know Shirley Copeland is behind all these murders, including the death of Mr Everett at the Bovey Castle Hotel, but we can't prove any of it.'

'We could bring her in for further questioning, really put the pressure on,' Jock suggested, retrieving Will's phone. Hearing its familiar ringtone, Jock passed it back, the device now sporting a large crack in the screen.

After finishing the call, Will addressed the group of despondent task force colleagues gathered in the briefing room. 'Guess what? Shirley Copeland has done a runner. The nightclub has been boarded up, and our Shirley is nowhere to be found.'

Jock placed a sympathetic hand on Will's shoulder. 'I guess we can't win them all. Frustrating as it is for all concerned, especially the victim's families.'

Will turned to face Jock. 'I will not let Shirley Copeland go unpunished for her crimes. Even if it takes the rest of my years in the force, one day, I will bring that bitch to account.'

***

Exeter, Devon, England
CID

Detective Constable Haig sounded out of breath, having ascended the steps two at a time. 'Glad I caught you, boss. Thought you'd like to be informed that Bruce Stamford's alibi checked out; he was definitely at BBC Radio Devon,

Broadcasting House, the night Mallory Wakefield was run down, not the Bristol Studio as one might assume.'

'Slow down,' Will Parker instructed. 'Are you sure about that, Haig? I was almost convinced our pin-up boy Bruce was involved.'

'One hundred percent, boss.' Charles had practiced this story, even starting to believe the lies he was telling. 'This whole incident resembles a classic hit-and-run scenario. Idiots out joyriding, probably teens, thrashing the old man's overpowered BMW around the lanes, out of control.'

'I have my suspicions; the car rounded the bend, no lights, well over the limit, the driver completely unsighted in the half-light, no chance in hell of avoiding impact, Mallory pitched onto the bonnet, dumped by the side of the road; the driver taking off at warp speed in a panic.'

'Right, well, thanks for the update. Night, Charles, and thank you.'

'No probs. I'll see you in the morning.'

Charles walked slowly back down the stairs into the cool evening. He needed a fix; beads of sweat were forming on his forehead. He felt sick.

***

Auckland, New Zealand
Nick Shelby's Family Home
August 1989

Nick fought to remain focused. His mother sat rocking in a chair in the next room; the bloodied body of his father lay nearby on the tiled floor of the adjacent bathroom. Helen bent over the table, head buried in hands, hysterical, screaming and sobbing simultaneously.

Nick grabbed hold of his sister's arm, dragging her outside into the cool night air. 'Helen, you need to relax. I can't think straight when you're in this state.'

'Think, think about what? We need to phone the police immediately. What is there to think about, Nick?'

Nick turned his sister around, forcing her to look at him. 'Helen, we can't let anyone get wind of this, not yet; it would destroy us all. I'm going to make this look like a suicide, alter the crime scene. I want you to take Mum upstairs and give her a sedative. Stay with her.'

'No, Nick, please.'

'Our father was violent. Basically, he got what he deserved. Mum needs our love and support; she doesn't deserve locking up. Now, please go inside and take care of Mum. I'll sort the rest.'

Nick glanced at his father's bloodied body, feeling no emotion. It wasn't the end; it was the beginning, the beginning of the rest of their lives.

Chapter Twenty-Three

New Zealand
Present Day

The manager of Bayview Nursing Home greeted them in the foyer, her face one broad smile. 'Welcome, Dr Shelby, and this must be your delightful mother, Ruth.'

'Yes, indeed.' Nick took in the overall appearance of the reception area: airy and bright.

Soft, unobtrusive classical music in the background; in a corner alcove, a large espresso coffee machine and water cooler. On one end of the long, curved reception desk, an outrageously oversized vase overflowing with native flowers, dominated proceedings.

Nick visibly relaxed, tension easing. Certainly not the crowded, chaotic, drab, and unhygienic accommodation resembling a boarding house, which he had been conditioned to expect.

'I'll get someone to collect Ruth's belongings, and we'll proceed upstairs to her second-floor room,' the manager suggested. 'I must say, Dr Shelby, fortuitously for your mother, this suite came up at the last moment; the previous resident vacated unexpectedly yesterday and moved back home. Perfect for her, one of our best. Sun most of the day, and of course, a lovely view overlooking the Bay of Islands, very relaxing.'

Ruth Shelby held tightly to Nick's wrist, triggering a moment of guilt. Ultimately, he knew this was the best solution; Ruth could no longer care for herself at home, Helen had to change jobs, chasing work down the coast as a nurse at a regional hospital in Hamilton, and Nick himself, a long time away, resided permanently in England for over fifteen years.

'Ruth will soon settle in,' the manager reassured him, sensing how difficult this was.

She walked them to the lift, pressing the button for the second floor. On exiting the lift, they turned a sharp right, entering a room tastefully decorated in a scheme of pastel pinks with cream furniture. Very safe, easy on the eye.

Nick noticed a modest bathroom with a washbasin, toilet, and shower in the corner. In the main bedroom, a spacious built-in wardrobe, a reasonably sized bed, a bedside table, and a chest of drawers to complete the picture.

'Ah, here we are.' The manager smiled. 'Get yourselves settled, and I'll have someone bring refreshments. No doubt you're both exhausted after that long trip up from Auckland.'

'I'm not staying in this dump,' Ruth announced when the manager walked out. 'I want to go home.'

'It's only for a short while,' Nick offered. 'We need time to renovate your house, Mum; it's looking a bit shabby.'

'I like shabby.'

Nick pondered what to do. He felt bad leaving his mother here. In the present moment, she seemed all too aware of what was happening to her. His mother walked over to the window, staring out into the lengthening early evening shadows.

'All that blood. What a shame he had to die, but it *was* for the best.'

Nick turned to look at his mother. 'Who died? Who are you talking about?'

'Your father, of course, but we must pretend it never happened, right?'

Nick felt a cold shiver run the length of his entire body. 'I really don't get…'

'Don't stress, Nicholas. I promise to keep our secret.'

Nick guided his mother to a chair. 'Mum, what do you remember?'

Ruth sat down, holding tightly to Nick's hand, her face devoid of expression. Suddenly, she looked up into his blue eyes with a questioning look. 'I'm sorry, have we met before? My name's Ruth. Who are you?'

Nick breathed a sigh of relief. For a fleeting moment, he'd assumed the past was coming back to haunt him. Helping his mother unpack, Nick convinced himself she would soon settle into her new home. Surely, there was absolutely nothing to be concerned about.

It was almost seven when Nick finally kissed his mother goodbye, walking with the manager to the front door.

'She'll be fine,' Mrs Woodford reassured. 'I believe you're heading back to London tomorrow, am I right?'

'Yes, things are piling up at work. Always the way.'

'We've got Helen's details, should we require anything. Your mother is in safe hands; try not to worry.'

'That's much appreciated, and thank you for finding her a room so quickly.'

'Pleasure.'

Nick shook Mrs Woodford's hand, about to step outside when she called after him, 'Oh, one more thing, Mr Shelby; has your mother ever shown any tendencies towards violence?'

'No.' Nick hastily disappeared back down the stone steps, into the warm antipodean night air.

***

Sydney, Australia
Eight Weeks Later

Fiona sat in the airport lounge, the twins close by, absorbed in watching aircraft movements through the viewing windows.

'So, you're really going,' Linton kept saying. 'I'm going to miss you, Fiona. We were starting to get to know each other, forming a wonderful working relationship; it's a shame.'

'Does anyone really know anyone?' Fiona was playing with the blue tag on her hand luggage. 'Look at me; I thought I knew Harvey Driscoll; it turns out I was horribly wrong.'

Fiona had been shocked to hear Harvey had orchestrated the helicopter crash in PNG, along with Ryder Albero, and was also ultimately responsible for, or at least an accomplice in, the death of Terry Coates, an innocent man killed for greed.

Linton had updated Fiona in relation to an ongoing international police investigation to track Harvey and Ryder, now notorious for carrying off one of the most spectacular

335

aviation bullion heists in history. Fiona knew it wouldn't amount to much.

Harvey was resourceful, the ultimate survivor, resplendent with all the necessary skills to vanish like a will-o'-the-wisp, leaving no trace, forging a new life for himself, carrying on as if nothing had happened.

'You can always come back to Australia,' Linton continued. 'Jaz will miss you; she's loved working with you at the lab, not to mention all your new friendships from the crash investigation.'

'It feels right returning to the UK. Besides, my boyfriend, Haruto, is moving permanently to England. I'm sick of long-distance relationships. It's time I settled down. I've loved my time in Australia, but it doesn't seem right staying here. I have a nephew who's growing up fast and siblings I miss. I'll be back to visit, Linton. Haruto and I will have a holiday here next year.'

'Cool. We can go for that sail up the coast to Pittwater I promised you. What about the twins? How do they feel about returning to England?'

'The boys are adaptable, remarkably resilient; guess it's the age. They're excited to be spending more time in Scotland with their father. It's important they have a father figure around. My work's demanding: I tend to get wrapped up in my job sometimes, almost forgetting they exist.'

An announcement was made for Fiona's flight. 'Well, I guess this is goodbye, Linton. Thanks for everything.'

Fiona and the boys rose, picking up their luggage, joining the throng, and making their way towards the departure gate. Linton bounded after them, swinging Fiona around to give her a warm embrace.

'It's been amazing working with you, Fiona Sinclair. Good luck. And remind me to keep out of your way if you're in possession of a gun. What you did out there in the national park was remarkable.'

Fiona grinned. 'I suppose I've earned my title, "The Scarecrow."'

'More than earned it. If you want a job as a marksman with the Feds, the job's yours.'

Fiona untangled herself from Linton's hug, producing her boarding pass to follow the twins down a ramp onto the plane, the headed scent of Linton's cologne lingering in her senses.

'To your left,' the flight attendant instructed, as they entered the cabin. 'You've been given an upgrade through to London, courtesy of the Australian Government. Enjoy the flight.'

***

Devon, England

Katie helped Mallory into the wheelchair, covering her knees with a crochet blanket. 'Right, where would you like to go? It's cold outside, but I did notice a nice sunroom along the corridor.'

'Splendid. Hope I won't fall asleep on you, considering the strong pain medication I'm taking. Plus, it's hard sleeping at night amid all the hospital activities: nurses and doctors coming and going, restless roommates, corridor lights.'

'Sounds like hell. Mind you, I've had Jason staying with me the past few nights. That young man insists on waking up at five every morning. I can't comprehend how James manages to stay sane.'

'He's cute though,' Mallory acknowledged. 'You'll be next to have a child. Your clock's starting to tick; don't leave it too late.'

Katie's heart sank, her recent miscarriage coming to mind. 'Not you as well. That's all I ever get from my mother. Me, I'm definitely a career woman. That reminds me, I hear congratulations are in order. You've made it to DI; you go, girl, what an achievement!'

Mallory declined an answer, allowing Katie to assist her out of the wheelchair into a comfortable cane chair in the bright sunroom, thankfully void of other visitors.

'Your family must be so proud, Mal. What does Bruce think about it all?'

'I think Bruce is too wrapped up in his own career to notice my progress.' Mallory attempted to shift into a better position to lessen the pain. 'My promotion means a move to either Yeovil or Truro; I'm not sure I want to work in either of those places, leaving behind friends and family.'

'Ooh, yeah, that's tough. Here, I bought some chocolates, the ones you like with the orange cream centres.'

Mallory's face lit up. 'There's a vending machine just outside; why don't you grab us both a coffee to go with the chocolates?'

Katie obliged, returning a few minutes later with two large coffees, placing them on the windowsill. 'What's on your mind, Wakefield? You seem distant. I realise you've been through a lot, but something's bothering you; I can tell.'

Mallory sipped her drink before reaching for a chocolate. 'I'm sure it's nothing; the night of the accident, when I went looking for Tonic, I had my small silver torch with me, the one I normally keep handy in the glovebox. After being admitted to the hospital, I asked Mum to grab a few items from my bedside table; a novel, packet of tissues, my favourite scent.

'Anyway, she came across the torch tucked away in the bedside drawer and brought that as well, thinking I might need it. I can't work it out, Katie; I distinctly recall having the torch with me when I was struck by the car. Why would it end up in my bedside drawer?'

'You must have two torches exactly the same; simple explanation.'

Mallory sighed. 'I guess so; I must be going mad. I was convinced I only ever had the one silver torch. The bump to my head must have done a fair bit of damage.'

'Nah, you're still the same old Mallory,' Katie reassured.

The women relaxed in comfortable silence for a while, glad to be inside the heated room, sipping their drinks, enjoying the view through the glass doors of the hospital grounds and the ornamental bridge over the pond at the bottom of the garden.

Eventually, Katie spoke, 'I almost forgot; Will's been asking after you. Do you want me to send him a message, providing an update on how you are?'

'Of course, please be discreet. I'm sure Bruce suspects something is going on between myself and Will. He's been distant of late.'

'Probably busy; I caught him on the radio last night. He's great; his quick wit had me in stitches, especially the segment last week on…'

Katie became silent, not finishing the sentence.

'What?' Mallory pushed.

'Oh, I don't know. Now that I come to think about it, the whole segment was a bit odd.'

Mallory put down her coffee, looking at her friend in earnest. 'Go on, please explain.'

'It was a twenty-minute chat, during which time listeners could phone in. The topic was on cheating partners. One question Bruce put to the listeners was: What length would you go to if you found your partner to be cheating on you? I can't help wondering if Bruce put the segment together in retaliation, which means *he* clearly knew about you and Will.'

'Katie, I think Bruce was the one behind the wheel when I was hit,' Mallory blurted out. 'I'm convinced Bruce tried to kill me.'

Katie looked at Mallory in horror. 'Surely not. I mean, he was probably angry; that's possibly why he slotted in the cheating partners piece; he wanted to let off steam, but I can't for one moment believe Bruce would deliberately mow you down. Anyway, the police will do a thorough investigation and check out exactly where Bruce was when you were struck.'

A solitary tear slid down Mallory's flushed cheek. 'Bruce is experienced at covering his tracks. He'll stop at nothing to hide something if he wants to.'

'If you have concerns, you need to converse with Will,' Katie persisted. 'He'll be able to clarify where Bruce was the night of the accident.'

'Out of the question. If for one moment Will thought Bruce was behind the hit-and-run, he'd kill him, literally.

Katie, I beg you, please don't say a word to anyone about this.'

'Mal, if you really believe Bruce is the scheming monster you make him out to be, why are you still with him?'

'It's complicated.'

'I don't see how.'

Tears started to fall in abundance, Mallory attempting to wipe them away with a napkin. 'I'm tired; I'd like to go back to the ward. Thank you for visiting.'

Katie reached for Mallory's hand. 'What's going on, Mal? What are you not telling me?'

'Like I said, it's complicated.'

Katie knew not to push the issue, instead silently helping Mallory into the wheelchair and back to the ward. Once Katie had left, Mallory turned onto her side and openly wept. It was a mess; the whole thing was a bloody mess, and she didn't have a clue how to sort it out.

***

Albufeira, Portugal

The woman positioned the wide-rimmed sun hat firmly on her head before reaching for the cocktail; already, she was starting to tan. Just the way she liked it. Noticing a short, stocky man in a white linen suit and straw cream fedora enter through the pool gate, she called out.

Waving acknowledgement, he came over to sit next to her under the shade of an umbrella, occupying the vacant sun lounge, the smell of garlic strong on his breath.

'Ah, thankfully you found me, Miguel.' She beamed. 'What took you so long? I thought you'd gotten lost. Would you like a beer?'

Her visitor nodded, smiling nervously. Removing the fedora and smoothing a pencil-thin black moustache, dark, piercing eyes anxiously scanned the "ex-pats" milling around the crowded pool deck.

'Senorina, I needed to ensure this arrangement is, how do the British say, genuine.'

Her laughter rang out. 'You can trust me 100%, Miguel. I have money, and plenty of it. I have managed and owned bars and strip clubs most of my life. I will make you a very rich man.'

Thankful to be out of the fierce midday sun, Miguel threw his jacket over the end of the lounge, taking a moment to wipe his sweaty brow with a white handkerchief. 'Yes, you seem a respectable woman, Sherry. Now, I need to see your passport, just to make sure we can proceed without issues.'

A British passport was produced, which Miguel studied carefully. Appearing satisfied, he passed it back. 'You and I will be happy in business, Senorina, I can tell. It is a great honour and privilege to be doing business with you, Sherry.'

'And the hacienda you have promised me. When can I move in?'

'It is ready for you now, Miss Sherry. I have installed an excellent security system at your request, and you have a bodyguard twenty-four-seven.'

'Thank you, Miguel. One more thing: my dogs, when will they arrive?'

'Your altercations will be here tomorrow, and please, what are their names?'

'Alsatians,' the woman corrected him. 'They are Alsatians, not altercations, and their names are Scotch and Soda.'

**

Exeter, Devon, England
CID

Will switched off his computer, reached for his jacket and keys, glad to be going home. Stepping out into the carpark, he was greeted by a pleasant evening: a clear, star-filled night.

Will stopped to quickly check his phone messages, pondering what to have for a late dinner; confronted by the prospect of a bare freezer, whipping something up at home was not an option. That Mexican restaurant recently opened in Exmouth; perhaps he could divert there and pick up a few dishes? He really wanted to drop by the hospital and visit Mallory, but on reflection, probably not the best idea.

Making his way to his car, Will thought he detected footsteps close behind. He stopped, turned around, failing to detect any body in the shadows of the sparsely populated carpark.

'You're getting paranoid, Will, you old fart,' he mumbled to himself.

Two muffled shots from a silenced automatic in quick succession, barely discernible in the stillness of the carpark, scythed through the humidity-laden March evening, striking home like the blows from a sledgehammer, Will slumping to the ground, his world descending into darkness.

**

Linton Ansley, alerted by the message on his phone, swivelled around and switched on the flip laptop, just in time to catch the live image of his federal police equivalent coming up on Zoom from Canberra, smiling broadly.

'Linton. You're looking well; it must be all that healthy sea air. Anyway, thanks for taking the call, and by the way, I appreciate the cooperation and help from your team in this PNG matter over the last year. The Commissioner sends his thanks as well.'

'Hi, Len. I'll pass it on. No problems at all.'

'Must apologise; haven't spoken for a while. Anyway, due to some major developments, I thought I'd bring you up to date on the current state of play.'

Commander Len Wildman, Australian Federal Police, moved briefly out of screen, returning with a file and bottle of mineral water.

'First and foremost,' Len continued, opening a file in front of him. 'The PNG Government has taken the decision, as of last Friday, to discontinue the investigation; reason not given. Hence, they have ceased to further pursue any recovery of the gold or potential prosecutions. I have a few ideas why, probably the same as you, but let's not go there.'

'We have a rough idea now of how events unfolded. Harvey appears to have been the mastermind behind the operation, cooked up with Solomon Leahy; Ryder was brought in at the last moment because of his specialist knowledge and experience. The plan being to split the proceeds three ways.'

'We still aren't certain if the chopper crash was deliberate or an accident. Nevertheless, the bullion was taken off intact, on schedule, from the atoll and onto a large cruising yacht at night and sailed to Thailand. Harvey and Ryder were probably not on board. There are no records of their travels or whereabouts for some time afterwards. They just disappeared.'

'Authorities traced the yacht's movements to Bangkok three weeks later, where it passed through customs without hassle. Around the same time, there is video and document evidence of a man matching Harvey's description, using his passport, turning up in Phnom Penh, where it's believed he held meetings with major players in the Asian gold market, mostly associated with jewellery manufacturing. After that, nothing.'

'So, he got rid of the bars?' Linton questioned.

'Our information from people in the gold business confirm; with the right connections, it would be no problem disposing of one tonne of gold. The physical market over there is huge. Because of the unorthodox nature of the transaction and for immediate payment, we presume Harvey and Ryder sold it at a 10% discount to the spot price. The gold probably ended up as 9 and 18 carat jewellery and small, retail ingots in the lucrative Indian and Southeast Asian investment markets.'

'Then the metal is no longer traceable,' Linton surmised.

'Correct. Now, regarding our friend, Solomon, you already know what happened there, but I'll fill in the gaps. Our intelligence is that Leahy promised a lot of important people a cut of the share of the proceeds for certain favours rendered and some bad debts he had accrued. It never happened. Harvey and Ryder split the cash 50/50 and vanished. About USD 35 million.'

'No honour among thieves.' Linton laughed. 'Couldn't happen to a more deserving creep. Sounds to me like a little payback in action. Incidentally, did the PNG Government ever come up with the ransom?'

Len shrugged. 'No one knows. Leahy is still missing, presumed hacked to pieces and thrown in the Bulolo River like his bodyguards in the Range Rover. This is PNG, old son; 700 dialects, 1000 tribes, 7000 cultural groups.'

'Now we know why the PNG Government is reluctant to continue investigation,' Linton replied. 'Half the people in positions of power up there are most likely up to their eyeballs in this mess. Who would have guessed?'

'As for Ryder, he didn't change his identity or go into hiding like Harvey,' Len Wildman continued. 'Purchased a villa some time ago on the Mexican island of Cozumel in the Caribbean. Living the high life, running a reef diving business, free of interference from the local police and authorities, presumably bought off with his newfound wealth.'

Our contact in the Mexican Federal Police sent us a copy of the front page of the local paper a few days ago. His villa was invaded late at night, Ryder tied to a chair. The maid who was present claimed the armed group kept asking, "Where is the doré, Señor?"'

'Frustrated, they left after asphyxiating him with a plastic bag tied over his head and ransacking the place. The police are downplaying it as a dispute with the local drug cartel, but somehow, oh, I don't know. Perhaps we'll never uncover the whole truth.'